PRAISE FOR KIERAN KRAMER'S
PRELUDE TO A KISS SERIES

"Will delight Regency fans looking to escape London's stuffy ballrooms. . . . Supremely gratifying, and readers will eagerly await future stories."
—*Publishers Weekly* (starred review)

"Charming and disarming love stories are Knightley's forte . . . sweet and sexy, humorous and tender—a delight." —*RT Book Reviews*

"Breathtaking . . . very sensuous . . . kept me reading past my bedtime." —Fresh Fiction

"Endearing . . . a pitch-perfect blend of comedy and sweetness." —Under the Covers

"A sweet romance . . . delightful." —Open Book Society

continued . . .

Also by Erin Knightley

The Prelude to a Kiss Series

The Baron Next Door
The Earl I Adore
The Duke Can Go to the Devil

The Sealed with a Kiss Series

More Than a Stranger
A Taste for Scandal
Flirting with Fortune

ERIN KNIGHTLEY

The Viscount Risks It All

A PRELUDE TO A KISS NOVEL

A SIGNET ECLIPSE BOOK

SIGNET ECLIPSE
Published by New American Library,
an imprint of Penguin Random House LLC
375 Hudson Street, New York, New York 10014

This book is an original publication of New American Library.

First Printing, January 2016

For more information about Penguin Random House, visit penguin.com.

ISBN 978-0-451-47366-0

Printed in the United States of America
1 3 5 7 9 10 8 6 4 2

Penguin
Random
House

To anyone who has ever had to bear the title of widow or widower. May you find peace and happiness as you move forward, while always holding tight to the love and memories from the past.

And as always to Kirk, the absolute love of my life. You make every moment richer simply by being by my side. Keeping me fed while I'm on deadline is simply icing on the cake ;)

Acknowledgments

I'm so blessed to have been able to work with my very talented editor, Kerry Donovan, since my debut. Thank you, Kerry, for all of your wisdom, insight, and tact (vital when working with us sensitive authors!). I'm a better author because of your guidance. Thank you as well to my lovely agent, Deidre Knight, and her team at the Knight Agency.

Many thanks to my friend Lainie, who didn't miss a beat when I cornered her with my out-of-the-blue medical questions. Also to Christi Caldwell, who allowed me a little window into her fourteen-month-old twin daughters' lives. Those two are heroines in the making!

My heartfelt thanks to you as well, dear reader. I'm grateful for each and every one of you, and I love hearing from you! You can find me on Twitter (@erinknightley), at facebook.com/erinknightley, or on my Web site at erinknightley.com. Happy reading!

Prologue

There she was.

Standing by the alcove, alone and searching the crowd. The filmy white fabric of her gown looked cloud-like against the blue velvet drapes behind her. She was beautiful, but that wasn't what made Gavin Stark, Viscount Derington's stomach drop at the sight of her. No, it was the fact that it was *her*, Felicity, the girl he knew better than any person in the world. More to the point, it was what he had come to say to her.

He'd seen her skinned knees, heard her laugh so hard she'd actually snorted, and comforted her as her tears had soaked through his best shirt following her mother's funeral. He'd seen her tired, angry, stubborn, and even frazzled, but she'd never been anything but beautiful to him. As far as she was concerned, they'd been the best of friends since they were children.

And as far as Dering was concerned, he'd been desperately in love with her since they were fifteen.

It had been five long years since he'd fallen for her, and yet, in all that time, he had never once been able to bring himself to say anything. How could he, when he knew that the moment he did, everything would change between them? No more easy, lighthearted afternoons beside the river. No more stolen conversations in the folly, or teasing debates about the merits of stowing away on a ship to the Caribbean when the first blanket of snow covered the Somerset landscape.

Dering—the nickname his friends had given him at school, which Felicity refused to use—knew that the moment he declared himself, everything would be different. It was a prospect that had scared the hell out of him, but time was of the essence.

His stomach rolled with a wave of nerves at the thought. Biting hard on the inside of his cheek, he straightened his shoulders. It was now or never. Her coming-out had been postponed first by her mother's illness, then by her mother's death, but in a few short months, she would be off to London to make her debut.

This, his break over Christmas between the Michaelmas and Lent terms, was the last time he would see her before she left. God knew the moment the *ton* got a hold of her, his chances would be destroyed. She'd be a diamond of the first water, an Incomparable for certain.

What was the overly tall heir to an earldom when there were dozens of rakish noblemen to be had? He couldn't take the chance. Further, he simply couldn't wait anymore.

Five years was long enough.

That thought finally pulled him from his invisible moorings and propelled him forward in her direction. He used his height and breadth to his advantage, gently but firmly bullying his way through the crush. He knew every last one of them there—his father entertained constantly and had instilled the importance of socializing in all his sons—but at that moment, none of the other guests meant a damn to him. There was exactly one person he wanted to see, and she had just noticed him coming toward her.

Felicity's lips spread into one of her adorable, overwide grins that made her entire countenance come to life. "Gavin," she exclaimed, wrapping her gloved hands around his and giving a tight squeeze. "I'm so glad you're here. I've been waiting for you for ages."

His mind instantly went blank as he leaned into her touch. Her fingers fit so well in his hands. Struggling to understand her meaning, he said, "Did I forget a meeting?"

Shaking her head, she pulled him the slightest bit closer so she could whisper by his ear. "No, but waiting for your return has been torture. Meet me in the library in five minutes?"

Dear God. In all of the scenarios he had dreamed up on how he could sweep her from her feet, he'd never imagined she might be the one to do the initiating. His Adam's apple bobbed against his suddenly tight cravat as he swallowed and nodded. "I'll see you then."

Her smile was swift and glorious, making his heart hammer in his chest. "Excellent. I think I shall go nonchalantly take a turn about the room." With a wink, she released his hands and slipped away, leaving him to stare after her and reflect that this might very well have been the greatest day of his entire twenty years on this planet.

Sucking in a deep breath, he set off to find a footman, or more specifically, a glass of champagne. No, make that *two* glasses of champagne. If his dream was about to come true, he damn well wanted to celebrate with the woman he loved.

Precisely three minutes later, he was pacing the marble

tiles of his father's prized library, his heart thundering with anticipation. In a few short minutes, Felicity would arrive. After all these years of wanting her so badly, but knowing he couldn't say a word for fear of risking their friendship, it was impossible to believe that the waiting would be over. The not knowing would be over. The moment was finally here for him to show her the man he had become, declare himself, and allow the pieces to fall where they might.

Hopefully, right into his waiting arms.

The door squeaked open. He turned just as she slipped inside, her cheeks pink and her eyes fairly glowing. Drawing a steadying breath—which failed utterly to calm his nerves—he set the drinks down on the nearest table and held his hand out to her. "There you are."

"Here I am," she responded with a grin. She hurried to his side and slipped her hands right back into his. He wished that the soft fabric of her gloves weren't there, so he could feel the heat of her skin against his, but that would come soon enough.

His mouth practically went dry at the thought.

"I've missed you," he exclaimed, not willing to hide the truth even a moment longer. It had been almost four months since he had seen her—far too long.

"And I you. Desperately," she added, tightening her grip on his hands.

Desperately. He nearly closed his eyes against the pleasure the word evoked. Could it possibly be that she felt the same way about him as he did about her? *Desperate* was exactly the word to describe the way he had felt these last few months, waiting to see her again. "Lissy," he started to say, but his voice cracked on the second syllable. Embarrassed, he cleared his throat and tried again. "Lissy, so much has changed of late."

She seemed to be humming with just as much energy as he was. She nodded, her pale locks swaying with the motion. "Yes, I know. *Everything* has changed. And there is no one with whom I can speak of it but you."

Yes! He had been going mad, not being able to talk to anyone about his intentions. His school friends would have mocked him for actually wanting to marry, let alone for falling in love. His chest tightened as he reached into his pocket, where he had stashed the betrothal ring he had commissioned. As heir to the earldom, there were literally dozens of jewels he could have chosen from, but he hadn't wanted them. No old family heirlooms for his Felicity; he wanted her to have something created just for her. Opal, surrounded by a cluster of diamonds to represent the moon and stars that he knew she loved so much.

The gold was warm to the touch as his fingers grazed the delicate curve. "I—"

"No, please, I can't wait another second." She bit her lip, looking as though she would burst if she didn't say whatever was within her. "Gavin, I'm in love!"

His ears roared with the surge of exhilaration that washed through him. They were the sweetest words he had ever heard. "Me, too," he rushed to say, relief and elation assailing him in equal parts. All this time, he had been so afraid she wouldn't return his regard, and here they were, declaring their love for one another. It was like a dream, even better than he had imagined in his very best scenarios.

Her eyes went huge, rounding to the size of twin guineas even as she laughed with delight. "You are? With whom?"

Dering froze like a rabbit in a snare. *With whom?* The words reverberated through his brain like a ricocheting bullet. If she didn't think it was her, then that could only mean . . .

She was in love with someone else.

His fingertips went numb as he stared back at her, thunderstruck. "You first," he said, only barely able to push the words past his lips.

She sighed gustily, her eyes briefly fluttering closed. "Oh, Gavin, he's wonderful. He's kind and handsome and smart, and I haven't told a soul yet, but we're getting married!"

The room dimmed from Dering's vision, fading to gray as he focused on her beautiful, beloved lips and the unbelievable words they had just delivered. "Married?" he whispered.

She nodded, her light brown eyes glittering in the room's dim candlelight. "He spoke to my father last night, and the announcement is to be made just as soon as the contracts are signed. I'm so happy, Gavin, I could burst."

As she wrapped her arms around him in an impromptu hug, her scent enveloped him, that soft hint of gardenia that had taunted his dreams for years, and he breathed it in even as the shock numbed his thoughts.

She was getting married. She'd soon belong to another man, and there wasn't a damn thing he could do about it. If she was being forced, that would be one thing, but she had uttered the one phrase that could keep him from declaring himself, consequences be damned.

She was in love. Felicity was in love, and it wasn't with him.

He had missed his chance after all.

Chapter One

Ten years later

I'm *so* glad you've decided to join us."

Felicity Danby turned and smiled to her brother-in-law's wife, Charity, as she came to join Felicity at the front window. The servants were busy loading the last of the trunks onto the carriage, which meant they were right on time for a noon departure, less than three hours hence.

"As am I," she said, directing her gaze back to the courtyard. It was more or less the truth. She was nervous and a tad anxious to be returning to Bath for the first time in years, but she felt confident in her decision to do so. A year and a half was quite long enough for her self-imposed isolation.

Although perhaps *isolation* wasn't quite the right word. She readily socialized with the villagers in their tiny little corner of England, which was about as southwest as one could go in this country without hitting water. But she hadn't yet been able to make herself travel north to visit the many friends and family who lived in Somerset. She just hadn't been ready.

Felicity shook her head and sent a wry look to Charity. "Frankly, I'm surprised you were able to adjust to my rather last-minute whim. I hope Hugh truly won't mind having two more females in his midst."

Between Charity, Charity's grandmother Lady Effington, Felicity, and Felicity's daughter, Isabella, the poor baron would be quite outnumbered—just as he was every day here in Cadgwith. He was a good sport about it, but this was to be a holiday for them. It was the anniversary of when they first met, after all.

And it truly had been a last-minute decision on Felicity's part. Charity and Hugh had been asking her for months to join them for the second annual Summer Serenade in Somerset music festival, and she had steadfastly declined until, out of the blue, she had changed her mind yesterday.

The idea of traveling to her hometown for the first time since her life had crashed down around her ears last year was intimidating. Here, everyone knew what had happened and the awkward expressions of sorrow and condolences were well behind them. Though she had proudly gone by Lady Cadgwith when she was married, the villagers all knew to call her Lady Felicity now. Bless her father for being an earl, because she vastly preferred her original honorific to the Dowager Lady Cadgwith distinction.

Ghastly term, that. *Dowager* brought to mind gray hair and squinting eyes and many well-earned wrinkles. No one under the age of sixty should have to use it, let alone under thirty.

And yet, here she was.

Charity, oblivious to Felicity's train of thought, shook her head decisively. "Of course he doesn't mind. You know he adores having you and Bella around."

A genuine smile came to Felicity's lips. She held true affection for her husband's younger brother, and she knew the sentiment was mutual. They had helped each other through dark times, as best they could, anyhow, and she loved him every bit as much as one of her own brothers.

When he had married Charity, Felicity had offered to move out, but Hugh wouldn't hear of it. Now she was so lucky to have a father figure for Bella, a dear friend in Charity, and a surrogate grandmother in Lady Effington.

"Besides," Charity added, sending her a mischievous grin, "we were operating on the assumption that you would eventually change your mind, so no plans needed to be altered."

Felicity laughed out loud at that. A bit cheeky on their part. "I'm not sure whether I should be flattered that you know me so well or insulted that apparently you think I'm flighty."

"Flattered, definitely," Charity said with a wink.

A movement from the drive caught their attention, and in unison they leaned to the right to see who was coming. Mild surprise lifted Felicity's eyebrows as she recognized the vicar's wagon.

"Well," Charity said, shooting her a knowing look, "it appears your presence may well be missed."

Perhaps she was right. Felicity certainly hadn't expected Mr. Anthorp to respond to her note this morning in person. They'd spent enough time together of late—doing charity work, sharing walks, organizing the Flora Day feast—that they'd developed a rather nice friendship, and she wanted to let him know that she would be gone and to wish him a happy summer.

Smoothing a hand down the lavender-colored muslin of her skirts, she headed for the front door. The air was warm and breezy, perfumed with the ever-present salty smell of the sea. She lifted her hand in greeting as he came to a stop and secured the reins before hopping down. Though he wore a sensible straw hat, the sun glinted off the silver strands liberally peppering the fine brown hair at his temples.

The corners of his eyes crinkled behind the round lenses of his spectacles as he smiled at her. "Good morning, Lady Felicity. It seems that you are to have an adventure."

"That may be too strong a word, I think," she said with a wry smile. "I simply came to the conclusion that it was past time to visit my hometown."

He nodded, a bit of somberness softening his countenance. "I am very glad to hear it. They will be happy to see you, no doubt." His smile was gentle, encouraging.

He knew exactly why she hadn't gone home since Ian's death. As a widower himself, he understood better than anyone the pain of facing those who knew a person before a great tragedy. Those people expected the person one used to be, not the person one was now. Felicity could barely remember the carefree, happy girl she had once been. It was a lifetime ago.

"Let us hope so," she said, only half joking. "You needn't have come to see me off, however. I know how busy you are on Saturdays." He always liked to study at home the day before his sermons.

He glanced around at the courtyard before offering her his elbow. "Why don't we step away from the bustling servants for a moment?"

She readily accepted, and he led her through the gates toward the rose garden overlooking the sea. From this vantage point, she could see Hugh cutting through the waves on his last morning swim before their departure. Seagulls cried noisily as they circled the sky above him, clearly unhappy at his presence.

The vicar cleared his throat, drawing her attention back to him. "Though I'm certain this trip will be a joyful one, I realize, from experience, that it may not be without its trials." He reached into his jacket pocket and pulled out a small leather-bound book. "I hope that this can bring you some measure of peace while you are there."

The gold leaf letters easily stood out on the black cover, spelling out the book's title: *Holy Bible.* A fitting gift, coming from a clergyman. Accepting the book, she smiled. "Thank you for such a thoughtful present. I'm sure it will be very comforting."

"I certainly hope so. It's a good size for traveling, so I thought it might come in handy for you should you find yourself overwhelmed during your sojourn."

He truly was one of the most thoughtful men she knew. "I probably shouldn't accept this, but I will, with much gratitude for your kindness."

A soft but sincere smile settled on his lips as he met her gaze. "You are quite special to me, Lady Felicity. I hope you know that."

She was coming to see that. She swallowed, not entirely sure how she felt about hearing of his affection for her. It was nice, spending time with him. He was fifteen years her senior, which, combined with his profession, lent him an air of wisdom and tranquility. After the turmoil of the last year and a half, she appreciated those traits more than ever. He filled that need in her to have a stable, calming presence in her life.

Looking down to the book in her hands, she gave a single nod. "Thank you, Mr. Anthorp. I value our friendship as well."

They talked a few minutes longer about the coming journey before he finally steered her back toward the house. Patting her hand affectionately, he said, "I look forward to your return already, but in the meantime, I bid you safe travels and a very happy reunion with your family."

In short order, he was back in his wagon, heading home, with Felicity waving after him. Charity walked outside, attempting to look nonchalant but failing completely. After offering her own wave to the vicar's retreating form, she said, "So will you miss him?"

"Do you know? I think I will," Felicity replied, surprised to realize it was true.

But it was only for two months. By summer's end, she would be back here where she belonged, breathing in the salty air and listening to the crashing waves that she loved so much, as well as sharing walks and quiet conversation with Mr. Anthorp. Bath might have been her hometown, and she was indeed looking forward to the visit, but Cadgwith was and would always be her true home.

"And who is it that you are most looking forward to seeing once we get there? I met several of your cousins already, and they seem like lovely people."

Felicity considered the question as they turned and headed back into the house. Thoughts of her childhood and adolescence in their sunny estate just outside of Bath drifted thought her mind, and there was one person in particular who stood out the most. "Gavin," she said, a broad smile coming to her lips. The very thought lifted her heart, soothing some of the anxiety that had gathered there.

"Gavin? Oh! Do you mean Lord Derington?"

Felicity nodded. She was the only one who called him by his Christian name. His schoolmates had nicknamed him Dering his very first year at Eton—a play on his daring manner as much as his courtesy title—but she'd always preferred the name she had called him since they were children.

It had been so many years since she'd seen him, but he was such a part of her memories from there, she could hardly think of her childhood without thinking of him. It had started out with her eldest brother Percy and him playing together—the heirs to two distinguished earldoms—but Percy never had been one to have much interest in others. What had started out with Felicity tagging along had turned into true friendship before long.

"Though we have written on occasion, I haven't seen him in almost a decade—dreadful timing with my visits and his time at his other estates—and I can hardly wait to do so." It was amazing it hadn't occurred to her before. With her old friend there, at least she would have one true ally.

"Well, then," Charity said, putting her hands to her hips, "it's a good thing that his is the first soiree we are set to attend. You can start the festival off right."

A relieved smile came to Felicity's lips at this fortuitous bit of news. Thank goodness. Having another friend in her corner who could bypass all the awkwardness she feared awaited her would be wonderful. As the worry faded, something else seeped in to take its place: excitement.

"Indeed," she replied, clasping the vicar's gift to her chest. With the help of her friends both old and new, perhaps this would turn out to be an enjoyable trip after all.

Setting his hands to his hips, Dering surveyed the scene before him, pleased that all of it had come together so well. His townhouse wasn't overly large, but enough people were packed into his drawing and music rooms to put one in mind of a proper London party, right here in Bath. Merely thirty or forty of his closest friends, of course.

The lighting was low, ostensibly in deference to the warmth of the June evening, but in truth to subtly encourage his guests to be a little daring tonight. What was the fun of summer if one couldn't relax the rules a bit?

"Quite the crush, it would seem," Theresa, Lady Kingsley, declared as she strolled over to him. Every last one of her generous curves were on full display tonight in a shimmering silver gown that was impossible not to notice.

He smiled and lifted his glass. "On the eve of the festival's opening, we must properly celebrate. Where is your champagne, anyway?"

Her laugh was soft and throaty, as seductive as a siren. "I've already had two glasses. You're not trying to get me foxed so you may have your way with me, are you?"

He offered her a wry smile. "I'm much too keen on self-preservation to try, Theresa." Her husband might have been as old as the pyramids and as lecherous as Lucifer, but Dering wasn't about to take chances with a married woman. Besides the obvious complications, he held too much stock in honor to dabble in such a thing.

She looked him up and down, taking her time as her gaze lingered on his chest. "A man of your impressive size and strength has little to worry about." Even as she said the teasing words, it was clear that she wasn't really serious. They had played this game for years, and it was exactly that: a game.

Smiling, he shook his head. "I do hope you'll save a dance for me tomorrow at the opening ball."

"Mmm, perhaps. *If* you are very fortunate." With a

wink, she sauntered off toward the desserts, clearly aware that he would be watching her go.

He chuckled lightly. He lived for nights like this. Nights where he could flirt harmlessly with worldly women, laugh with friends, and immerse himself in the energy of the gathering. Silence was not his friend. Idleness drove him mad, and peaceful settings made him shifty. He thrived in the noise and movement and bustle of a roomful or even city full of people.

Better to be with others than alone with his thoughts.

Marcus Trough, a friend and frequent rival at the card tables, paused at Dering's side, sliding a knowing grin his way before directing his famous blue gaze back to Theresa. "Good to see Lady Kingsley looking so well." He was in full rakehell form tonight, with his brown hair dipping across his forehead in the way he was convinced women loved and his jacket cut so close to his form, Dering suspected he could have seen the impression of the man's navel, were he so inclined to look.

"As always," Dering replied easily. "Glad you could make it out, old man. I didn't think a music festival would be quite your cup of tea. Or whiskey, I should say."

"After the buzz about it last year? Had to see for myself what it was about this place that could convince Radcliffe and Evansleigh to succumb to marriage in the space of a month."

Dering snorted. "It was something to behold, I'll say that much. My mother was deuced disappointed that a similar fate didn't befall me. Getting old, to hear her tell it. Me, not her."

Trough laughed, shaking his head. "It's a wonder we can still chew our food, if our mothers are to be believed. Old girl told me just last week that if I waited much longer, she feared she may not live to see her first grandchild. She's not yet fifty, mind you."

Chuckling, Dering patted his friend on the shoulder. "To our mothers," he said, lifting his drink and tossing back the rest of it. Trough did likewise, and with a salute, set off into the crowd, no doubt in search of a proper prospect to woo. Or perhaps it was an *im*proper prospect he sought. The man thrived on female company. Not that Dering blamed him. Truth be told, he himself was on the lookout for a good match this year. He was fast approaching his thirtieth birthday, and, though he'd never say as much to his meddling mother, it was past time for him to get on with the business of heir making.

This wasn't the first time he had thought about taking the plunge. He'd briefly considered his longtime friend Charity Effington last year. Her loveliness, mild temper, and extraordinary talent in music had seemed a proper match for his tastes, but she'd gone and fallen in love with the baron. He was happy for her—for them both—but he had no interest in making a love match.

As long as he lived, he would never make himself so vulnerable again.

As if summoned from his thoughts, Charity herself entered the room, her hand settled comfortably on the arm of her husband. Her dark copper hair was pulled back in a becoming chignon with soft curls framing her freckled face. Grinning broadly, he strode over to greet them. He hadn't been certain they would make it in time, given the rainy weather they'd had this week, so he was thrilled to see them.

As he raised a hand in welcome, his gaze shifted to the blond woman who stepped in just behind her. Almost before his brain realized who she was, Dering's heart slammed to a stop, taking with it all the air in his lungs.

Felicity?

What on earth was she doing here, in his house? He hadn't even known she was coming to the county, let alone to his home. Shock held him momentarily rooted to the ground, hand up and mouth half-open, before some sane, blessedly rational part of him pushed through, propelling him back into motion. Before he could get a true thought in his head, Charity spied him and broke out in a wide smile.

"Dering," she exclaimed, coming forward to greet him with both hands extended. "How wonderful to see you again."

It took every ounce of his willpower to focus on her and not the vision from his past that was just behind her. His mouth stretched into something he hoped looked like a smile as she clasped his hands and kissed his cheek. "And you," he murmured, his voice seeming to come from somewhere outside his body. Having restarted, his heart was thumping nearly loud enough to be heard over the din of conversation around them.

How could Felicity be here? He hadn't seen her in ages, despite her efforts to visit him when she was in town over the years. He had purposely avoided her, not wanting to see her in the beginning, when she was a glowing newlywed, and then later when it had just been easier to stay away. He'd put his ridiculous adolescent love behind him, and it wasn't something that he wanted to think about now.

Unfortunately, the choice was proven to be out of his hands as Charity leaned back and gestured to Felicity. "I do hope you received our note," she said, completely unaware of the turmoil within him as he continued to smile politely. "We didn't hear back from you, but I know you and Felicity are old friends, and more to the point, I know that when it comes to parties, your philosophy has always been the more, the merrier."

Dering cocked his head. Note? He had been too damned busy today to bother with sorting out the correspondence that was piling up in his study. What he wouldn't give to go back in time and read the bloody mail in order to give himself a heads-up. Although would it have been better or worse to know that she was here in Bath and would make an appearance this evening? Would he have been able to stand the suspense, knowing she could arrive on his doorstep at any moment?

Impossible to say.

Drawing in a fortifying breath, he turned his attention fully to Felicity. His stomach somersaulted as their gazes met after so long apart. Even though he didn't want to appear overly interested, he couldn't help but take in every inch of her face. She'd matured since he'd last seen her—her cheeks were less round and the corners of her eyes showed the first sign of laugh lines—but she was unmistakably the girl he remembered. He wouldn't have thought it possible, but those small changes in her only served to enhance her beauty.

When she broke into a wide smile, the air left his lungs in a rush.

God, but he remembered that smile. He remembered those light brown eyes, the color of strong tea with a dash of cream. He remembered the way her hair smelled and how her voice sounded when she was happy. Did it sound the same now?

Drawing a much-needed breath, he dipped his head

and said, "It's been an age, Felicity. I hope you are well."
By some miracle he sounded almost normal. Hopefully
no one would guess he was so affected by her unexpected presence, least of all her.

Her smile tilted into a wry impression of itself. "Is
that the greeting I get after ten years?" She shook her
head as though sorely disappointed. "Do come here
and greet me properly. You are, after all, the one person
in the city I have been looking forward to seeing most."
Leaning forward an inch, she added in a mock whisper,
"Don't tell my cousins I said that."

Swallowing against the stubborn lump in his throat,
he stepped forward, unsure of what a proper greeting
between them even looked like after all these years.
Gingerly, he reached for one of her hands and brought
it to his lips, pressing a quick, featherlight kiss to the
leather at her knuckles. The teasing scent of gardenia
wafted to his nose, and he inhaled before he could think
better of it.

It was the scent of all his favorite memories . . . as
well as the worst one.

She squeezed his hand as he lowered it, her eyes
bright with obvious affection. "Much better. Now perhaps we can take a turn about the room, so that you
can explain why you have been such a dreadful correspondent these last few years."

His wits were slowly coming back to him, enough that
he could see how bad an idea that would be. He needed
a moment to gather himself. It had been almost a decade;
there was no reason why she should still affect him so
strongly. He was past all that. Her presence had blind-
sided him, and he just needed time to get himself together.

"How I would love to, but I have quite a bit to tend

to at the moment. Please do enjoy yourselves, and perhaps we can find a moment a little later?"

Mild surprise showed in both women's faces, but neither of them challenged him. Pretending he didn't see the
disappointment in Felicity's dimmed smile, he offered
them a brief nod, murmured a greeting to Cadgwith, then
plunged back into the crowd, hoping to lose himself in
more ways than one.

He might be a coward, but he was a prudent one.

Chapter Two

"It's about bloody time you got here."

William Spencer, Duke of Radcliffe's, eyebrows shot clear up his forehead at Dering's rather shabby greeting. His wife, May, pressed her lips together, but Dering could see surprised amusement sparkling in her bright blue eyes.

"Well, good evening to you, too," the duke responded mildly. "I doubt you missed me that keenly since our meeting yesterday, so am I to assume something unpleasant occurred in my absence?"

"You could say that," Dering replied, dragging a hand through his hair. "Might you be amenable to leaving your lovely wife for a bit to join me in my study for a drink?"

He knew full well that Radcliffe didn't drink anything stronger than the wine that was readily available on any passing servant's tray, and Radcliffe knew that he knew that, so it didn't take any time at all for his friend to grasp Dering's desperation to speak with him alone. "Certainly," he replied, then turned to his wife. "Might I abandon you to your friends for a few minutes?"

May, who was resplendent in a crimson-and-gold gown and elegantly plaited hair, didn't hesitate at all. "Of course. Good to see you again, Dering," she added with a knowing smile before heading off to find her friends. Exceptionally fine woman, that one. His friend could scarce have done better in choosing a wife.

Once in his study, he shut the door and waved Radcliffe over to where a pair of leather chairs sat prominently in the center of the room. The duke pursed his lips, not making any move toward the chair. "No need to get cozy. Is something amiss?"

Dering gave a curt nod. "It is indeed." He stalked to the sideboard and pulled out his favorite brandy. Pouring a glass that was entirely too generous even by his standards, he took a long drink before setting it aside and pouring a glass of wine for his friend. Handing over the goblet, he reclaimed his own drink and began to pace.

The duke watched him make a few circuits before finally crossing his arms. "Shall I wait for you to wear a hole in the carpet, or would you like to go ahead and tell me what the devil is going on?" The question was mildly spoken, without ire or annoyance. Radcliffe was as bemused as he was curious.

Pausing midstride, Dering drew a breath and spread his arms. "She's here."

The duke tilted his head, watching him closely. "*She* being . . . ?"

"*Her.* The bloody girl who broke my heart."

For the first time in their entire acquaintance, Radcliffe's jaw actually dropped as he stared back at him, stunned. "She's here? Now? Did you invite her?"

He was the only other person on the planet who knew of the whole debacle ten years ago. He'd been there at university when Dering had returned, brokenhearted and bereft. They had spoken of it exactly once, when Dering was deep in his cups and self-pity, and never directly brought it up again.

Until now.

"No, I didn't invite her. I damn near fell over my own dropped jaw when she walked though the door. The worst part about it is that she thinks we're still friends. Everyone does."

The duke shook his head, his brow knitted as he tried to make sense of Dering's rush of words. "If you didn't invite her, how is she here?"

Dering exhaled and dropped into the nearest chair. What a mess. Setting his drink on the table beside him, he ran both hands over his hair. "She came with Charity and Baron Cadgwith. She's his sister-in-law."

Radcliffe blinked a few times before the import of his words sunk in. "Lissy was *Lady Felicity*? The Earl of Landowne's daughter?"

Nodding once, Dering leaned forward, his elbows on his knees as he scrubbed his hands over his face. "Or the Dowager Lady Cadgwith, if you prefer."

"Well. That *is* a problem," Radcliffe agreed. "She'll be as thick as thieves with Charity by now, who will be equally as attached to May and Sophie, which means there is little chance you will be able to escape her this summer. Unless you intend to hole up here for the remainder of the festival." He paused. "Assuming you wish to escape her?"

"Yes. No." Dering shook his head. "This is ridiculous. I am a grown man, and am well past the stage of adolescent infatuation and heartbreak. There is no reason I should be so affected by her presence other than the fact that it was a complete surprise."

It was the only explanation. He had gotten over Felicity years ago. He'd been infatuated with a dozen women since then, danced with hundreds, and flirted with more than he could count. He'd learned that, outside of the bubble of his youth, there was a whole wide world out there with females aplenty with whom to share enjoyment and attraction. *Mutual* attraction. He had no intention of getting caught up in a one-sided love affair again so long as he lived.

Yes, it had to be the surprise that had him so off-kilter.

Coming to sit in the chair beside him, Radcliffe sighed. "An understandable reaction, given the fact you were taken off guard."

It was a diplomatic response, for which Dering was grateful. He could have easily rehashed what a blubbering idiot Dering had been that night he'd poured out his woes to Radcliffe over a bottle of blue ruin. Or there were the weeks of sullen moping that had been followed by some rather poor choices in company, the latter of which had resulted in Dering's father traveling to Cambridge to set him straight.

Drawing a deep breath, Dering nodded. "Yes. Exactly. We are both adults, and there is no reason why we cannot interact as such."

"Precisely."

"Absolutely." He was a grown, responsible man. He could damn well act like one around an old friend, no matter how embarrassing their past was.

The two of them sat in silence for a few moments, Dering momentarily lost to their shared history, to the feelings he'd endured that night when Felicity had announced that she was in love and about to marry.

"So," the duke said at last, his tone even, "shall we return to the party?"

"Yes, of course. My apologies for the outburst."

Radcliffe leaned forward and gave him a brotherly pat on his shoulder. "No apologies necessary. I know full well how badly she hurt you, however unintentionally. If there is anything I can do to make this easier for you, just say the word."

Gratitude bloomed in his chest as he sent his longtime friend a grateful smile. "You've already done it. I appreciate both your discretion and your ear. Now let us return to the festivities and pretend that I didn't just blubber on about a female like some Friday-faced fool."

They both stood, set aside their unfinished drinks, and headed toward the door. "I know a thing or two about being a fool when it comes to a woman," the duke said, sending him a wry glance. "Are you certain you'll be all right?"

Dering gave a mirthless laugh. "I will be fine." And if he wasn't, well, hopefully his acting skills were up to scratch.

So far, things had gone surprisingly well at this, Felicity's first true social event since Ian's passing. By some stroke of luck, she didn't know very many people at the party. A few familiar faces here and there, but other than Hugh and Charity and their close acquaintances, she was blessedly anonymous. After having conversed for a long while with Charity and her delightful friends Sophie and May, she had stepped back from the conversation so they could discuss the upcoming concert they were performing later in the week.

Gavin's home was well suited to entertaining, with strategically placed conversation areas in the corners of the two main rooms while the bulk of the space was open for mingling. She rather liked people-watching, which wasn't something she could easily do in their little town, where everyone knew everyone else. It was an indulgence to simply be a fly on the wall. After finding a footman with a tray of drinks, she stood off to the side with her glass of sherry and glanced around the room.

It was an interesting collection of people. Musicians, peers, ladies, opera singers, and even a few foreigners filled the two front rooms nearly to bursting. There was a clear air of celebration, with the other attendees laughing, drinking, and generally making merry. She couldn't remember the last time she had attended something like this. It was . . . invigorating. Exciting, even. The sense of optimism for the coming days of the summer festival was both palpable and infectious, and she found herself smiling.

"Lady Cadgwith?"

Without thinking, she automatically turned around, her eyebrows raised in question. A slim, tall brunette with pleasant features and a ready smile approached her.

"I thought that was you. My family owned the bookshop that you used to frequent before you married and moved away."

It was enough to jog her memory. "Miss Hedgecock! How nice to see you again. You are looking very well indeed." Felicity could clearly recall the woman as a girl only a year or two older than herself, smiling at her from the other side of the counter whenever she stopped in to peruse the well-stocked shelves.

Dipping her head shyly, she said, "It's Lady Ware now, actually. Married for three years this March, with a wee one in the nursery."

Felicity hadn't heard that Sir Geoffrey had married. A bookish academic who must be in his late fifties by now, the baronet had always seemed destined to remain a bachelor. It was probably a very nice match, considering their shared love of literature.

"How wonderful," she replied, truly meaning it. As nonchalantly as she could manage, she added, "And actually, it's just Lady Felicity now. My husband passed a little over a year and a half ago."

But, of course, there was no nonchalant way to say such a thing. Just as she feared, Lady Ware's eyes widened as her hand flew to her throat. "Oh my, I am so very sorry to hear that." All traces of joviality had vanished as she shook her head slowly, her features schooled in sympathy. "You poor, poor dear."

Felicity forced a smile, hating the pity that bled into the other woman's voice. "Thank you. I appreciate the sentiment. And like you, I am blessed with a child. She's just over fourteen months old, in fact."

Instead of lightening the mood, her words only served to further distress the baroness. "Born after her father's death? How absolutely tragic for you both! I can't even imagine."

Dread settled like a stone in Felicity's stomach as she cast about for something that would defuse the situation. People were beginning to notice the conversation, turning curious gazes their way. She nearly groaned when she saw that there were actual tears brimming in Lady Ware's eyes.

"There you are," a deep, resonating voice interjected at Felicity's side, and she nearly wept with relief. Gavin had returned at last, and his timing couldn't have been better. "I hope you don't mind my stealing Lady Felicity for a moment, Lady Ware. It's been years since we've seen each other, and I find I am exceedingly anxious to catch up."

If she could have kissed him without causing a scandal, she would happily have done so. Not waiting for the woman's response, Felicity said, "It was so lovely to see you again. Do enjoy your evening."

Placing her hand to the viscount's sleeve, she gladly allowed him to lead her away. He skirted around the room, keeping his pace slow and steady.

"Oh, bless you, you wonderful man, for coming to the rescue. That was *not* going well."

He kept his eyes trained ahead as he nodded. "Given your stricken expression, it seemed rather obvious that you were in need of a savior. Luckily for you, that's always been my specialty."

Though his words were teasing, his manner was somewhat detached. Not unlike how he had originally greeted her. She wasn't sure what, exactly, she'd been expecting from him, but somehow this wasn't it. In her mind, she had envisioned a happy, heartfelt reunion where the years would melt away.

A silly thought, now that she examined it. It had been nearly a decade since they'd seen each other. He wasn't likely to be the same unreserved, unabashedly extroverted boy she remembered. Heaven knew she wasn't anything like the girl she had once been.

Still, even just being in his presence reminded her of the lightness of spirit she once possessed. "Rescuing women from uncomfortable situations? Oddly enough, I can believe it. You always did have a knack for saving the day."

"Did I?"

Her lingering unease began to fall away as she soaked in his protective presence. "Don't tell me you don't recall the flipped rowboat incident of oh-seven?"

He chuckled, the sound a low rumble in his chest. A

chest that was easily twice as broad as she remembered. When had he filled out so much? Last she remembered, he had been as tall as he was now, but a good two stone lighter. It shouldn't really surprise her. He was a man now, whereas back then he had been barely more than a boy.

"Oh yes," he replied, his lips quirking up as he nodded. "Well, if Gregory Cox would have realized the folly of his plan before setting sail, he could have saved himself a dunking. Which, by the way, I maintain was an accident."

She laughed at the memory of the boy emerging from the waist-deep water, his hair in his face and his less than honorable intentions thoroughly thwarted. Gavin had offered to hold the boat steady as Gregory stepped in. It might have gone better for him if Gregory hadn't confided his intention to row to the middle of the lake with her then refuse to row them back unless she kissed him.

It seemed like they were so young, looking back, but she had met Ian only two years later. She drew in a slow breath, lingering on the memory of the day they had first laid eyes on each other. They'd accidentally collided as they both hurried to Collin's Sweet Shop for shelter from an unexpected rainstorm, and when she'd looked up to apologize, his gorgeous blue eyes had stolen the breath right out of her. Within three months they were married, and in their entire marriage, they never spent a single night apart.

It felt so strange to be here in Bath without him. The last time she had come had been two years ago, when they had been losing hope that she would ever conceive. They had been married almost eight years at that point, and their lack of children certainly wasn't for lack of trying. She had teased that perhaps she just needed to take the famous waters and, knowing that she really just needed to spend some time with her family, he readily agreed.

Whether it was the waters, or the change of scenery, or the fact that it took their minds off the effort, something about the trip must have done the trick, because she had returned home pregnant with Isabella.

At the thought of her sweet daughter, born four months after Ian's death, the baroness's face came back to her. Would the people here think Felicity was someone to be pitied? *Was* she someone to be pitied? The thought lay heavy on her chest, and she put a hand to it as though there were a physical pain that could be eased with a touch.

All at once, the crowd felt like it was closing in on her. Her lightheartedness of earlier had evaporated, and with the memories of how things used to be pulling at her, she really needed some air. Her smile felt strained as she turned to Gavin. "I know this is your party, but would you mind terribly taking me somewhere quiet to breathe for a moment? Or just point me in the direction of a place I can go."

His eyes cut to her, really seeing her this time. Unmistakable concern reflected in their dark depths. "Yes, of course. Follow me."

He led them down the corridor to a room that appeared to be his study, but instead of offering her a seat, he opened the French door at the back of the room and invited her outside. The garden was small, barely more than the size of the townhouse's front rooms, but the walls were high, offering blessed privacy and quiet.

She closed her eyes, breathing in the fresh, rain-scented air, wishing that she could smell the ocean.

"Are you all right?" His voice was soft and soothing. Familiar.

She nodded, just a small bob of her head. Exhaling, she opened her eyes and looked up at the sky. It was still too early to properly see the night sky, but there was a sprinkling of stars, fighting their way through the dusky light. She focused on them, finding comfort in their presence. "Just . . . a little overwhelmed. I'm sorry."

He didn't respond. Instead, he went to the small wrought iron bench at the foot of the flagstone path, shed his jacket, and laid it across the bench. "Come sit," he said, the command gentle but firm.

Now that she was away from the crowd, embarrassment at having dragged him away from his own party heated her cheeks. "You should get back to your guests. I'll be fine out here alone."

"You are my guest. And I'm sure you will be fine alone, but you don't need to be." He patted the bench. "Now come sit."

A ghost of a smile came to her lips. Once upon a time, she would have set her hands to her hips and refused, for no other reason than to vex him. Teasingly, of course. It was the way they had been together, never taking anything seriously.

But she didn't want to vex him. And more to the point, she didn't really wish to be alone. She had had enough time alone in the past year and a half to last a lifetime. All she wanted was to have a quiet moment with a dear friend.

Wordlessly, she came to sit beside him. His coat was warm beneath her, and the air smelled of hints of his shave soap generously flavored with brandy. It was a comfortable scent. One that was male, but not overwhelmingly so.

In the falling dusk, he turned to look her in the eye. "I know it's been a while, and I've already said as much in one of my letters, but I just want to say out loud that I'm sorry for your loss, Lissy. It was a damned shame."

She nodded, smiling briefly before dropping her gaze to her lap. The grief was so familiar by now, it had become part of who she was. It was like a low, constant noise in the background to which one simply became accustomed. "Yes, it was. I hate that you never got to meet him. You would have liked him, I think."

"I imagine I would have. If nothing else, he made you happy, so he couldn't have been all bad."

Leave it to Gavin to make her smile. But just as quickly as it happened, it melted away, leaving the familiar dull ache behind. Sighing, she turned to meet his inky, dark eyes. "I thought by now things would be better, and they are much of the time. But sometimes, it hits me anew and I'm back to that day again."

She hadn't intended to talk about it. People occasionally asked how she was doing, but they all expected the same answer: *Fine. Better every day. Thank you for asking.* No one wanted to hear that it never truly got better.

He leaned back, angled enough that he could comfortably meet her gaze. "Would you like to tell me about him?"

Dering could hardly believe the words had left his mouth. He had never wanted to know anything about Ian Danby before. It wasn't that he wished the man ill, because he never had. It just stung to know that the baron had been the better of the two men, so to speak. Whether anyone knew it or not, Dering had lost the woman he loved to a rival he hadn't even known existed until it was too late. How could he dislike the man when it was Dering's own damn fault?

On the other side of that coin, Dering didn't have to

like him, either. By avoiding him, the man was neither villain nor hero; he was simply an abstract thought who Dering could pretend to ignore.

But all of that was a moot point now. The poor bastard had up and died, and whatever Dering and Felicity's past, all Dering wanted to do was ease an old friend's pain.

Her smile was sweet as she cut a glance to him. "You really want to hear about Ian?" At Dering's nod, she said, "What do you want to know?"

He gave a light shrug. "Whatever it is you would like to tell me."

Biting her lip, she squinted off into the middle distance, clearly considering what best to share. At last, a real smile stretched her lips. "He was terrible at cards. In a decade, I don't think he ever won a game."

Dering almost laughed. He knew how competitive she was at cards. She hated to lose almost as much as he did. In fact, it was through their games that he learned never to risk what he couldn't afford to lose. He briefly wondered if she still had his gold watch fob. She'd taken devilish delight in wearing it after he'd lost it to her right before he had left for Cambridge. "Perhaps he was graciously allowing you to win."

She rolled her eyes, a spark of affection flickering to life behind her chestnut gaze. "Extremely doubtful. That would have been pandering, and that was something Ian never did. If there was something at which he could defeat me, then he happily would. Billiards, for example. He won most of the time, but every now and then I would edge him out."

"After all the time I spent teaching you the trick shots, you should have won every time." He clearly remembered leaning over the table close beside her, eyeing her aim and adjusting the angle as needed. Her brother Percy had sat with his nose buried in a book in the corner of the room, completely oblivious to Dering's oh-so-subtle attempts to accidentally on purpose brush against her bare arm or the curve of her hip.

He cleared his throat, pushing the memory back to where it came from. He didn't need any more reminders of what an idiot he had been.

"Let's just say he knew how to distract me," she said with a private little grin.

Definitely not something he wanted to think about. "What do you miss most about him?"

She exhaled, slipping her hand up to rub the back of her neck. "The taste of his kiss. The way he used to tease me about my terrible sense of direction. The warmth of his voice when he told me he loved me."

The words painted such an intimate portrait, Dering diverted his gaze back to the sky in order to distance himself. Those were her special memories, and knowing the way he had once felt about her, hearing her speak of them felt like an intrusion. Not that he begrudged her the right of saying them. He had asked, after all.

But this little tête-à-tête had gone far enough. She no longer looked upset, which had been his goal. In a tone that conveyed that he considered the conversation to be over, he said, "It's clear he was well loved. For such a terribly short life, it sounds as though it was an exceedingly well-lived one."

Nodding, she blinked away the moisture that pooled in her eyes, her smile little more than a determined curve of her lips. "Well, then. I do believe I have stolen you from your guests for far too long. I won't have your friends left bereft of your company on my account."

She stood, and he followed suit, taking a moment to shrug back into his jacket. He was proud of himself. They'd held a perfectly reasonable conversation. It really had just been the shock that had caused him to react so strongly when she arrived. Yes, he had enjoyed her company, but there was nothing wrong with that.

"I'm sure they somehow managed without me. Shall I escort you back to your friends, or would you like to stay here? It's private access only, so you won't be disturbed."

"Very tempting, but I don't want to worry Charity," she said, linking her elbow with his. As they started to walk back to the house, she gave his forearm a little squeeze. "I've missed you, Gavin. Letters between friends just isn't the same as true conversation."

"I've missed you, too," he replied. It was the truth. Further, ever since he'd lost her for lack of speaking up, he had been determined to live life out loud. He spoke his thoughts, he took more chances, and he reached for the things he wanted. Always keeping in mind, of course, how much he was willing to risk. Never too much money at the card table, never acting in a way that compromised his sense of honor, and certainly never risking his heart again. Mutual attraction and pleasure were much more to his tastes these days. "Though absolutely no one calls me Gavin anymore. Dering will do quite well, if you don't mind."

Rekindling a friendship was fine, but it was best to maintain some boundaries. He had been a different person back when she'd called him that, and he didn't want to be reminded of that hen-hearted pup. Yes, his pulse might still pound at the sight of her, but she was a beautiful woman. Any red-blooded male would have the same reaction.

Sighing, she shook her head and grinned. "If you insist. I do hope we can see more of each other while I'm here. You remind me of a part of myself that I had forgotten."

He knew the feeling. Opening the door and waving her inside, he gave a little shrug. "Based on how last year's festival went, we'll likely be running into each other frequently. You may well be sick of me by the end of it."

"Impossible," she said with a wink. "There are lots of things and people that I could tire of, but you could never be among them." As they reached the study door, she rose to her toes and pressed her lips to his cheek in a quick, affectionate peck that he felt through his entire body.

Other than sucking in a soundless breath through his parted lips, he worked not to show any reaction to the innocent kiss. Innocent-to-*her* kiss, he amended. Because, God help him, no matter how evolved he thought he had become, every part of his baser self came roaring back at that simple touch. For the space of a second, when her lips had met the sensitive skin beside his mouth, he was right back to being that desperately-in-love adolescent.

Bloody hell.

Smiling tightly, he said, "Enjoy your evening, Felicity. I'm going to pour a drink from my private stash before returning, so please carry on without me."

With a nod and a grin, she was gone. Pushing the door closed, Dering leaned his forehead against the cool oak and groaned. Without a doubt, this was going to be a very long summer.

Chapter Three

"Good morning," Charity said on a yawn as she made her way into the breakfast room. Her pale blue morning gown complemented the room's ivory-and-blue color scheme perfectly. The dappled sunlight angling through the trees in the back garden gave the room a warm, cheerful glow but could do little to disguise Charity's slightly green complexion.

Felicity smiled back sympathetically. Though very few others knew, Charity was expecting their first child in the spring. "Feeling a bit under the weather this morning?"

As excited as she was to be an aunt, she could still sympathize with the less than enjoyable effects of pregnancy. The reward was worth it a thousand times over, but that didn't make it any easier when one was in the thick of it. She hugged Isabella a little tighter, pressing a kiss to the top of her downy head. Such a sweet, sweet girl. Her daughter squirmed in response, so she eased her hold and offered her a bit of apple.

Most women of their rank would be appalled at having a baby at the table, but Felicity loved sharing meals with her daughter, and she was fortunate that the rest of the family indulged her. Breakfast at the breakfast table, luncheon in the nursery or outside, then a light supper followed by reading fairy tales with Isabella in her lap until the baby fell asleep. It was a routine they followed day in and day out, and Felicity was hoping to disrupt it as little as possible while they were in Bath.

"This morning? This *month* is more like it," Charity replied with a half grin, half grimace. She paused to blow kisses to Bella before continuing to the sideboard. "Usually the middle of the night is worst, but this morning hasn't been very fun, either."

She perused the light buffet, her nose wrinkled in distaste at the selection of eggs, meats, and beans to the left. Finally selecting a piece of toast and a few apple slices from the less offensive right side of the spread, she slipped into the chair across from Felicity. "I must say, though, that after hearing of your troubles in your first few months, I think I have been pretty fortunate thus far."

Felicity cringed at the memories. "It was rather miserable, if I'm honest. Poor Ian handled things so well, but I was an absolute mess." He'd rubbed her back and pressed washcloths to her neck more times than she cared to remember while she sat with a chamber pot clutched in her lap. He'd been so excited for the pregnancy, he hadn't batted an eye at such ignoble tasks.

Adjusting Isabella to the other side of her lap, she offered Charity an encouraging smile. "I only wish I had your pianoforte skills, so I could have kept my mind and hands busy. Have you finished the lullaby yet?

At this, Charity perked up. "Almost! I keep thinking the ending needs to be sweeter, more tender, but other than that, I'm very pleased with it so far."

She was the most talented pianoforte player and

composer Felicity had ever met. She played as though she'd been born to it, coaxing music from those black and ivory keys that seemed otherworldly in its beauty.

"I'm sure it will be spectacular. Actually, perhaps that's why things have gone as well as they have. The baby is probably already a music lover."

"Mm, then it appears that we are in the right place. I can hardly wait for the opening ball tonight. Or the rest of the festivities, for that matter. Dering's party last night was the perfect way to ease into things, didn't you think?"

A smile came to Felicity's lips as she nodded. "I enjoyed it, for the most part. I'll admit it's hard to get used to being in a crowd again. At one point, I had to seek a few minutes solace in the garden."

"Is that where you went? I forgot to ask where you had gotten off to on the ride home." Charity had actually fallen asleep shortly after the carriage started moving, so they hadn't yet discussed the evening in any real depth. As she poured a cup of tea, she added, "When you disappeared last night, I admit, I briefly wondered if you had hailed a hack and snuck home."

Isabella reached for the plate, and Felicity intercepted her with a bite of scrambled eggs. Turning her attention back to Charity, she offered a rueful grin. "I may have been tempted. But when I finally had a few minutes alone with Gavin—Dering—it made for a lovely evening."

"I'm so happy to hear that! What did the two of you talk about?"

The warmth from their time together still lingered. It did her heart good to finally have him back in her life. "It was a short conversation, but a poignant one. We spoke a little of memories, talked of the coming festivities, and even touched on Ian. He never met him, you know."

Charity rounded her eyes, her teacup halfway to her lips. "Really? I wasn't aware there was anyone in this country who Dering doesn't know one way or another. I once met an Austrian prince in London who had been in the country less than a week and already was looking forward to grouse hunting at his new friend Dering's northern estate."

That sounded exactly like him. He and his father had never met a stranger. Felicity hadn't been shy growing up, but she was certainly more reserved than Gavin had ever been. She shook her head, chuckling. "He's changed since the last time I saw him, but that outgoing nature is the same as always."

Lady Effington glided into the room then, her silver hair already neatly in place. "Good morning, darlings. What is it we are chatting about this morning?"

She held her hands out to Isabella, and the little girl squealed in delight. The sound made Felicity grin. She lifted the baby up, knowing how much the dowager adored holding her. As far as the two of them were concerned, they were grandmother and granddaughter, and Felicity couldn't be happier for the joy they so clearly brought each other.

Sitting down at the head of the table, Lady Effington ignored the food in favor of making faces at Isabella that made them both laugh.

"We were just discussing Lord Derington's party," Felicity said, speaking loudly enough for the older woman to hear easily.

"Oh, such a handsome young man," she said, her attention wholly on Isabella, who patted her cheeks as the older woman spoke. "And a nice young man, at that. I'm still surprised he didn't offer for you, Charity, but it's a lucky thing since obviously it wasn't meant to be."

Felicity nearly dropped her teacup. "Offer for Charity?" She turned her widened eyes to the lady in question. "Was there an expectation?"

Charity gave a dismissive little flip of her hand. "He was never truly serious. Besides, I was holding out for love while he had no such intention. I think his only real criterion for a wife is that she be of good humor."

Well. The things one learns at the breakfast table. "Is he looking for a wife, then?" Such a thing would be expected and completely normal, but for some reason it rather stunned her.

And what was this nonsense about not looking for love? Had he not proclaimed to her that he was in love once upon a time? Yes, he had later teased that it was with the barmaid at the tavern in Cambridge, but she was never certain he was being truthful. He had been so passionate at the time, but she had been so beside herself with excitement over the betrothal, she had never properly pursued it.

She frowned. Now that she thought about it, that wasn't very well done of her.

Peeling the skin from an apple slice, Charity nodded. "He is, I think. He said as much to Hugh last year, when he spoke of his intention to court me. He is to be thirty this year, after all, so I imagine he feels the need to settle the matter sooner rather than later."

Felicity made a face. "Don't remind me. He and I share a birthday, so we shall be plunging into the next decade on the same day." Even as she teased, she couldn't help but be a bit disconcerted by the revelation. Gavin, married? Impossible to picture.

"Oh yes, I forgot! Well, since you're both here, we shall have to host a joint soiree to celebrate."

"Heavens, please do no such thing. You know I hate being the center of attention." The last thing she wanted was an event in her honor. The thought of having a houseful of people there, lifting their glasses to her and expecting her to laugh and be merry—to be that vivacious girl she had once been—was enough to make her shudder.

Charity fluttered a hand as though waving away the suggestion. "Yes, of course. I wasn't thinking. Perhaps a day trip, instead? Thomas, Sophie and Evan, Radcliffe and May, Hugh and I, and whomever Dering would like to invite? I think that could be a wonderfully fun outing."

The idea wasn't half-bad. It had been so delightful to finally meet Charity's friends yesterday after hearing so much about them. Sophie was just as sweet and vivacious as she imagined, and May as witty and forthright. Felicity was definitely looking forward to spending time with them in a little more private setting.

"I think that could be lovely. There aren't too many places of interest outside of Bath, but there are some ruins about an hour away that I remember visiting as a child and thinking them very grand."

Excitement brightened Charity's whole face. "I think that sounds like great fun. Let's see, your birthday is in a fortnight. We could depart just after breakfast, and be home by dusk. Would you want Isabella to come along?"

Felicity glanced to her daughter, who was giggling as Lady Effington pressed kiss after kiss to her outstretched hands. "I would, but I think it might be a bit too much for her. Let me try some long outings to the river and Sydney Gardens first and see how she does. In fact, we may walk the waterfront on our way to visit my cousin today."

The fast clip of approaching footsteps announced the arrival of Richardson, their butler, as he strode into the room with his usual purposeful manner. "Pardon me, ladies, but we have an unexpected visitor this morning."

Felicity's younger brother popped around the corner, his pale eyes gleaming with delight. "Good morning! I hope you don't mind, but I got in late last night and didn't want to waste any time seeing my favorite sister and niece. You, too, Charity and Lady Effington. The more females, the merrier, I always say."

Happy laughter bubbled up inside her as she stood to greet him. "Thomas! I thought you weren't arriving until later this week. How did you know I was here?"

She had seen him only six months ago, but she had missed him in the interim. There was something about him that always made her feel better when she was in his presence. Despite his being six years younger than her, they had always been close.

"I joined a late-night game of cards with the stragglers at Dering's party and he let me know the good news." He swallowed her up in a great hug, squeezing her ribs until she squeaked. "I'm so damn proud of you for coming up, Lissy. Pardon my language," he added with a wink toward Lady Effington.

The older woman chuckled and shook her head. She had easily been won over by Thomas's charming nature since first meeting him at the festival last year. He might have been the most irreverent vicar ever to walk the earth—certainly night and day from Mr. Anthorp's quiet, reflective behavior—but he was so sweet at heart, it was easy to overlook.

"Do be careful, young man," the dowager chided, her voice mild despite its usual high volume. "Little ears do the most listening, especially when little mouths are learning to talk."

He dipped his chin in a nod of deference. "Right you are, my lady. Come here, little Issy," he said, plucking the baby from the dowager's arms. "Don't listen to your naughty old uncle. He does tend to loosen his tongue when he is away from his ever-vigilant and impressionable flock. I shall fully repent by day's end, I assure you."

Isabella, obviously having no clue what he was nattering on about, clapped her hands and babbled right back at him. He nodded solemnly. "Thank you, princess. Your forgiveness means the world."

Felicity smiled watching them. Though their coloring was completely different—Isabella had inherited her father's dark hair, while Thomas had pale blond hair like Felicity—she could see a bit of familial resemblance in the smile. That was the only part of her daughter that even remotely looked like Felicity. Those beautiful sky blue eyes of Isabella's were directly from her father, as were her sweet dimpled cheeks. Felicity considered it a gift that her daughter carried such visible reminders of Ian. Someday she would appreciate that.

As Thomas handed Isabella back into Lady Effington's waiting arms, he turned his attention to Charity. "Where is that husband of yours? Not still abed, I hope."

Her smile was soft as she shook her head. "No, he

decided to head to the baths this morning. The journey here was taxing, to say the least."

Felicity grimaced. Knowing how these things sometimes affected him, she should have thought to ask about him before now. "He's not feeling poorly this morning, I hope?"

Shaking her head, Charity smiled. "No, thankfully. But he figured it was best to head off any effects before they made themselves known. It's been a while since he's had an attack, and he'd like to keep it that way."

So would Felicity. It made her heart ache to think of the years he had suffered so terribly from the wounds he sustained in battle. Things were much better now, but it was understood that the pain would never leave him completely. She was so grateful that her suggestion last year for him to come to Bath for treatment had turned out so well. "Good thinking. Does he plan to attend the opening ball tonight?"

"No, definitely not. Though I'm not certain if that is in deference to his injuries or if it's that he just hates balls." Charity's lips tipped up in a fond grin as she rolled her eyes. "I'm inclined to believe the latter."

Thomas spread his arms. "Does this mean I'll have two lovely ladies on my arms tonight?"

"Oh, I think I'll skip the ball tonight," Felicity said, as she retook her seat. "Charity and her trio's concert sounds like a better way to ease into the festival. I hadn't realized Hugh wouldn't be going, so I'm glad the two of you can attend together."

Thomas reached over and stole the uneaten scone from Felicity's plate and took a bite. "Nice try," he said as he chewed. Swallowing, he added, "I've never been to a ball with you, and I am determined for us to share the experience."

She started to protest, but then stopped, tilting her head as she considered his words. It was true: They never had been to any sort of society event together. He was so much younger, and she lived so far away, it had simply never happened. Still, it would be absolutely packed tonight. Just the thought of it made her want to curl up on the sofa with a book. "There will be plenty of events that we can attend together. Once things get under way, we'll decide on something and go, just the two of us."

Charity pushed back her barely touched plate and settled back in her chair. "Why don't the three of us go together an hour after it starts, enjoy the incredible orchestra that I know will be there—truly, you don't want to miss it—then after a dance or two, or even just a game of cards, you and I can come home and leave Thomas to his own devastatingly charming devices."

Thomas flashed her a bright smile. "I knew you were one of my favorite people for a reason." Turning his attention to Felicity, he added, "A fine plan, in my very important opinion. What do you say? Shall I meet you here at eight?"

His sweet, boyish face was so pleading, Felicity caved almost at once. She adored her younger brother, and never had been very good at telling him no. Actually, with the exception of Percy and their father, no one had ever been good at telling him no. It was probably why he could be so irreverent and still be so loved by his parishioners.

"Very well, if you insist," she said, shaking her head. Before he could get too cocky, she added, "And in return, you shall escort Isabella and me to our cousins, the Potters. They are expecting us at one o'clock, so that leaves plenty of time for us to prepare for the ball."

Martha was a lovely woman, but she could easily talk a person's ear off. It was best to visit with reinforcements, if possible. Thomas wasn't the least bit perturbed. Coming to his feet, he gave a sharp salute. "It will be my pleasure. They were jolly good sports last summer when they let me stay with them for part of the festival until Father was able to rent the townhouse."

"Excellent. When is Papa planning to arrive, anyway? He made a passing reference to it in his last letter, which is one of the reasons I decided to come. I gather it won't be until July?"

Leaning forward to rest his forearms on the back of the chair he just vacated, Thomas lifted his brow. "The good earl shall descend upon us the first week of July. But that's not all, dear sister. He's asked Percy to join us as well. Any prayers you would like to send up for my patience and sanity and mindfulness of that annoying 'Thou shalt not kill' commandment would be very much appreciated."

Felicity sent him a sympathetic look. Poor Thomas. She and Percy had been neither friends nor enemies growing up, more or less just tolerating each other, but her older brother had distinctly disliked Thomas. Where Felicity was putty in his hands, Percy seemed to get annoyed by every little thing their younger brother ever did. It was exhausting, watching the two of them bicker. "I'll do my best."

"The elusive older brother," Charity mused, cupping her tea in both hands. "I've heard bits and pieces about him, but owing to the lack of visits or correspondence, I wasn't entirely sure he existed."

Thomas snorted. "Oh, he definitely exists. He'll be more than happy to demonstrate his impressive intellect and complete lack of tact for you, I'm sure."

"Thomas," Felicity said with mild reproach. "He's still our brother, and like it or not, we must be nice."

Charity stood and came around the table to pat his shoulder. "Well, if you find you would rather be nice to him from afar, I'm sure we can find room for you here if need be."

Hugh stepped into the room then, his scarred eyebrow lifted. "Remind me not to leave you alone again," he said, wry humor coloring the deadpan statement. His sandy blond hair was damp and his cheeks were flushed, but overall he looked relaxed and happy. "I'm sure Thomas can fend for himself."

Charity lit up at the sight of her husband, and she went to his side and gave him a quick kiss on the lips. "Now, now. He didn't leave you to fend for yourself when you needed help, and I won't do so to him. Without him, I may very well have had a different future without my husband."

"I would have come to my senses sooner or later," the baron grumbled. Still, he offered an easy smile to Thomas. "However, you do know that you are always welcome. In moderation," he added with a completely straight face.

Giving a little mock salute, Thomas said, "And with that, I shall be on my way. Shall I meet you here or at the Potters' house, Felicity?"

With the lovely sunshine beckoning outside, her initial idea of walking with Bella by the river still sounded lovely. As reluctant as she had initially been to come, she was anxious to share this city with her daughter. "I'll meet you there at one."

* * *

Mornings were never, nor had they ever been, Dering's favorite time of day. It was nearly eleven o'clock, and still his eyes were gritty and his head fuzzy despite his having been awake for hours. It had always been his curse: He couldn't bear to go to bed when there were parties to attend and card games to join, but no matter how late he returned, his body would never let him sleep in. He always thought it had something to do with the quiet. Too many unwanted thoughts and undesired dreams came with the night.

Yawning hugely, Dering stepped out onto the pavement outside his townhouse and surveyed his surroundings. The weather was typical enough, with more clouds than sunshine in the sky and a soft warm breeze blowing from the west. But nothing else about the morning was typical. It was exceedingly clear that the city was on the cusp of a huge celebration.

Carriages, horses, carts, and wagons all jockeyed for position in the teeming streets. Pedestrians filled the pavement, some hurrying to their destinations while others strolled, taking in the sights. Banners were strung over the street while hanging flower baskets lined nearly every available foot of the black wrought iron fences bordering the pavement.

Despite the lingering effects of the previous night, a smile tilted up the corners of his mouth. In a matter of days, the entire town had come to life. The whole place was as shiny as a new halfpenny, and he loved it.

Once the ball opened the festival tonight, things would grow even more frenzied. He could hardly wait. Plunging into the hubbub, he headed off toward Sally Lunn's for a late-morning bun, his favorite of all Bath's delicacies.

By the time he reached the shop, he had greeted and

chatted with no fewer than a dozen acquaintances. Having been roused from his groggy state by both the exercise and conversation, he was feeling considerably better. The place was beyond busy, and the line extended nearly to the door.

Mrs. Langley, who was filling orders with efficient ease, looked up to see him and grinned. "Morning, Lord Derington."

He lifted a hand in greeting at the same time a woman two places up turned. Much to his surprise, he found himself looking straight into Felicity's welcoming gaze.

"Dering," she exclaimed, all smiles. "How lovely to see you this morning. Although I don't suppose I should be surprised."

She stepped aside and let the gentleman between them switch places with her. Her pale purple gown was very pretty, with cheery sprigs of lavender printed across the bodice. *Not* that he was looking at her bodice. Studiously meeting her eyes, he grinned. "See? Did I not tell you we were bound to see each other frequently? And no, never be surprised by my love of a proper bun."

She rubbed her hands together, her expression bordering on gleeful. "I'm so excited. It's been years since I've had a decent bun. Mrs. Kew, the best baker in Cadgwith, bakes some wonderful breads, but the tender delicacy of a bun truly escapes her."

"A travesty. As for me, I may or may not have attempted to bribe Mrs. Langley to share the recipe with my cook, so I could partake when I'm at our other estates, but she steadfastly refused."

"You mean to tell me that she somehow withstood the patented Gavin Stark charm *and* wealth? She must have the fortitude of a granite statue."

He chose to take the comment as a compliment. "I know. I'd be impressed if I weren't so blasted annoyed."

Laughing softly, Felicity shook her head. "It does a man good not to get everything he wants. Builds character, I'm sure."

If that was the case, then most of his character building had occurred a decade ago. These days, he made a point of pursuing the things he wanted. Oddly enough, he had her to thank for that. "I'm pleased with my current level of character. Thank you. Although I wonder: If being denied what he wants builds character for a man, what builds character for a woman?"

She spread her arms. "Women are born with character. And I am well aware that I have neatly backed you into a corner. You must agree, or risk appearing ungentlemanly."

Chuckling, he nodded. "Very well. I will stifle any urge to disagree."

It was their turn at the counter, and Dering gestured to the offered selection. "What would you like? Plain or cinnamon raisin? I shall very generously, with my copious charm and wealth, treat you to your roll."

"One of each, actually. And I can't let you do that, Dering, though you are a dear to offer. This is to be my treat for my daughter."

The statement shouldn't have startled him as much as it did. He knew she had a child. He knew the girl was here, but he certainly had never thought of her in the flesh. "You must be the one with the granite fortitude if you can make it all the way home without partaking in the treat."

Her smile was so sweet, so maternal, it made his lungs hurt as he struggled to breathe normally. "She's across the way in the waterfront park with her nursemaid. She fell asleep, and I thought it would be a fun treat for when she wakes up." Felicity paused in order to complete the transaction, then turned back to face him with her paper-wrapped buns in hand. "Won't you come meet her?"

Something inside of him rebelled at the idea. It didn't make any sense—and he sure as hell didn't want to analyze the instinct—but he didn't want to think of her as a mother. "Three of your plain, please," he said to Mrs. Langley before offering a brisk smile to Felicity. "Bad timing, I'm afraid. I was just indulging a craving before an appointment. Will I see you at the ball tonight?"

The enthusiasm and joy of only moments ago visibly dimmed as she gave a small nod. "Oh. Yes, I'll be at the ball, but only for a moment. Charity and Thomas insisted I come. The compromise is that I don't have to stay long."

"Long enough for a dance?"

The thought of holding her in his arms for their very first dance had his blood racing. Would she be as graceful as he imagined? He prided himself on being an exceptional dancer, something that initially surprised people because of his size. Oddly enough, it had been boxing that helped teach him to be light on his feet and to move with fluidity. He liked the idea of surprising her with a grace that had been wholly absent in his youth. Much more than he should.

She lifted a shoulder as she headed for the door. "I don't dance anymore. However, it may be long enough for a card game. Good day, Dering. Enjoy your treat."

Doesn't dance? Disappointment leached the tension from his shoulders as he watched her step outside onto the pavement.

"Lord Derington?" Mrs. Langley held out his purchase.

Smiling distractedly, he paid her and made his way to the door. Felicity was just slipping out of sight, headed toward the waterfront. As far as he was concerned, she had issued a challenge. A woman like her, so young and lovely but with a sadness that existed just below the surface, needed to dance. She needed to experience a few moments of joy, of *fun*, and simply allow herself to be swept away.

The pain that he'd glimpse last night certainly wasn't going to be cured with a dance. But if he could give her a handful of minutes in which she could lose herself, then that would be a win.

Nodding resolutely, he started back toward his house. Tonight, so help him, he would get her to dance.

Chapter Four

Eyeing the packed ballroom, Felicity was half-impressed, half-intimidated by the grandness of the scene before her. She'd been to the Assembly Rooms several times in the past, and had even danced in the handsome Ball Room a time or two, but she had never seen the space quite like this before.

Overhead, the famous crystal chandeliers glittered with reflected candlelight, throwing both light and little rainbow prisms to every corner of the huge space. Flowers were everywhere: hung from the chandeliers, draped from the balcony railing, and cascading from overflowing baskets lining the deep windowsills above. It was truly gorgeous.

The orchestra was already playing, and the light and lively music filled the entire building, somehow managing to rise above the noise of the crowd as they laughed and greeted one another. In a word, it was loud. Exceedingly so. For many, it was surely a feast for the senses, but to Felicity, it was close to overwhelming.

Charity seemed delighted as she bobbed her head in time with the music, searching the crowd for the duchess and countess. She looked stunning tonight, in a spectacular Eton blue gown that complemented her hair and made her eyes seem more blue than gray. The cut of the gown accentuated her delicate, slender build, making her appear almost ethereal.

Looking down at her own gown, Felicity sighed. She had had two choices: Wear her proper ball gown, which was almost four years old, or wear a more current fashion that was not quite formal enough. She had gone with the latter, wearing a pretty but somewhat plain lavender gown. She'd added her mother's diamond-and-amethyst necklace and hair combs, and Lady Effington had contributed a lovely pair of satin gloves along with her amethyst bracelets, but Felicity still couldn't help but feel out of place among the exquisitely dressed attendees.

Thomas, looking so very dapper in his navy blue jacket and smart, buff-colored breeches, rubbed his hands together and grinned. "Are we going to linger in the doorway, or shall we go enjoy the celebration?"

Patting his arm, Felicity said, "You are more than welcome to go join in the fun. I think I will go see about some refreshments."

Charity abandoned her search and turned worried eyes Felicity's way. "Is it too much? We can go find a quiet corner in the Tea Room and chat until you feel more comfortable."

It was sweet of her to offer, but Felicity didn't want to impede her friend's enjoyment of the ball tonight. "No, but thank you. I'd feel better if the two of you enjoy the music while I go help myself to something to drink. And look," she added, spotting the Duchess of Radcliffe's tall, willowy frame through a break in the crowd, "I do believe that's May, right over by the door to The Octagon."

Charity glanced toward her friend, then back at Felicity, clearly torn. "Come join us."

Shaking her head, Felicity said, "I'm more than capable of seeing to myself. You know very well how self-sufficient I am."

As much as she loved living with Hugh and Charity, she was a private person. The vast size of the house made it possible to still maintain plenty of independence, and she relished the peace that came with it.

"Of course, you are right. Well, if you change your mind, please do come join us. I know the others would be thrilled to see you again."

Nodding, Felicity turned and made her way toward the Tea Room at the other side of the building. She had to admit, the music really was superb. It had been years since she'd heard a proper orchestra, and she found herself humming along as she wove her way through the crowd.

"Lady Felicity?" An older woman with silver-threaded hair and kind green eyes smiled at her with a bit of hesitance. She wore a lovely pale gray gown with a silver overskirt that shimmered in the candlelight.

"Mrs. Overton," Felicity said at once, remembering her from her many visits with Felicity's mother when she was alive. "How do you do?" She hadn't seen the woman in years, but she had always been a very kind person.

"Very well, thank you. I hope that you are. I heard of your sad news, and wished to convey my condolences." She glanced around, looking a little unsure. "Probably not the most appropriate time for me to say so."

She had a gentle way about her that made Felicity feel more at ease than she normally was when people offered their sympathy. "Thank you. I appreciate the sentiment."

"Well, those of us who have been through such a loss

know that it is present no matter where one goes. I am glad to see you joining in the festivities, however."

Her heart tugged at the sadness that tinged the other woman's voice. It was hard to detect, but as one who knew what buried pain felt like, Felicity recognized it in others. "My apologies. I hadn't realized you were widowed as well."

When Felicity's mother died twelve years ago, many of her friends had drifted away as well. Papa wasn't interested in maintaining relationships for sentimentality's sake. Though he was a good man and dutifully fulfilled his social requirements, he wasn't one to host gatherings or invite guests over for parlor games. And by then, Felicity had been nearly grown, anyhow, so his goal was to see her married. He was blessedly indulgent, thankfully, with the young baron from an obscure village who had captured his daughter's heart. Although she had long suspected that he was relieved to be spared the hassle of the marriage mart in London.

Mrs. Overton nodded, her gaze briefly dropping to her hands. "My husband passed a little over three years ago. He was quite a bit older than me, but somehow it was still a shock." Looking up, she smiled brightly and said, "But let us talk of better things. I hear you have a daughter?"

They linked arms and strolled toward the Tea Room, chatting of Isabella and of Mrs. Overton's four grandchildren, all of whom were under the age of five. Though the rooms were still just as crowded and noisy as when she had arrived, Felicity gradually relaxed and began to enjoy herself a bit. Her mother's old friend was a calming presence, as well as an exceptionally pleasant companion.

When Felicity laughed at her description of her grandson's first pony ride, Mrs. Overton tilted her head and smiled. "You reminded me so much of your mother just now. Did you know that you have the same laugh?"

Did she? Pleasure at the comment warmed Felicity's heart as she shook her head. "I didn't. Although I remember hers quite clearly. It was one of my favorite things in the world."

"Well, you should laugh more often. It will be like she is right there with you."

She grinned, loving the thought. "Perhaps I will. I think I need a bit more laughter in my life, anyway. Part of the reason I decided to come here this summer is because I realized I was allowing myself to become too cloistered. I absolutely love living in Cadgwith, and it is very important to me that Isabella is raised in the place where her father was known and loved, but she needs to know my family as well, and the place where I was raised."

After Felicity married, her father had sold the house he had bought as a wedding gift to his bride. Mama was from Bath, and had dearly wished to maintain close ties to her family. Though Felicity no longer had a place to call home here, she still considered Somerset to be her hometown. The people here, both family and friends, were part of who she was.

As she lifted her teacup to her lips, she spotted Gavin walking through the crowd. He was easily visible, thanks to his height. She couldn't help but smile a bit. If nothing else, she was glad to have been able to see him again on this trip. He brought out a bit of the old Felicity, and though she would never be that person again—wasn't even sure she wanted to be, in fact—it was nice to have that connection to the past.

"Recognize someone?" Mrs. Overton's brows lifted as she followed Felicity's gaze.

"Only Lord Derington," she said, setting down her cup. "Do you know him?"

Chuckling, the older woman nodded. "But of course. I don't know anyone who doesn't know the Starks, the viscount included." She tilted her head, a fond smile lifting her lips. "Your mother was convinced the two of you would marry."

Felicity was very glad she had just set down her fragile teacup. Gaping at her mother's old friend, she said, "I beg your pardon?"

Her parents had been much more lenient than most when it came to her friendship with Gavin. Of course, they hadn't really known the half of it. With her mother's illness, they had had other things to worry about. Between Percy's frequent presence, their meeting up in the woods between their estates, and even the times she snuck out at night, Felicity had been able to downplay the closeness of their relationship.

Or so she had thought.

"Charlotte was sure that the two of you would be a wonderful match. Your father had wanted to reach out to Carlisle for a betrothal agreement, but she was determined that the decision would not be made for you."

Her mother had championed her? How had she not known that? Her parents' marriage had been arranged practically from birth, and they'd not only liked, but deeply respected each other. Now Felicity wondered. Did her mother wish she had found love in her life? *Had* she found love and been unable to act on it?

"I had no idea," Felicity murmured, her gaze sliding back to Gavin. Her mother had thought them a good match? It was such a foreign thought, she barely managed not to make a face. But he was *Gavin*. Things had never been like that between them. He was a great friend back then, and she was happy to still call him one now.

Turning her attention back to Mrs. Overton, she said, "I'm so grateful to her for not allowing someone else to make the decision for me, because I was fortunate enough to have found a true love match. It's a shame she never met my husband." It was something she had thought frequently over the years, but she'd had no idea how much she actually owed her mother.

The older woman patted her hand. "I remember your young man quite well from the wedding. He was very handsome, and you were so smitten with him. I'm glad you had him for the time that you did."

"Me, too," she said quietly, meaning it with all her heart. Whatever she had been through since his death, she wouldn't have traded their life together for anything on earth.

When she glanced up, she happened to meet Gavin's gaze at the exact time he looked toward her. A huge smile stretched his lips as he quickly dismissed the man he was talking to and started toward her. His dark brown jacket and bone-colored breeches looked very well with his dark hair and eyes. Striking, in fact.

"Mrs. Overton, what a delight to see you again. You are looking beautiful as ever."

The older woman's cheeks flushed with pleasure as she shook her head. "You flatter me, Lord Derington. I was just about to take my leave. Won't you keep Lady Felicity company?"

He dipped his head solemnly. "You may count on me, madam. The question is, will you have me, Lady Felicity?" He turned mischievous eyes her way, clearly playing with her.

Mrs. Overton's words suddenly popped back into her mind. Had her mother really thought they were suited? For some reason, the thought made her cheeks warm, and she quickly nodded to try to hide the reaction. "Yes, of course," she said brightly, coming to her feet. "Dering and I are dear friends, after all. Thank you, Mrs. Overton, for such delightful conversation. I do hope to see you again soon."

She smiled, sincerity softening her eyes. "Nothing would please me more. Good evening to you both."

As she walked away, Felicity turned her full attention to Gavin. "What a lovely conversation that was. I can't believe I never thought to visit any of my mother's old friends."

"She is a fine lady, to be sure. She and my mother are still friends, though they don't visit as much as they once did. After her husband died, she spent several years outside of society. I'm glad to see her here."

Shifting his position so he could look around, he said, "Speaking of rejoining society, what would you say to setting aside your reservations and having a dance with your oldest, dearest, and most handsome friend?"

The last part of his sentence made her laugh, even as she shook her head. "That was an admirable try, but no thank you. I will, however, play a game of piquet with you if we can find a table in the Card Room."

"I know enough people in the right places that there's always a table for me." He crossed his arms and angled his head, considering her. "I'll make you a deal. I'll play a game with you, but only if you'll dance with me."

"Aren't we tenacious. But the answer is still no."

"All right. Then we'll play for it. If I win, you'll dance with me."

Why was he so fixated on getting her to dance? It wasn't as though they ever had before. Still, he'd chosen his terms cleverly. He knew full well that she loved a game with real stakes. Especially since she had so often trounced him at the card table. She pursed her lips. "And if I win?"

He spread his arms. "Whatever the lady wants."

"Fine," she said, lifting a challenging brow. "If I win, no more asking me to dance."

His nose wrinkled in displeasure. "You'll only be hurting yourself. I merely want for you to forget the world for a moment and have a little fun. Would that be so bad?"

He certainly knew how to take her off guard. He made it sound as though she were some closeted old matron who needed a knight in shining armor to rescue her from her dotage. She had fun. Plenty of it. Well, enough of it not to feel as though she was missing out. Dancing simply no longer held interest for her.

"Thank you for the thought, but you are making a bigger issue of it than it needs to be. There are plenty of other ways to enjoy oneself."

The smile he gave her was pure wickedness. "Don't I know it."

"Gavin," she exclaimed, rounding her eyes in admonishment. Pausing to look around, she lowered her voice. "I won't have you teasing me like that, you fiend."

It was impossible to stifle his laugh. Her cheeks had gone bright pink in a way that made him want to know *exactly* what she was thinking. It was a bit of teasing straight out of their past. Well, a bit more risqué than anything he'd said back then, but she had the freedom to interpret any way she chose, and she obviously went to the wicked.

"What? I was merely agreeing that there are many ways to enjoy oneself. What exactly did you think I meant?" He blinked with feigned innocence, welcoming her to say exactly where her mind had gone.

She leveled a patently disbelieving gaze up at him. "I know what you meant," she said, not in the least bit fooled. "Now then, do you want to play or not? I certainly haven't got all day."

There was the Lissy he remembered so well. He loved when she left the polite, distant Lady Felicity behind and gave him glimpses of his old friend. Holding out his arm, he gave a single nod. "I do. I just hope you are prepared to lose. And by *lose*, I mean win, because I know you'll be happy if you simply allow yourself to relax for a moment."

She slipped her fingers onto his arm. "I am quite relaxed, thank you. In fact, I am looking forward to trouncing you. There are few things more *enjoyable* than that," she said, emphasizing the word purely to vex him, he was sure, "and it's been an age since we've played."

"Yes, it has," he agreed, placing his hand over hers as he picked his way through the crowd. His heart had kicked up the moment her hand had touched his sleeve, and it was all he could do not to press her fingers more firmly to him. It was intoxicating, having her on his arm like this. He couldn't help but think of the way he had craved contact between them when they were younger. Every fiber of his being had hungered for a single touch, a brush of her skin against his, even the whoosh of her skirts brushing his leg.

God, but he had been such a fool for her back then.

If only he could have seen the self-possessed, bold man he would become. If he could have had even an ounce of the confidence he boasted now, he would have taken her by the hand, pulled her ever so slowly to him, and captured those beautiful lips of hers with his own.

Even now, a decade later, the thought made his mouth go dry.

What would it be like to kiss her? They were both so different from the way they used to be, but she was still his Felicity. In the time between her unknowing rejection and now, if there was a woman he wanted, he pursued her. He'd yet to encounter a woman he was attracted to who hadn't responded favorably to his advances.

It could certainly happen, but he'd been fortunate so far. More to the point, even if a woman wasn't interested, at least he had made his intentions known. Felicity was the one and only woman in his life he'd ever wanted who hadn't wanted him back.

Drawing a long breath, he set aside that particular thought. He didn't want to think about things he couldn't have with her. What he could have was an enjoyable evening of cards and, with any luck, a real dance with her. Raising a hand to the Card Room attendant, he gave a quick nod. The man instantly recognized him and sprang forward to help.

In a few moments, they were seated in a small table in the back corner, a deck of cards between them. Taking a deep breath, he pushed away the noise and activity around them and focused on the task at hand. There was only one acceptable outcome for the game, and he intended to have it.

Gesturing to the cards, he said, "Ladies first." The real fun was about to begin.

Chapter Five

"You can't be serious!"

Felicity scowled down at his cards, looked back at hers, and groaned. "How on earth did you have that hand? The odds are ridiculous."

Blast it all, how had he done that? She'd never seen anyone get all twelve tricks like that. She had been leading with eighty points to his fifty, but in one fell swoop, he'd gotten a capot, and the resulting sixty points had won the whole blasted game.

He sat back in his chair, triumph written all over his face. "It must be my lucky night. And it must be *your* lucky night, since now you have the marvelous opportunity to dance with me."

Leaning forward, he lifted one side of his mouth in a smug grin. "You do realize you could have just told me you wished to dance after all. You needn't have let me win."

Now he was just trying to get a reaction out of her. She crossed her arms in a very unladylike manner, refusing to rise to his bait. "No one likes an arrogant winner."

He waggled his eyebrows. "Better than a sore loser."

She wrinkled her nose at his taunting, but came to her feet anyway. No matter how much it pained her—and, heavens, did it pain her—he had won fairly. "I'm a terrible loser, as you well know, and an even worse winner. It's a wonder you decided to play with me at all, after the watch fob incident."

"Aha! You do remember that. Whatever happened to that, anyhow? I still lament the loss of that thing."

It was actually tucked in her jewelry box at home. She had been devastated when he first left for Cambridge, knowing that he was truly leaving her behind. It shouldn't have been worse than his going to Eton, but it certainly was. University was only one step away from a man leaving his family behind for good. When he lost the watch to her in one of their last games, she had squirreled it away like a little magpie. It had felt like having a part of him with her meant that he would always come back.

She waved a hand airily, not quite willing to share that particular truth with him. "I'm sure it's around somewhere."

He made a face as he came to his feet. "Heartless wench. You're fortunate I like you far too well to allow you out of our bet." He extended a hand, obviously more than a little pleased with himself. "Shall we dance?"

The true significance of the win sank in then, and she swallowed, pushing against the first hints of panic. She had made the bet. She had absolutely no one to blame but herself. She thought of the last time she had danced, and the dread settled that much more heavily in her stomach. Damn it all, why had she agreed to this?

But it was too late now. A bet was a bet, and she had as good as given her word. Drawing in a long, deep breath that did nothing to ease her dismay, she nodded.

* * *

Winning had never been so sweet. Dering stood there, heart racing, waiting for her to slip her hand into his. He had never been so glad in his life for his connections than he was at that moment: The conductor was an acquaintance of his.

One who would gladly play the waltz Dering planned to request of him. He hadn't waited half his life for a dance to have it be a reel or quadrille. This was to be a dance with the two of them, and no one else.

With no small reluctance, Felicity plopped her hand in his. She allowed him to lead her across the crowded room and through the door into The Octagon, though she might as well have been a prisoner heading to the gallows. He almost chuckled. She always had been a rather sore loser. When they reached the foot of the stairs that led to the orchestra's alcove, he held up a finger. "One moment, please."

Dashing upstairs, he skirted around the musicians' seats to where Mr. Basildon stood, competently leading the group. His baton swished this way and that as he coaxed them louder before gently pulling them back to softness. His timing was impeccable, as metered as a metronome.

Not wanting to throw him off, Dering stood off to the side, waiting to be noticed. It took longer than he expected. After two minutes, Basildon signaled the end of the song with a dramatic inward swoop of both arms. Applause rose from the ballroom below, an interesting occurrence for a ball, but this was as much a concert as a dance.

After taking a quick bow at the balustrade, the conductor turned and blew out a breath. "Lord Derington," he said, sending a fleeting smile his way before taking a gulp of his drink. "What brings you into my domain, good sir?"

Spreading his arms, Dering said, "What else but a woman, my friend?"

Basildon laughed as he swiped a small towel over his bald head. The heat up here was oppressive compared to below, and it was fairly warm down there. "I should have known. I'm guessing a waltz should be next?"

"The longest one you know."

He shuffled through his sheet music for a few seconds until he found the one he wanted and held it up. "Change of plans," he said to the orchestra before him. "The good viscount wants a waltz, so a waltz he shall have."

Grinning, Dering placed a handful of coins on the man's music stand—excessively generous by anyone's measure. "You have my gratitude, sir. Just give me a minute to make my way to the Ball Room."

Dipping his head in a brief bow, he said, "As you wish, my lord. Your patronage is, as always, greatly appreciated."

As Dering descended the stairs, he rubbed his hands together in anticipation. After all these years, he would finally have the chance to hold her in his arms. He was determined to make it a dance that Felicity wouldn't soon forget. He could hardly wait to see the evidence in her lovely eyes of the joy that he was certain it would bring her. With any luck, she wouldn't be saying *I don't dance* again for a very long time.

His allowed his gaze to settle on her as he made his way down. She stood just where he had left her, with one hand on the banister and the other one pressed to her middle. With her corn silk hair piled in a mass of curls at the top of her head, he had a lovely view of the back of her neck. It was long and slender, and elegantly accentuated by the sparkling gemstones draped across it. He had an unexpected vision of pressing a kiss to the pale skin at her nape, and a surge of desire flooded him at the thought.

When she turned her head, he caught a glimpse of her expression and slowed. All teasing and good humor seemed to have fled. *What the devil?* Her mouth was pressed together in a firm line, and her fine features were tense with unease.

It certainly wasn't the look of a woman simply displeased with having lost a bet. He knew that particular look well. Was the thought of dancing with him really that abhorrent? It was such a small thing. It was supposed to lighten her up a little, not distress her.

When she saw him, she lifted her chin and offered up a swift smile, but there was no sincerity in it. "There you are," she said, her voice strangely even. "I was beginning to wonder if you were coming back."

His didn't smile back as he approached her. "Is everything all right? Other than the ignominy of losing to me, I mean."

With so many people around, it didn't seem the proper place to have this conversation, but there wasn't anyplace he could think of that would offer more privacy.

The forced smile faded as she gave a small shrug. "I shouldn't have agreed to the bet. But that's my fault, not yours. You won, and it is your right to collect your spoils."

Her response didn't do a thing to ease the feeling that something was genuinely wrong. He knew the orchestra would be starting the waltz any moment, but this didn't feel right. Crossing his arms, he said lightly, "I've never forced a woman to dance with me yet, and I'm not sure I wish to start now."

She pressed her eyes closed for a moment, and when she looked back at him, the shimmer of tears glazed her eyes. His stomach dropped at the sight. What had he done to cause such a reaction?

Giving her head a small shake, she said, "I'm sorry. I'm being silly, ridiculous even, but . . ."

As she trailed off, searching for words, Basildon's voice rang out from his alcove as he announced the waltz. A flurry of activity followed as the dancers rushed to adjust to the change.

Dering stepped closer to her and waited until she met his gaze. "Tell me what's wrong. Perhaps I can decide whether you are being ridiculous or not."

Her eyes were as clear and bright as well-aged brandy, but the distress in them made his chest tighten. "It's just that the last man I danced with was my husband. It's hard to let that go."

Her words were like a kick in the stomach. *Bloody hell.* Blowing out a breath, Dering held out his arm. "Come with me."

Hesitantly, she wrapped her hand around the crook of his elbow. Damn it all, he'd never intended to upset her. He had only wanted to bring her a little excitement and joy. And some for him, as well. He had assumed she didn't want to dance because she didn't want to allow herself the chance to feel young and free again. He understood that being a widow must be difficult, and thought that she needed someone to give her permission to enjoy life again.

But clearly things weren't as simple as that.

Taking the lead, he guided her through the people packed into the main corridor. He kept his gaze straight ahead and his stride purposeful so that no one would attempt to waylay them, and successfully led them straight out the front doors into the warm night beyond.

There were considerably less people in the courtyard. Darkness had finally won out over the late-summer evening, with a handful of tiny stars just visible through the low light of the city.

He turned to face Felicity, who watched him with widened eyes. Was she really so surprised that he wouldn't force her to dance? Sighing, he dragged a hand over his hair. "You needn't look so astonished. I'm not going to trample the memory of your husband by forcing you to dance with me. It was a stupid bet, and can be undone easily enough."

The look she gave him made his heart ache. It was an uncomfortable mix of sorrow and gratitude, reminding him of just how recently her husband had died. To him, a year and a half seemed ages ago, but to her, it was obviously still fresh.

"I feel like such a fool," she said, her voice quiet in the night. Soft strains of the waltz carried from the hall, providing an ironic backdrop for their conversation. "I should never have allowed my competitive nature to get the best of me, and I certainly shouldn't have done anything to make you feel bad. You didn't do anything wrong."

He gave a soft snort. "Other than pushing the issue in the first place?"

Her lips curled up in a hint of a smile. "Other than that. You were just being a friend. I know you want me to be more like my old self, to simply break out of this melancholy that still has a hold on me, but it's just not that easy."

Rubbing a hand over the back of his neck, he nodded. "I know. And I'm sorry. I do hope you can forgive me for being such an insensitive lout."

"Only if you can forgive me for not honoring our bet." She nibbled at her lip for a moment, thinking. "What else can be your prize?"

He waved a dismissive hand. "No prize necessary. I was able to play cards with you again, and that is reward enough." Lifting an eyebrow with mock severity, he said, "Let this be your lesson to never risk that which you aren't willing to lose." Apparently that was a lesson that everyone had to learn for themselves.

"Lesson learned, I assure you. However, I'm afraid I must insist on a forfeit of some sort. I may be a sore loser, but I am a fair one. What else would suit your fancy?"

It felt like a loaded question. But now that the dancing request had turned into such a disaster, he was slow to want to suggest anything that might be touchy for her. Which left . . . what? Strolls through the park? A night at the opera? He couldn't seem to think of a single thing that would serve as a decent stake. Whatever it was, he didn't want it to bring forth any memories of her lost husband.

Tilting his head back, he stared at the meager starlight above them. Blinking with inspiration, he grinned and glanced back at Felicity. "How daring are you willing to be?"

Her eyes narrowed as she eyed him with a hint of caution. "I'm not sure. What do you have in mind?"

"Go tell Charity and Thomas that I'm leaving early and have offered to take you home. I'll have the carriage brought round in the meantime."

She stared at him as though he had quite lost his mind. "You are aware that though I may not be a debutante, there are still rules for acceptable behavior, yes?"

He rolled his eyes. "I'm not taking you to Gretna Green, for heaven's sake. Have a little faith in me, please?"

For a moment, she didn't say anything. He could practically see the wheels turning as she thought through his odd request and decided whether or not she was willing to go along with it. Just when he was sure that she was going to decline, she gave a quick bob of her head. "Very well. I'll be back in a moment."

Blowing out his pent-up breath, he grinned and nodded. "I'll be waiting."

Chapter Six

Hands pressed to her mouth, Felicity shook her head in wonder at the sight in front of her. "I can't believe it! It looks exactly the same."

Gavin leaned against one of the elegant pillars, his mouth tipped up in an indulgent smile. "Stone does tend to weather well," he quipped, earning an eye roll from her.

His father's Somerset estate was less than four miles from the outskirts of Bath, but they might as well have been a hundred miles away. None of the city's lights or sounds polluted this place. It was quiet, save for the frogs chirping by the lake a hundred paces down the hill, and the only light came from the three-quarter moon that still hung low in the sky.

This was the meeting place of their youth. The folly was a ridiculous little building with no real purpose other than to decorate the landscape. It didn't even have a roof, which made it worthless in both sunshine and rain. But the one thing it was wonderful for was stargazing.

How many nights had they lain on their backs on the mosaic floor, staring up at the dawning stars and marveling at the changeable nature of the moon? This spot was less than a half mile from her old house, and only three-quarters of a mile from Gavin's house—one of many that his father owned. Back then, she could have walked the path blindfolded.

She smiled, wrapping her hands around her waist and breathing in the smell of the dewy country air. It was nothing like the salty air back in Cadgwith, but it was equally as sweet. "It doesn't just look the same; it *feels* the same. I feel as though I've stepped back in time a dozen years or so. If your silhouette were a little less bulky, I could believe it."

"*Bulky?*" He pushed away from the pillar and waved a hand down his frame. "I'll have you know that this is lean, hard-earned muscle, my friend."

She laughed at his affront, shaking her head. "*Bulky* is not a synonym for *fat*, for pity's sake. I'm well aware that you are in exceptionally fine shape." One look at the man was all it took to know he worked hard for his physique. He always had been fond of physical activity. She suspected it was something he could accomplish that had nothing to do with his family's wealth or status.

"Exceptionally fine, you say? I do like the sound of that." He gave a waggle of his eyebrows that was obviously meant to make her laugh. "For what it is worth, I know what you mean about it feeling the same here. The house has changed quite a bit thanks to my mother's love of renovation and redecorating, but this place is of little interest to anyone but the groundskeeper. Believe it or not, I haven't been out here in years myself."

"I thought that might be the case, seeing how you have your own townhome in the city now. Between that and your other houses, I doubt you have much reason to come here."

"So many places to be, so little time," he said with a little half grin. "My parents and at least one of my brothers will arrive early next week. Mother wanted to give the city a chance to 'get itself sorted out' before coming to visit."

"I'm so glad! I saw your parents a few years ago, but your brothers are as elusive as you are." The second-oldest, Eric, had been sickly as a child and had rarely left the house, and the other two were young enough that they were still in the nursery when Gavin and Felicity were teenagers. She saw them so infrequently growing up, it had never occurred to her to keep up with them as adults.

"I'm sure they will all be delighted to see you." His voice was soft but deep, like a velvety dark chocolate mousse. "Just as I have been. Now then, shall we take our positions?"

She nodded, and he unfurled the blanket he had taken from the carriage. Positioning it in the center of the circular structure, he waved her over. "My lady," he murmured, holding out his hand.

The absurdity of the moment almost made her laugh. There he was in his finest evening attire while she wore her diamonds and satin gloves, the both of them about to sprawl on the ground like children.

He cocked his head. "What's so amusing?"

"I was merely thinking that we are a tad overdressed for the occasion."

Looking down, he gave a little chuckle. "Quite a step up from what we used to wear." He shrugged out of the tight-fitting jacket and swung his arms a bit. "Much better."

On a whim, she pulled off her gloves, taking care not to disturb Lady Effington's borrowed bracelets. The night air seemed almost cool against her bare arms.

"Oh, that feels heavenly. Gloves are the most ridiculous of accessories in this sort of warmth."

"Not half so ridiculous as a cravat styled in the latest fashion. Why ever would one want to have full mobility of one's head and neck, anyway?"

Felicity grinned as he pulled at the offending piece of clothing. "Oh, you think *that's* restrictive? You can't imagine the discomfort of these blasted stays. They surely were invented by a man who has no particular like or regard for women."

Gavin let out a crack of surprised laughter. "I cannot believe you just mentioned your unmentionables to me."

The heat of a blush swamped her cheeks. What had possessed her to say such a thing? Thank goodness for the darkness. "We are both adults," she said matter-of-factly, as though she went around discussing her underthings on a regular basis. She couldn't even claim the influence of drink, since she had had nothing but a glass of sherry during their card game well over an hour earlier.

"If you say so," he replied, obviously still amused. "Now, shall we do a little stargazing, or would you rather tell me about your chemise while you're at it?"

Forget the darkness—her cheeks were probably glowing with the heat of her blush now. Nodding primly, she held out her hand for him to help her down. When his fingers met hers, it was with the shocking reminder that she'd divested herself of her gloves, and so, apparently, had he. His hand was warm and slightly callused, scraping against the smooth skin of her own palm. She shivered at the sensation.

He lowered her gently, with all the care he might have afforded a priceless piece of porcelain. Once she was settled, he lay down beside her, leaving only a few inches between their arms.

This time when she breathed in, the whisper-light scent of his shaving soap flavored the air. She smiled as she stared up at the sky. Despite the scattered clouds, the heavens were readily visibly in the inky darkness. "Lovely," she breathed, almost light-headed with the pleasure of the moment. In her mind, this was the very definition of comfort and happiness.

It was impossible to think of a place she would rather be than right there at Gavin's side, gazing up at the stars. "Ready?" she asked, her gaze already searching the heavens. They were fortunate that the breeze had blown away the last of the clouds that afternoon.

"Mmhmm," he murmured, the sound little more than a soft rumble in his chest.

Raising her arm, she pointed to the first constellation that stood out to her. "Corona Borealis."

Gavin lifted his hand and slid it back and forth a few times before coming to a stop. "Libra."

Groaning, she pushed his arm several degrees to the west. "That's Libra." Pointing to the zigzag-shaped one above it, she said, "Serpens."

"North Star," he said confidently.

"Not a constellation, but I'll accept." Making her next selection, she pointed. "Delphinus."

"Scorpio," he said, indicating a cluster of stars to the west.

"You mean Virgo," she said, with a roll of her eyes. "Be serious."

"What? They're both astrological signs. That's close enough."

Wrinkling her nose, she said, "That's like saying a

guppy is interchangeable with a shark because they're both fish. Now come on, concentrate."

"Yes, ma'am," he replied, suppressed laughter in the words.

"All right, then. Let's see." She trailed off as she flicked her gaze around the inky expanse above them. When she saw the little cluster of stars to the east of Corona Borealis, she grinned. "Hercules."

"Right here," Gavin quipped, earning a light smack on his shoulder from her.

"You are incorrigible," she said, but any sternness was lost to her mirth.

"What? I assumed you were addressing me. It is what they call me at the boxing saloon, after all."

"What, was Samson taken?" Even as she teased, she really wasn't surprised at the moniker. He must be rather intimidating to his opponents. She briefly wondered if he ever lost a match, but decided not to pursue the question. Picturing him bare-chested in the ring didn't seem like a prudent thing to do.

"Alas, I haven't the hair to pull it off."

"Ah yes, of course. I should have guessed." With a brief smile, she turned her focus back on their game. Pointing almost straight up, she said, "Ophiuchus."

He put his hand directly next to hers, the fine lawn of his sleeve grazing her bare forearm. "Gemini."

"*Gavin,*" she exclaimed, nudging him playfully. "For heaven's sake, Gemini is a winter constellation. Honestly, you should be ashamed of yourself. When was the last time you even looked at the stars?"

He rolled his head to the side so that he could face her, and she followed suit. His eyes were so dark, they were little more than black disks in the pale expanse of his face, but she could still sense the fondness in them. "Probably the last time I was here with you."

A decade ago? Her brow furrowed as she said, "How could that be? You loved stargazing."

He gave a small shrug, his eyes not leaving hers. "I loved the company," he said quietly. "The stars were merely a bonus."

Oh. Her stomach gave a little flutter at the thought. Turning her attention back to the sky, she pondered that. She had loved being with him, too. It was an easy friendship, one that seemed to come effortlessly between them. They could talk, or simply be quiet. They could see each other several times a week, or not for months at a time. No matter what, the friendship between them thrived.

Until she left.

When he left, things had changed, but not terribly. It wasn't until she married and moved away that she truly lost him. She had expected more of him. It had been years since she'd thought of how she'd felt when that first letter had gone unanswered. And then the second. When he finally had written back to her third one, it was with a detachment that had initially shocked her. Over the years, she grew used to it, but that first time, it had really hurt.

"Gavin?"

"Hmm?"

"Why did you walk away from our friendship?"

Though he hadn't expected the question at that moment, Dering didn't pretend not to know what she was talking about. He didn't want to break the mood between them—this was the most enjoyable evening he'd had in years—but he couldn't ignore the question. Sighing, he gazed up at the indigo sky. "You married. It didn't seem prudent to maintain a correspondence with another man's wife."

"It wouldn't have been like that."

He could hear the hurt behind the words, and he had to stop himself from reaching out to her. He never could stand the thought of her being anything but happy.

"Not to us. But who's to say how he would have felt about it? I didn't want to cause any strain in your marriage. We had memories, great ones, and that was good enough."

She sat up and wrapped her arms around her knees. If not for the elegant gown and jewels, he could have imagined her to be eighteen again. "For you, perhaps. When I moved to Cadgwith, I didn't know a single person. They saw me as an outsider in the beginning, and I could have really used your friendship."

The words dinged his conscience. Pushing up to a sitting position, he said, "I thought you were blissfully happy. Your letter gushed with praise for your new husband and home. How was I to know anything was amiss?"

"You would have known if you had written me back. And you should have known it would be a difficult transition, no matter how excited I was to make it. You were supposed to be my friend, yet you couldn't see that I needed you."

It was a profoundly unfair statement. She was the one who had left, and she had taken his happiness, however inadvertently. She had broken his heart. She had gotten everything she wanted, and he was the one who was left breathless, attempting to make a *difficult transition*.

What she said went both ways. She was supposed to

be his friend, yet she hadn't even suspected that he was bloody well in love with her.

The magic of the night was completely broken. He stood and brushed at his clothes. "I'm sorry I wasn't the friend you thought I was," he said, his voice neutral. "But we all move on in life, and I think it's safe to say that we both have." He reached down to grab his jacket and shoved his arms into the sleeves.

Her brow was furrowed as she looked up to him. "Yes, clearly." The words were soft, but left him feeling chastised. Again, not fair.

But he was still a gentleman. He held out his hand to her to help her up. After a moment's hesitation, she slipped her bare hand into his. Her skin was petal soft and cool to the touch, a stark contrast to his warm, roughened palms.

He refused to feel self-conscious about it. Though it wasn't the norm for his set, he enjoyed lifting weights and rarely wore gloves while doing so. Some thought it made him too bulky, but to him, there was nothing more invigorating than besting his previous lifting records.

She seemed as light as the air around them as he pulled her to her feet. He stepped away quickly, not wanting or willing to react to her closeness the way he always did. It had been enjoyable throughout the night to experience that rush of desire in the pit of his stomach whenever their hands brushed or, better yet, when they had lain beside each other like lovers in bed.

Not love, of course. Just desire, his favorite of all emotions. Unfortunately, she had just reminded him of exactly where those sorts of feelings led when it came to the two of them: disappointment and pain. He was a rational man these days. He wasn't ruled by his passions or fears like he once had been, so he could walk away before he risked too much.

He made quick work of refolding the blanket while Felicity pulled on her gloves and adjusted her gown. When she was finished, she offered him a brisk smile that was little more than a polite stretch of her lips. "Thank you for the glimpse of our past. As lost bets go, I could scarce have done better."

"I aim to please," he said, purposely glib. "Shall we be off? I'm anxious to return to the ball, as I am sure there is still much enjoyment to be had."

Felicity nodded, and they headed back to the carriage in a much different mood than when they had come. It was a good reminder, really. She had never been the one for him, and that held true even now. His pleasure was to be found elsewhere, particularly in the parties and gatherings of the *ton*.

At least then there were no expectations or disappointment.

Chapter Seven

Surrounded as she was by so much wonderful company, Felicity should have been thoroughly enjoying the afternoon. After being treated to a brilliant rehearsal by Charity, Sophie, and May—an experience Felicity had been anticipating ever since she heard of the unusual pairing in their unlikely trio of pianoforte, oboe, and zither—she had been invited to join them at May's home for some tea and conversation. The day really couldn't have been better.

Except for the fact that she felt badly about how things had gone with Gavin two days ago. As such, it was impossible to truly enjoy anything today.

Yesterday, she had still felt somewhat justified about the conversation that led to the abrupt departure. It was a legitimate question, asking him about his reasons for more or less turning his back on the friendship. Lying on the ground, looking up at the stars as they had in their youth, had really driven home how far apart they had come to be.

She barely even knew him anymore.

But what she felt guilty about was what had followed.

It was unfair to assert that he should have *known* that she needed his friendship. That he should have anticipated what it would be like for her to leave her family and her home and start anew in Cadgwith. The more she repeated the conversation in her head, the worse it sounded until now, here she was, surrounded by some of the most interesting and lovely women she had ever met, and she could hardly even follow the conversation.

"Did any of you see Dering last night?" The question was out of her mouth before she even knew she was going to say it. She immediately pressed her lips together, knowing Dering had absolutely nothing to do with whatever they had been discussing. The particulars of their concert, perhaps?

"I'm sorry," she rushed to say, feeling like an idiot. "I only ask because he mentioned his parents are coming, and I forgot to ask when. If you'd spoken to him, I thought maybe he might have said something about it."

Though the explanation sounded pitiful to her ears, the others seemed to take no issue whatsoever.

"William and I stayed in last night," May said, her blue eyes giving away perhaps a little more than she intended. Felicity pressed her lips together against a knowing smile. She remembered those nights from when Ian was alive. "Dering is a frequent visitor, but the last I saw him was at the ball, and it didn't come up."

Sophie's dark curls swayed as she nodded. "Me, too, I'm afraid. I didn't see him until he came back later in the night, but we danced sometime before midnight, and I don't recall him saying when they'd be here."

The flash of jealousy that zipped through Felicity's heart at Sophie's words was so unexpected, she put a hand

to her chest. Absolute absurdity, of course. She had no
intention of dancing with him or anyone else, and he was
free to enjoy anyone's company that he wished. He had
deposited her on her doorstep at eleven o'clock that night.
She didn't think he'd truly go back to the ball, but obviously she was wrong.

Not that it was any business of hers.

"Same for me," Charity added. "Although I didn't
even last as late as Sophie."

Felicity nodded, not wanting to dwell on Gavin lest
one of them start asking questions. She certainly had
no intention of explaining their night beneath the stars
and her subsequent unwise comments. "Well, you all
outlasted me. I haven't been to a ball in years, and I can
happily go that long without another one."

"Nonsense," Charity said, fluttering a slender hand
through the air. "You just need to acclimate to having
people around. By the time the final masquerade is upon
us, you'll know more people and it will be more fun.
Speaking of which, we need to commission a proper
gown for the occasion."

"I'm *so* glad you said that," May said, cutting her
gaze to Felicity. Enthusiasm was written all over her
beautiful face. "My husband and I are introducing a
new line of specialty fabrics that have been embellished
with embroidery from the very best hands in the world.
I have a bolt of burnt coral silk with copper accents that
I would *love* to see with your coloring."

Sophie grinned over her teacup. "I highly recommend
giving in to her now. She'll not give up, and what's more,
you don't *want* her to give up, because she truly does have
the eye of a master when it comes to fabric. As evidenced

by my new gown," she added, waving a hand down her skirts. The buttery yellow fabric was lovely, especially against the crisp white sash and hem.

"Hmm," Felicity said, torn between the idea of wearing something so gorgeous and giving up the lavender and purple half-mourning colors she'd been wearing since hanging up her widow's weeds seven months ago. "I don't know. I only just came out of half mourning last month. I don't know if I'm ready to be donning anything so colorful just yet."

Charity set down the remainder of her shortbread and sent Felicity a sympathetic look. "You are of course free to choose when you're ready to wear normal colors again, but I do hope you'll consider May's offer. I think it could do a world of good for your spirits to feel pretty again."

Felicity blinked, taken off guard by the comment. She hadn't felt *not* pretty. She simply hadn't thought of it in a while. How she looked just didn't seem important anymore. But still . . . "Do my spirits seem low to you?"

"No, I didn't mean that," Charity said, placing a hand over Felicity's. "I do know that there is still great sadness in your heart, though, and I just meant that wearing beautiful things often brings us joy."

Nodding, May leaned forward in earnest. "Yes, that's exactly the way I feel about fashion. I actually chose not to even wear mourning clothes when my mother died. A love of fashion was something we shared, and I wanted to look and feel nice to honor her. Something I don't imagine I could have gotten away with if I had been in England at the time."

Lifting her teacup for a sip, Felicity pondered that. She had never imagined that looking and feeling nice

would be a way to honor someone else. She thought of
Ian, who had particularly liked to see her in forest
green. She and Mr. Anthorp had already discussed at
length how their respective spouses would want them
to be happy in life, but she had never considered how
mourning and half mourning wear might affect that.

"Do you know, Ian never did like the color purple.
Or pink, for that matter. I'm not sure how it's supposed
to honor him that I continue to wear it."

Here she thought she was being a respectful wife,
but upon further examination, it was actually a little
absurd. It was supposed to signal to the world her continued devastation over her husband's death, but why
should she be concerned with the world's opinion? She
knew how she felt, and nothing as silly as clothes were
going to make her miss her husband any more or less.

May pressed her hands together. "Does that mean I
can go fetch the fabric?"

Smiling, feeling oddly free, Felicity nodded. "I
believe it does. And if you have anything in green, I'd
like to see that as well."

Now that she'd solved a problem she hadn't even
realized she had, she moved on to the one that had been
bothering her all day. She really had treated Gavin
poorly. He'd been so gracious in not forcing her to
dance, and then to take her out to view the stars like
that . . . She bit her lip. Yes, she'd been in the wrong,
and she needed to let him know that she was sorry.

As May dashed off to find the fabric, Felicity turned
to Charity and Sophie. "I know your concert tomorrow
night is going to be quite an event. I wonder, what is
on the agenda for this evening? Anything particularly
exciting?"

"Oh yes," the countess answered, her dark eyes brightening considerably. "Tonight is the dueling sopranos from Italy. Apparently they will be singing both in harmony and canon in order to compete for the audience's favor, and the winner—although I'm sure there really won't be a loser—anyway, the winner will perform opposite the premiere tenor in the world at the gala in Sydney Gardens in a few weeks."

It sounded promising. Gavin would likely be at the one of the most anticipated events of the festival. "That does sound interesting. I think I might actually attend."

"Evan and I will definitely be there. Opera is one of our favorite things." Sophie's blush made Felicity raise an eyebrow, but she didn't say anything.

Charity smiled at Sophie before turning her attention to Felicity. "After spending the last three nights out, I'm going to stay in this evening. I feel like playing some of Hugh's music tonight."

Felicity knew what that meant. Music could be a trigger for the baron's episodes, but when Charity played the dark and tender music meant just for him, it always brought him peace instead. That further cemented Felicity's intention to spend the evening out. The two of them could use some time alone together, and she knew that Lady Effington had plans to play cards with an old friend tonight.

As soon as she got home, she would write Gavin and inquire if he would escort her to the opera event. She wished she were more certain than she was that he would agree, but if he didn't, it would only mean she would have to seek him out in another way. She had thoroughly spoiled things between them, and she was determined to see them set right.

* * *

As he slowed the carriage to a stop in front of Felicity's rented townhouse, Dering tried to ignore the odd hint of nerves that flickered through him. He hadn't expected her to write him. And he certainly hadn't expected her to ask him to accompany her to the opera event tonight. But what he was most surprised by was the fact that she had asked that they have some time alone.

That had definitely gotten his attention.

Despite his efforts to lose himself in the merriment of the festival, their parting had weighed heavily on him. It wasn't how he wanted things to be between them. What's more, no matter how much she aggravated or provoked him, there was something between them that he couldn't seem to walk away from.

Hence his agreement to be here.

Thankfully, after yesterday's drizzle, it was another fine day outside. He had borrowed a phaeton from a friend so that a driver wouldn't be necessary, but it would have been uncomfortable in inclement weather. His barouche offered extravagant comfort, but certainly not privacy, since it required a driver.

As he climbed down to the pavement, the white lacquered door swung open and Felicity stepped out, a broad smile in place. "Good afternoon," she said, nodding to the butler as he closed the door behind her. Dering wondered if she caught the man's censorious look. It wasn't quite the thing to meet a man on the street in front of the house like this. "Charity is practicing, and I didn't wish for her to be interrupted. I hope you are well."

He tried to be detached and urbane, but damned if the sight of her smiling up at him like that didn't just go straight through his resolve. She was his weakness, plain and simple. Something he should have come to terms with before accepting her offer.

"I am, thank you, and I hope you are," he said blandly as she approached. It was hard not to notice the way her elegant eggplant-colored gown called attention to her narrow waist. As she walked, he could just perceive the fullness of her hips against the narrow drape of the skirts. It was beyond distracting.

In the best and worst way.

She was beautiful. Womanly. Certainly not the young debutante she once was, but he found he preferred her the way she was now. Of course, he was much older now than he was when he'd last seen her, so it stood to reason that his tastes had changed.

Or had they?

She was still Felicity, after all.

Shaking himself from his wandering thoughts, he offered his hand to assist her into the carriage. "Since you indicated that you wished to have a little privacy, I thought we could take a circumvent route around the city. I had already invited some friends to join me in my box since the event is being held at the theater, so there is little chance of privacy there."

He very properly handed her up in the carriage, but didn't miss the warm smile she offered him.

"Thank you. That will be perfect. I hope that I'm not intruding upon your plans, though."

Once they were both settled, Dering flicked the reins and set them on their way. "Not at all. I tend to enjoy company, so most of my friends know that my general rule of thumb is the more, the merrier."

She smoothed both hands down her skirts. "Yes, I remember Charity said as much. I'm glad that you have so many friends in your life. It's clear that you are very well liked."

He gave a light shrug, keeping his eye on the street. Cadgwith had found a place that was far enough away from the center of the city to be relatively quiet, so the road wasn't overly busy. "Well connected, at least. I have my father's talent for socializing, so I am rarely without words when talking to people. There really aren't that many whom I would consider close friends, however. That's something I reserve for a select few, and I don't take the distinction lightly."

He assumed that was why she wanted to meet with him, so it seemed best to go ahead and bring it up. No use beating around the bush.

She turned to face him, her eyes partially shaded by her bonnet. "I know. And I wanted to say that I'm sorry. It wasn't fair for me to say what I did the other night. Those were old frustrations that I haven't thought about in years, but for some reason I allowed them to come to the surface. Our friendship was a special moment in time, and if it wasn't meant to last forever, that doesn't make it less meaningful to me."

On a whim, he turned onto a side street that he knew led to a dead end by the river. At the end of the street, he pulled back on the reins and turned to face her directly. The wind had reddened her cheeks and added shine to her eyes, both of which only served to make her look that much more lovely.

"I agree," he said quietly. "That relationship was wonderful, and will always be a part of who I am today. And though we may not—and perhaps should not—be able to recapture how it used to be, that doesn't mean that we can't form a new kind of friendship now."

She brushed a few strands of hair from her eyes as she met his gaze evenly. "So we begin anew?"

He smiled, loving those beautiful golden brown eyes of hers. "Not quite anew," he said, setting a hand over hers and giving it a squeeze. "I don't wish to go back to calling you Lady Felicity and pretending I don't know the things that I do about you. But I do think that this can be a fresh revival for us. A redefining, of sorts."

Even as he said the words, he couldn't have denied the way his heart beat faster with her directly by his side like this. Here he was, attempting to remake their friendship, and yet, for some reason, his eyes briefly fell to her lips, imagining a kiss to seal the deal. The thought brought with it a surge of awareness.

God, what was wrong with him? Must he be a glutton for punishment when it came to her?

She pressed her lips together in a sweet half smile and nodded. "I'd like that. Though I do miss calling you Gavin. It's how I think of you."

She thought of him? He knew full well that she didn't think of him the way he thought of her. She didn't imagine what his lips felt like, or how sensitive the skin of his neck was. She wasn't sitting there with her heart nearly beating out of her chest, imagining what he would do if she just threw caution to the wind and kissed him.

Wetting his lips, he worked to paste a normal-looking smile on his face. "No one calls me that. People would wonder about us if you did. We wouldn't want to give anyone the wrong idea."

It was clear to him that was nothing going on here. She wasn't feeling the same tension he was—that undeniable, nearly cosmic pull between them that made his lungs forget how to breathe.

"No, of course not." She smiled softly before turning her gaze out over the river. It was slow-moving here, so the sound of the water was barely audible above the distant sounds of the city. "We've been lucky that no one ever did get the wrong idea about us. It made the way we behaved seem . . . less wrong, I think."

His brow creased. "You thought we were wrong?"

She pulled her bottom lip between her teeth, worrying it for a moment. "Society would have thought it was wrong. We knew it was innocent, but in the eyes of the world, it would have been beyond scandalous."

Innocent. His intentions were never quite that. He'd always wished for more. Even now, he wanted more with her. "Society will think what it wants to think. I'm glad we didn't listen. I'm glad we risked what we did."

His only real regret was not risking more, sooner.

He swallowed and looked out over the river, trying to let his heart find a sustainable rhythm. How was it possible that he had started the day wanting to maintain as much distance as he could from her, and here he was, contemplating slipping his arm around her shoulders and drawing her in for a kiss?

"I'm glad we did, too."

He could hear the affection in her voice. If nothing else, she was happy in his presence. Shouldn't that count for something? Unable to stand not touching her anymore, he reached over and covered her hand with his. "Thank you for writing me today. I would hate to lose you again."

He slipped his fingers beneath her palm and lifted her hand to his mouth. When he pressed his lips to the backs of her knuckles, he lingered for a heartbeat too long, wishing all the while he could peel away the leather and feel her skin beneath his mouth.

* * *

Felicity drew in a swift breath, surprised by the sudden drop of her stomach. It was a fleeting sensation, one that was gone almost before she felt it. When Gavin released his hold, she rubbed her one hand with her other, not exactly sure what the devil had just happened.

It was, after all, just a simple, friendly kiss. Nothing at all out of the ordinary, and for heaven's sake, it was only Gavin. Exhaling, she sent him a slightly unsteady smile. "I agree completely."

It had clearly been too long since she'd had normal contact with a gentleman of higher society. Back in Cadgwith, men did not go around kissing the hands of women. Theirs was a simple fishing community, where greetings were familiar and affectionate, but not generally physical.

As Gavin took the ribbons back in his capable hands and guided the carriage toward the main road, Felicity cleared her throat, attempting to clear her mind in the process. It was good that she was getting back into the world again. She'd gone too long in her little bubble. And more than anything, she was glad that Gavin was here with her. Things had gotten out of hand thanks to her dredging up old history, but today, they started again.

A fresh start. Wasn't that exactly what she needed in general?

Starting right that moment, she resolved to open her mind and her heart to life again. It went right along with her decision to wear real colors again. Coming to Bath had been the first step, and she was so glad she had done so. From now on, she was going to do more of the things that made her happy, and that pushed her limits.

"Gavin?"

"Yes?"

The steady clip of the horses' hooves echoed the beating of her heart. "Later this week, will you do me a favor?"

"Anything," he said without the slightest hesitation.

"Take me to play billiards. I'm not particularly good at it, but it's something I used to love, and it's just one more thing that I haven't done these last two years. I know you enjoy playing it, so would you mind?"

It seemed a simple, silly thing, but that was rather the appeal of it. Something she liked to do, for no other reason than it brought her joy.

He glanced to her with much more seriousness than she expected. "Whatever you want, your wish is my command."

Chapter Eight

The four days between Felicity's request and the agreed-upon assignation had been pure torture for Dering. First, he'd had to sit through the dueling operatic performances with her sitting mere inches away from him in the darkness, with little more than his friends' presence and his dwindling willpower holding him in check.

Next was the much-anticipated concert performed by Charity, Sophie, and May, where they'd sat with Thomas between them, frustrating him to no end. More often than was prudent, he caught himself glancing her way, wishing she was sitting beside him. It had been a marvelous performance, and certainly the audience had shown enthusiastic approval, but damned if he had heard even half of it.

This was what happened when one denied one's desires. He wanted her, and it was making life both exquisite and miserable.

Well, tonight would be his chance to lay his intentions on the table. He was attracted to her, pure and simple, and he didn't want to ignore it or deny it anymore. In fact, he had a plan.

Felicity wanted to play billiards, and their choices were limited. She could come to his home, but that was a bigger risk than he was willing to take. Any unmarried female that showed up alone at his house would lead the neighbors to one conclusion, and one conclusion only. Not what he wanted for them.

He could invite himself over to Radcliffe's palatial house, and make use of their table. Perfectly acceptable, assuming the duchess was about. Unfortunately, having others around wasn't what he had in mind.

So he had come up with the perfect solution: his parents' estate. They weren't due to arrive for a few days yet, and certainly no one would notice if he and Felicity took a drive out there. There were enough staff present preparing the place that it would be minimally acceptable if anyone did somehow discover their presence, but he highly doubted it would become an issue.

Best of all, he would have her all to himself.

Alone, he was free to say things he normally couldn't. And if it turned out that she was open to his affections, well, he couldn't be in a better place.

With that thought rattling around in his head, he knocked on her door. The butler answered almost immediately, welcomed him with an economy of words, and led him into the morning room.

When Dering walked into the room, smile already in place, he wasn't at all prepared for what he saw. Felicity stood by the window in a dark p rple gown, bathed in the afternoon light. She was beautiful, but that's not what brought him to an abrupt halt.

It was the baby in her arms.

The little girl was all smiles as she reached out to the

glass, her chubby hands slapping against its smooth surface. She had dark hair and pale skin and looked absolutely nothing like her mother.

A lump lodged in his throat. In a space of half a second, the abstract became real. Felicity was a mother, and this little girl was the child of her husband.

The butler announced him then, capturing Felicity's attention. She smiled, her face as luminous as he had ever seen it. "Thank you, Richardson. Good afternoon, Dering. Come, meet Isabella."

As she walked toward him, the baby curled shyly against her chest, watching Dering with uncertain blue eyes. Felicity kissed the girl's head and said, "Say *How do you do?* to the nice man, Bella."

Those huge blue eyes blinked twice before she said, "How do do." Her voice was airy and light, barely more than a whisper.

"Lovely to make your acquaintance, Miss Danby," he answered, forcing a grin.

Patting the baby's back, Felicity sent him an apologetic smile. "We lost track of time looking at the birds in the fountain outside. Richardson will be fetching the nursemaid, so we'll be able to go shortly."

He nodded, mainly because he could not think of anything to say. Felicity looked as happy as he had ever seen her, standing there with her child in her arms. There were no hints of sadness or grief hidden in her eyes. Just joy. Peace.

That was a good thing—a great thing, really—but he was still trying to reconcile the way he always thought of her, and the woman standing before him. It struck him, more poignantly than ever, that she had given birth to this child without her husband by her side. She was solely responsible for overseeing her upbringing, for hiring trusted servants, and for making sure no harm befell her.

What strength she must possess. What fortitude. Even as he struggled to come to terms with this new maternal image of her, he was assailed with newfound admiration for her.

He allowed his gaze to settle on the girl, searching for some hint of Felicity. "She looks a lot like Cadgwith."

She smiled. "That's because he looks a lot like his brother. Different coloring, but the shape of the eyes, the mouth, and the chin are so much alike."

It was almost possible to imagine the girl wasn't even hers. That she was holding a niece, or a friend's baby. "It's a shame she didn't get your eyes. The color is so warm and lovely. Not that the blue isn't very pretty," he added, not wanting her to construe the comment as an insult.

"Her eyes are my favorite thing about her," she said, tucking a finger beneath Isabella's chin and smiling down at her little face. "They are the very image of Ian's. We have only one decent portrait of him, but the artist did an exceptional job of capturing the exact color of his eyes. I'm happy she'll be able to look at that painting and see herself in her father."

Thankfully, the nursemaid bustled in, saving him from trying to think of a response. It was hard to describe the way he felt at meeting the baby, and frankly he didn't want to dwell on it. He stood to the side and waited while Felicity kissed her daughter's plump cheeks before handing her over. When the servant had left, she turned to Dering and spread her hands. "Now then, are we ready

THE VISCOUNT RISKS IT ALL   101

to go? I'm anxious to discover if I will be as sore a loser at billiards as I am at cards."

"God, let us hope not," he quipped, earning a laugh and a smack to his shoulder.

"That wasn't very gentlemanly of you," she said with mock affront, hands going to her hips.

"Am I supposed to be gentlemanly? That will take all the fun from the day."

She pretended to seriously consider the question, before giving a quick shake of her head. "Hm. I imagine you are probably right. Very well, I give you a pass. Whatever happens within the bounds of our game shall be exempt from any normal rules of society. Anything said—including goading, gloating, teasing, and salty language—will be between you and me and the ghastly cherubs on the ceiling."

He very much liked the sound of that. "I'm happy to say my mother had them painted over years ago. I suppose whatever happens will be our little secret."

As he led her outside to his waiting barouche, he savored the build of anticipation. Meeting her daughter might have momentarily thrown him, but in the scheme of things, it really didn't matter. Felicity was who he wanted. He knew that, in the light of truth, this summer was likely all they would have. She would go back to her seaside home, and he would go back to his investments and estate business, and all of this would someday be an exceedingly fond memory.

But he had waited a lifetime to make his intentions known, and he wasn't going to wait any more.

There it was again.

That buzz, that soft hum of awareness that came

from nowhere, but made her sit up and take notice. It happened when he settled down beside her, sitting just a little closer than was strictly proper. But he was a big man, and it stood to reason that he would take up more space on the bench.

As he signaled the driver to go, Felicity drew a calming breath, trying to disperse the oddness of the moment. "Well, then," she said, wanting to fill the silence. "I'm hoping I can remember how one even holds the cue. If I remember correctly, it's been over two and a half years since I've played."

His smile was sly as he shook his head. "That has all the makings of an excuse before you've even stepped foot in the billiards room. Fear not. I have every confidence that you'll remember everything the moment you line up your first shot. At least, that's how it seems to work for all the other sharks out there."

"Shark!" She narrowed her eyes at him even as she laughed. "I'm no swindler, I assure you. In fact, there will be no betting or stakes whatsoever, so such a thing would be impossible."

She had certainly learned her lesson last time. This was to be for the pure enjoyment of the game. And the company. The thought made her smile up at him, pleased to be able to spend the day with him without expectation or agenda.

When he met her gaze, his midnight eyes held suspicion. "What is it that has you smiling? What are you scheming over there?"

"Not a single thing," she said, purposely infusing her voice with suspicious innocence. "Just because a woman is smiling, it doesn't mean she is up to something."

He raised a single dark eyebrow. "Are you certain?"

"Quite," she said, the word couched in stifled laughter. "Now do behave. Trust me when I say I am simply looking forward to a pleasant afternoon."

"Ah. Then we have similar goals, I see."

"Except that I have the distinct impression that you will be the one scheming to win."

His lopsided little grin reeked of smugness. "No scheming involved. Just pure, honest skill. Where did you think I got all of my calluses?"

She almost shivered at the memory of his roughened palms scraping gently against her own. "Truly? Wait— you are teasing me."

He gave a negligent shrug. "Perhaps. I suppose we will find out."

Turning a little in her seat so she was facing him more fully, she said, "No, tell me the truth. How did you roughen your hands? It's difficult to imagine you engaging in manual labor. Your mother would have a fit."

His lips quirked up in a pleased little grin. "Do you really wish to know?"

She nodded, more than a little curious.

"You're sure?"

"Yes, please," she insisted, loving how easy it was to tease and banter with him.

Silently, he extended the arm closest to her straight out in front of them. Slipping his other hand beneath her wrist, he lifted her hand and placed it, palm down, on his upper arm. Then, he curled his arm up, making his biceps bulge to a hard knot beneath her fingers.

Her lips parted as her heart unexpectedly leaped in her chest. *Good heavens.* Meeting his expectant gaze, she said, "Lifting weights?"

"Precisely," he replied, relaxing the pose and dropping

his arm back to his side. "There is something very . . . elemental about the exercise. It's exhilarating. In Mother's eyes, it's *almost* as bad as manual labor, but not quite."

That made her laugh. As much time as Felicity and Gavin spent together in their youth, she had rarely seen much of his family. He either came to her house, where her mother's illness often precluded her from leaving her bedchamber and her father was always busy with one important thing or another, or they met in one the grounds between their estates.

On the occasions that Felicity had visited his house, Lady Carlisle had been something of a force of nature. A good woman, to be sure, but she could be intimidating when she put her mind to it. Probably a good skill when one has four sons and an earl for a husband.

"Well, if your mother couldn't persuade you from it, I'm sure it must be something you are passionate about. And I must admit, the effects are certainly imposing. I couldn't help but imagine that your boxing opponents must think twice before engaging you in a match."

Her words brought an endearingly pleased grin to his lips. "A more flattering compliment, I cannot imagine."

"Was that a compliment?" she asked, raising a single eyebrow.

"To a man, absolutely. Or at least to *this* man. It's hard work, literally the sweat of my brow, and an acknowledgment of that dedication is pleasing." He crossed his arms, regarding her thoughtfully for a moment. "What would be your most valued compliment?"

It was a question she had never thought to consider. Still, the answer came almost immediately to her lips. "That I am a good mother." Since Isabella had started life one parent down, it was Felicity's greatest wish that the parent she had left was the best she could be.

"I'm sure that is a given. What else?"

She wrinkled her nose, "I'm not in the habit of fishing for compliments."

"And I'm not in the habit of flexing before friends," he said, his deep voice soft with wry amusement. "Humor me."

An odd conversation, to say the least, but it wasn't in any way uncomfortable. Glancing to the farmland and forest around them, she gave the question due consideration. "I think one of the highest compliments one can give is to say someone is kind."

His chest rumbled with a low chuckle. "Spoken like a person who has never had a Season."

"Oh? And why is that?"

"If you had, you would have known that the most sought-after praise would be for beauty, then sharp-bordering-on-acerbic wit, followed by excellent fashion and graceful dancing."

She couldn't help but make a face at the list. "Do you know I never missed having a Season, but I was curious as to what it would be like. After hearing that, I can definitely say that I'm happy I didn't have one."

Of course she had imagined what it would be like to attend the storied balls and entertainments of the Season. It was hard to picture what London was like, with the incredible bustle and practically inconceivable size. To her, the Assembly rooms were incredibly lovely and grand—as were the rooms in her family's own estates—but from what she heard, the amount of opulence and wealth packed into one small area was spectacular.

It was odd to think that, as an earl's daughter, she had never actually experienced any of the things normally afforded a woman of her status.

"I'm glad you didn't have one, too," he said, surprising her. "I'd hate to think of the *ton*'s cynical outlook tainting you."

"But why, then, do you love it so much? You make it sound superficial at best, mean-spirited at worst. How is that appealing to you?" She knew he thrived on company and parties, but from what he described, she couldn't picture someone as deep and genuine as he was enjoying that sort of environment.

Dering shrugged. "If you are already cynical, as I am, and have an understanding of the dangers of trusting people with more than you'd be willing to hear announced from a balcony in the middle of London, then there is still much to be enjoyed. There is an energy to the gatherings that can't be replicated anywhere else. The people of the *ton* can be great fun, so long as you know the limits of the friendship."

Felicity could see the first flicker of sadness in his eyes. His life had always seemed exciting, but the way he described it now, it sounded . . . hollow. Her heart squeezed at the thought. She wanted him to be happy. She always had. She had assumed that with all the friends and activity in his life, he was.

Now, she wasn't at all sure.

Looking down at her hands, she fiddled with the edge of her glove. He was a wonderful man. Handsome, clever, amusing . . . Turning her gaze back to his face, she said, "Gavin, why have you not yet married?"

The question earned her a half scowl, half grimace. "Where did that come from? Lud, you haven't been talking with my mother, have you?" He shook his head. "It's on the horizon, but all in good time."

She, of all people, knew how fleeting "good time" could be. "We are very nearly thirty, Gavin. Dering," she corrected herself quickly. "I can tell you with absolute confidence that there is no guarantee that any of us will wake up tomorrow."

He blew out a short breath and met her eyes, the corners of his mouth tipped up in a sober smile. "I know you can." He set his hand over hers, the warmth instantly soaking through her gloves. It was one of the most comforting sensations she had ever experienced. With the driver's attention straight ahead and nothing but an empty road and undeveloped land around them, she allowed herself to lean into him.

She breathed in his familiar scent, savoring the contentment she felt at his side. He didn't protest. After a moment, when they had turned onto the lane that served as the mile-long drive to the house, he released his hold on her hand and swung his arm around her, allowing her to settle against the firm wall of his side.

Her stomach fluttered a bit at the sensation, but it was certainly only because such a position was rather taboo. But given the distance before they reached the house, the likelihood of encountering anyone was almost nil, so she stayed right where she was.

"Lissy?"

"Mmhmm?" she asked, liking the way she could feel the rumble in his chest when he said her name.

"I'm glad you came back."

She smiled, just a fleeting little tilt of her lips as she relaxed against him. She was, too. More so than she could have ever anticipated. It was freeing, breaking the rules like this with him. In a few minutes, they would be at the house and she would continue to break the rules as they played the game she had been looking forward to for days.

And if she was already thinking about the drive home at his side, well, some things were better left unexamined.

Chapter Nine

Dering could still smell the hints of gardenia clinging to his jacket like a memory as he led Felicity
through the maze of corridors to the billiards room at
the back of the east wing of the house. Mrs. Littleford, the
housekeeper, had been rather surprised to see them. He
had explained that he had wanted to show off the renovations while they both had a free day, before the
chaos of the family's arrival.

The older woman had always been easily charmed,
and it helped that she remembered Felicity. She'd waved
them on with a long-suffering sigh, clucking about how
much she still had to do before the others descended upon
the house. By a stroke of luck, the east wing was already
in order, so there was very little chance of them being
disturbed. Exactly what Dering had been hoping for.

Now, as they neared their destination, the hollow
echo of their footsteps was the only sound, a potent
reminder of just how alone they would be.

Christ, but he could hardly think straight.

The feel of her soft curves settled against his side had
been sweet torture. He had thought she might protest
when he'd laid his arm around her, but she'd surprised

him by relaxing into him instead. Sweet bliss. To feel her tucked against him like that, as natural as if they'd done it a hundred times, had been beyond intoxicating, and he already ached to wrap his arms around her again.

He drew a steadying breath. He needed to get his runaway thoughts back under control. If he acted like an overeager youth, it was sure to put her off. If he could just be himself, there was an excellent chance that things would happen naturally, just as they had in the carriage.

When he opened the door to the billiards room, it took a moment to adjust to the dark interior, since the heavy scarlet drapes were all pulled shut. He moved to the back wall and opened the series of five broad windows, letting the light pour in.

"This looks beautiful," she said, glancing around at the oak-paneled walls and ceiling. "Your mother did an exceptional job with the renovation."

He nodded, setting his hands low at his hips and looked about the room. "A vast improvement over the gold filigree and heavenly mural that were once in here."

The new color scheme included rich, bold reds and muted bronzes and greens that felt much more appropriate to the purpose of the room. The pale blue-and-gold wallpaper that had once decorated the space seemed more suited to a lady's bedchamber than a game room. Where once pale watercolors of seashores had been, now paintings of the grounds of their various estates hung from the wall, as well as a few of the family's much-beloved dogs. Ruby-colored King Charles spaniels for his mother, stout hunting hounds for his father.

She nodded. "I agree. Though I'm glad to see you kept the same table. It really is very handsome."

He strode to the austere mahogany billiards table and pulled the cover off, revealing a deep red baize where the traditional green had once been. "We were able to convince her to keep the table itself, but only if we agreed to having the color changed. Not the best hue when you consider the target ball."

He lifted the ball in question from the corner pocket and tossed it in the air. It was almost the exact same color as the wool. She smiled, coming forward to grab the painted sphere from his hands. "Well, let us see how it affects the game, shall we?"

Offering a short bow, he said, "I accept the challenge. Let me just get the cues." He walked to the display cabinet his mother had commissioned to hold the collection of cues and maces that went with the table.

She ran her fingertips along the bumper, making a circuit around the table. "I think a few practice rounds are in order, if you don't mind. I want to at least have a fighting chance at playing a decent game when we begin in earnest."

He handed over one of the slender leather-tipped cues and set the three balls on the table. "Take as much time as you like. I've got all day."

"Do you?" she said over her shoulder with a grin that bordered on mischievous. "And here I was under the impression that you had a very full social calendar."

He did, actually. He had planned to attend the "Setting Poetry to Music" demonstration that evening, but the moment Felicity had made her request, those particular plans had been shoved to the back of his mind. If he was late or didn't show, his friends would shrug it off and make merry without him.

Sending her a wink, he said, "I always have time for

you, my dear. Now then, do you need some lessons, or would you prefer to practice in peace?"

She waved him off. "I'll practice on my own for a few minutes, if you don't mind."

Nodding, he set his own cue aside and went to the globe-shaped cabinet that held a small selection of spirits within. He selected the brandy—always his first choice—and poured himself two fingers. "Any for you?"

She glanced over and shook her head. "Not yet. I'm already operating at a disadvantage. You, however, should pour yourself a little more."

The quip made him laugh. He leaned against the back of the sofa and watched her as she studied the table. "Yes, that does seem only fair."

Her focus was wholly on the game now. She circled the table, eyeing the possible setups before finally settling on an easy first shot. As she leaned over, he froze, his drink not quite to his lips. It was one hell of a view. She had tucked a small bit of lace in her bodice, which blocked any obvious view of her breasts, but it had just enough sheerness to show the full, round shape and the shadow of her cleavage.

He took a quick drink. Too quick, in fact. He swallowed noisily, barely managing not to choke on the liquid. Thankfully, by the time she had taken the shot and glanced over to him, he had managed to recover. "Not bad," he said mildly.

"Bad, but not terrible," Felicity countered, shaking her head. She had gotten close to the pocket at least. She went around the table and lined up her shot again. This time when she leaned over, he was presented with a view of her backside. It was swathed in several layers of fabric, but still.

He knocked back the rest of his drink, set down the empty glass, and pushed away from the sofa. "Would you like a refresher course?"

She shook her head, sending him a determined grin. "Not yet. I may still remember how to do this."

"Are you sure? I can already see what you are doing wrong."

"I'm quite certain that you can. But give me a moment to figure it out." She returned her attention to the table, and he sat back and watched as she took a few more shots. She got the target ball in once, but really, that was more or less an accident.

Finally, he reached out, caught the back of the stick, and pulled it from her hands, making her turn around with an indignant lift of her brow. "Enough," he said before she could protest. "I know you are very independent, but I'd like to be able to start the game before nightfall."

She made a face at his exaggeration, but didn't object. "Fine, fine. Show me what I am doing wrong, oh ye of masterful skills."

Her sarcasm made him grin. She had wanted to play for fun, but that competitiveness was already coming out again. "What do you want to do, a cannon or hazard stroke?"

Inspecting the layout of the three balls, she said, "A hazard?"

"Are you asking or telling?"

"Telling. I think," she added, giving him a wink. "It seems like the other cue ball is my best bet."

He nodded. He would have tried for a cannon, since he was confident a shot at the right angle would easily tap both balls, but if she wished to try for a pocket, that was fine by him. "All right. Start by getting into position for the shot."

She dutifully obliged, bending over the table and positioning her cue directly behind her ball. He stepped close to her side, ostensibly to view the angle. She turned her head to look at him, her eyebrows raised in question. "Does this meet with your approval?"

Did it ever. "Indeed," he said, his voice a little hoarse. She was close enough that it would take little more than leaning forward to touch his lips to the curve of her jaw. He didn't, though. Not yet. He wanted to see that light of attraction in her eyes before he made such a bold move. The exact right moment would come soon, he was confident of that, but it wasn't there yet.

By an act of will, he straightened. "Now, the main problem I saw in your practice shot was that you weren't following through. If you stop your cue's momentum, you stop your ball's momentum."

"So keep moving forward even after the ball has been hit?"

"Precisely."

She nodded, pulled back her stick, and took her shot. This time, she followed all the way through. The good news was that she managed to hit the ball she aimed for. Unfortunately, it was with so much force that it hit the pocket, skipped up, and dropped onto the thick rug with a thump.

Slapping her free hand over her mouth, she stifled a horrified laugh. "Follow-through, indeed! Perhaps I should stick to my own methods."

He gave a soft snort as he went to retrieve the ball from the floor. "How was I to know your strength? You were supposed to give it a firm tap, not catapult it into the drawing room."

"Let that be a lesson," she said, a single blond eyebrow raised. "I'm stronger than I look."

Of that, he had no doubt. Walking back around the table, he stopped directly in front of her and held up the cue ball. "Try again. And remind me never to stand on the opposite side of the table when you are taking a shot. I don't fancy a bruised rib or blackened eye."

Rolling her eyes, she took the ball from his fingertips. "Very amusing. I think you can scratch *billiards instructor* from your list of accomplishments."

"You didn't give me a proper chance," he countered, leaning a hip against the side of the table. "Perhaps you'd learn better by demonstration."

She cut a half-teasing glance his way as she set the ball back on the table. "Perhaps I'd learn better without your interference."

"Oh, really? Very well, let's see what you can do."

"Certainly. If you'd be so kind as to move."

He stayed exactly where he was, half teasing her, half just wanting to stay at her side. "Why? I'm not in the way of the shot. Unless you find my presence too distracting, of course."

She wrinkled her nose at him. "Yes, I do, actually. A very large man standing directly in my way is not exactly conducive to concentration."

"Isn't it? You must just be overly sensitive. Go on, make your shot. Show me how much better off you are without my instruction."

Rising to the challenge, she squared her shoulders. "Very well. But I should warn you, turnabout is fair play."

"Planning on having a large man stand in my way?"

"No," she said, the word muffled in laughter. "But when you least expect it, I will distract you."

One could always hope. Nodding, he gestured for her to continue.

As she leaned forward, he leaned down with her. She cut her eyes toward him, lightly exasperated. "Yes?"

"Nothing. Carry on."

She pursed her lips, gave him a lingering look, then turned her attention to the table. This time, her shot was much more controlled, with just the right amount of follow-through to send the red ball straight into the pocket. It was a smooth, perfectly tempered shot, really.

He narrowed his eyes in suspicion as she grinned triumphantly. "You were saying about not being a shark?"

Utterly pleased with herself, she gave a delicate shrug. "I told you I just needed to reacquaint myself with the game. Your turn. Assuming you'd like a practice shot before we begin."

He was so happy to see how much she was enjoying herself. He loved to see her smile, even if it was at his expense. Swinging the cue to his shoulder, he did a complete circuit around the table, looking for the best view. When he decided on a shot, he bent forward, lined up his cue, and carefully primed the shot three times. Just when he went to snap it forward, Felicity magically appeared at his side, her big brown eyes settled directly on him.

The shot went wide, missing the target altogether.

Her laugh was pure wickedness as he stood and glared down at her. "That was sorcery, woman. How did you sneak up without me hearing?"

"Did I? Well, it sounds as though you need to pay more attention to your opponent. For the record, I'm not nearly as distracting a presence as you are. I would wager you have at least five stone on me."

"Five stone?" He scoffed. "It's seven stone if it's a

pound. You can't weigh more than a bag of feathers. I wager I could span your waist with my hands, if I try." And oh, how he wanted to try.

She gave a short laugh. "Perhaps, but only because your hands are so large. You could probably span Prinny's waist."

"Not so large as that," he said, holding up his right hand. "You make me sound like some sort of mythical character."

"You were the one who compared yourself to Hercules," she said, her brown eyes dancing. "And let us put this into perspective." She set her bare hand against his, palm to palm. Her fingertips just reached the second joint of his fingers.

Smiling, he laced their fingers together and squeezed. "Not so very different as you claim." His voice was soft, a cross between gentle teasing and a light caress. "Still a comfortable fit."

Her grin ebbed to something softer, more intimate as she met his gaze. His stomach tightened at the look in her eyes. It was subtle, indescribable, but still something deep inside of him responded to it. He shifted closer, letting his head dip down, slowly closing the short distance between them.

"Well, well," a deep voice from the doorway intoned. "Isn't this a cozy scene?"

Chapter Ten

Dering could have happily murdered his brother in that moment. Felicity had yanked her hand away as though burned, putting a good three feet between them in the process as her widened eyes went straight to their visitor.

Eric stood leaning against the doorjamb, a lazy, amused, *knowing* grin slanted across his damn face. Thank God he hadn't come later, when he might have walked in on something a little more compromising, but Dering would have preferred he not show up at all.

Crossing his arms, he sent him a warning glare. "Eric," he said by way of curt greeting. He loved his brother, but he could have wished him to Australia right about then. "What the devil are you doing here?"

He looked moderately well, which was good. He was Dering's closest brother in age, just three years his junior, but he had spent so much of his childhood sick in bed with his asthma that they weren't as close as they might have been. He was a bit pale, which was normal, but at least he wasn't as willowy as he had been the last time Dering had seen him.

Eric spread his hands, unconcerned. "I was somehow

under the impression that when our parents asked me to come, they intended for me to actually come. Mad leap of logic, I know." He pushed away from the door and strolled toward them. "Good afternoon, Lady Felicity. It's been far too long since I've had the opportunity to stand in your lovely presence."

Dering scowled. If his brother thought he could come and casually flirt with her, he was about to discover otherwise.

Felicity, on the other hand, didn't seem nearly as displeased as Dering felt. In fact, she looked downright welcoming. Holding out her hand, she said, "So nice to see you again, Mr. Stark. We were just about to play a game of billiards, if you'd like to join us?"

Eric lifted her hand—her ungloved hand, the bastard—and brushed a kiss to her knuckles.

"I'm sure he'll be wanting to rest from his journey," Dering interjected, laying a hand to his brother's shoulder and squeezing hard enough to get his point across. For some reason, the warning only seemed to make Eric's amusement that much more apparent.

Not wanting to give him a chance to disagree, Dering added, "And I was merely surprised by your arrival. Mother indicated that you would all be coming early next week."

Eric shrugged. "Yes. Well, we all know how pleasant it is to travel with Mother. I decided to come up a little early so I could travel at my own pace. Plus, I was anxious to see what pleasures the festival had to offer. It appears there are many." He gave a sly half smile that accentuated the indentation in his left cheek.

Damn the man for coming to the obvious conclusion about Dering's intentions with Felicity.

Patting him firmly on the back, Dering gave an impatient smile. "There are indeed. Why don't you go get settled, and we can discuss the upcoming events over dinner? Say, eight o'clock?" That would give him a good four hours to enjoy the afternoon with Felicity, take her home, and be back with time to spare.

"Actually," his brother said, drawing out the word as he tortured Dering with the possibility he would insist on staying. Dering squeezed his shoulder a little harder, making him give a half laugh, half cough. "That sounds perfect. The journey was terribly exhausting, after all. I'll probably go upstairs and sleep for the rest of the afternoon. So very tired," he added, obviously mocking Dering now.

"Excellent," Dering said, releasing his hold on the man's shoulder. "Tell Mrs. Littleford of our dinner plans, and I will see you at eight."

Stepping away from Dering's reach, Eric bowed to Felicity. "It was a pleasure, my lady. I hope to see you throughout the summer. Perhaps we'll even have a chance to talk."

"I certainly hope so," she said, offering him a broad smile.

Felicity breathed out a long, quiet breath as Dering's brother turned and left the room. She had been equally vexed and glad for his intrusion, which in itself was vexing. She wasn't even sure what had happened earlier, but when Dering's fingers had laced with hers, a part of her had nearly melted in delight. A delight that wasn't necessarily found between friends.

It had been so long since she'd enjoyed the touch of a man. Not in a sexual way—though, obviously, that too—but in the casual way that one grows used to when living with a man. The holding of hands, the brushing of arms, the embraces of welcome or parting. It was something that could only be shared with a person of whom one was particularly fond, someone held in very high regard and with a high level of trust.

She hadn't realized just how much of her still craved that kind of touch.

The thing was, she wasn't altogether certain it was right that she share that sort of thing with Dering. Was she, in a way, using their friendship? Abusing it? He just made her feel so wonderful. It was something that was very hard to step away from. She wasn't sure if she wanted to, even if she probably should.

Blast, she hadn't expected things to get complicated between them.

With him, things were supposed to be simple. Easy. And they were, most of the time. It was effortless to fall into the old ways with him, when they had known each other inside and out. She worried the inside of her cheek as she turned back to face him.

"Perhaps we should call it a day," she said, keeping her tone light. "I wouldn't want to disturb your brother's rest."

His jaw set in a hard square. "No, we absolutely should not. Eric will be an entire house away, and will be more bothered by the maids than by us. Furthermore, you said you wanted to play billiards, and by God you shall play."

Her smile was completely genuine as she met his dark, determined gaze. "Well, if you insist. However, *I* must insist that we keep our hands to ourselves, lest another of your brothers make an unannounced arrival."

She was almost disappointed when he nodded in

agreement. "Whatever the lady wishes. Just be glad that there are no bets in place, because you are most certainly about to lose."

For the rest of the afternoon, they played as competitively as ever, teasing and taunting all the while. It was fun. Carefree. It reminded her of the way she used to feel, before her world had been turned upside down. More and more she found herself feeling *normal*. The old normal, not the new one. The new normal meant living with a constant knot in her chest, feeling like she could lose everything all over again in the snap of a finger. The old normal was happiness and security and rosy outlooks.

It was easy to feel as though nothing bad could happen when someone as imposing as Gavin was by one's side.

When she arrived back home, the sound of pianoforte music filled the house, its merry tune making her smile. She made her way to the morning room that served dual purpose as a music room and found Charity sitting at the stool, no sheet music to be found, her fingers flying over the keys as she played a sweet and light composition.

Lady Effington was situated on the sofa, her skirts hidden beneath a light throw while Isabella sat in her lap playing with a pair of wooden blocks. They both seemed as happy as clams.

Coming around to where they sat, Felicity smiled. "It appears that Bella talked you into breaking her out of nursery prison again," she said, winking at the dowager as she lifted Bella into her arms. She smelled of sweet milk and lilac, the latter thanks to Lady Effington's favorite scent.

The music ceased as Charity turned around and smiled in welcome. "Did you have a lovely time?"

Felicity had been somewhat vague when saying that she and Dering would be spending the afternoon together. Charity wouldn't have thought twice of their choice of activities, but for some reason Felicity hadn't wanted to share. They would probably make a fuss over how happy they were that she was enjoying herself, and she didn't want to make it into more than it was.

"Certainly. Oh, and Dering's brother Eric arrived this afternoon. He's looking so well, I'm happy to say."

Charity smiled. "That's great to hear. He had a very rough time of it growing up, but he seems much better ever since leaving home." Coming to her feet, Charity walked over the tea tray and poured herself a cup. She offered one to Felicity, but she shook her head.

"I don't think I realized he moved out. Where does he live now? Don't they worry about him having an episode if he's on his own?" One of the most awful memories of her childhood was when they'd found him gasping for breath in the garden, nearly blue from the lack of air. Lady Carlisle hadn't let him back outside for a month after that.

She hugged Isabella even tighter just thinking about it. The idea of something happening to her daughter like that was enough to make her break out in a sweat. Bella seemed perfectly healthy, of course, but then again, so had Ian. One minute he had been enjoying dinner with her, and the next . . . he was gone. Some sort of horrible reaction, the doctor had said. Some people were simply intolerant of certain things, and there was no way to know why.

Which was just about the most terrifying thought of the whole thing.

Charity shrugged, oblivious to Felicity's sudden turn

of thought. "I'm not exactly sure. A set of rooms in London, perhaps? He's determined to live on his own, so if his parents worry, I'm not sure there is much they could do about it."

Shaking her head, Felicity looked down at Isabella and wrinkled her nose at her. "You must always do as your mother says, do you hear me? I expect you to stay safe and sound at my side until you're thirty."

"No," her daughter said, the word exceedingly firm.

Felicity laughed out loud and swayed from side to side. These days, that seemed to be her favorite word, no matter the question. "All right, then. In that case, I insist that you run away to Scotland with the first handsome boy that turns your head."

"No," Bella said again. This time, Charity and her grandmother laughed as well.

Chuckling, Felicity kissed her on the nose. "I do believe it is time for someone's supper." She glanced to the other women and said, "I'll see you a little later. Thank you for entertaining Bella for the afternoon."

"Absolutely our pleasure. Hopefully the nursemaid doesn't mind that we keep stealing her away. Oh," Charity exclaimed, raising her hand as a thought occurred to her. "How could I have forgotten? A package came for you today. It's upstairs in your bedchamber. I can't wait to hear what you think."

A package? She wasn't expecting anything, but her friend's grin made it clear that she knew something Felicity didn't. Nodding her thanks with a suspicious half grin, she headed upstairs to her room, taking Isabella with her. She was too curious to wait until after dinner.

As she entered the light and airy space, she paused,

certainly not expecting the sight that awaited her. There on her bed were not one, but two huge neatly wrapped packages with a note tucked beneath the green satin ribbon tied around the one on the right. What on earth was this all about?

Setting Bella on the plush, pale yellow rug that covered much of the room's hardwood floors, she pulled open the note.

With love from your friends.

With an inkling of what it might have been slipping through her mind, she carefully unwrapped the first package, then quickly undid the other. *Oh my.* Before her lay two glorious gowns, both in the most vibrant of hues. One was deep green, with gorgeous gold trim and delicately embroidered leaves embellishing the high waist and flounced hem. The second was a stunning deep coral, almost orange gown. It was so beautiful, so rich in both color and fabric, she held it up to her and did a little twirl. She recognized the fabric as the one May had showed her, but it was even more lovely in its final form.

She caught a glimpse of herself in the full-length mirror as she spun and paused. She almost didn't recognize the woman looking back at her. Her cheeks were flushed, her eyes bright, and the smile was broader than anything she'd glimpsed from herself in ages. The gown was a perfect reflection of how she felt since coming here. No longer interested in donning the sweet pastels of youth or the dull lilac and lavender of mourning. This was the color for a woman who wanted to be happy again. More than happy: joyful.

She would never stop mourning Ian. No gown or bauble could change that, and she wouldn't want it to.

But she would stop loitering in the background of her own life. She'd honor both Ian and her daughter by embracing the time she was given on this earth.

Starting tomorrow, she would step out into the world with her head held high. And, she thought, hugging the gown to her body, she would do it with color.

"My apologies for ruining whatever private little moment you were having with Lady Felicity. I do hate being where I'm not wanted."

Dering set aside the days-old copy of the *Times* he'd been reading as he waited for his brother and leaned back in his chair. "The prodigal child returns, and at the worst possible time."

"Prodigal?" Eric scoffed. "You make my life sound much more interesting than it is."

"Interesting enough to keep you away for long stretches at a time," Dering said mildly before taking a sip of his brandy.

"Your memories are of freedom. Mine are of oppression. Doesn't exactly encourage family dinners and games of charades by the fire."

Dering's forehead creased as he sent his brother a censorious look. "You have memories because you lived. At least give them credit for that."

Allowing a small nod as he pulled out his chair, Eric said, "They did their best. I think the doctors were full of hot air, but that's just coming from the seven-year-old who was forced to smoke every night and vomit every day."

It was an old grudge, one that Dering was well aware of, but that he knew there was nothing to be done for. His parents loved Eric and had done everything in their power to keep him healthy. The treatments might have seemed more barbaric than the actual illness, but they had consulted the best doctors money could buy and felt they had no choice but to follow those doctors' orders.

"I hope you've got that out of your system now so that you can be pleasant when the others arrive." He set the glass down and sighed. They didn't always get along, but he was happy to have him here. His timing could have used some work, but nevertheless, it was good to see him. "I am glad you decided to come. And I know Mother will be thrilled."

Eric pressed his lips together in a tight smile. "Yes, it's out. Hopefully this visit will tide them over for a while. And speaking of visits," he said, settling back in his chair with a shrewd smile, "Lady Felicity?"

Dering gave a light shrug as a footman came in with the first course of their meal. The steam rising from the onion soup he set before them was deliciously fragrant. "She is a longtime friend. You know that. We had a whim to play a game or two, so we did."

"I should have friends like that," Eric deadpanned, dipping his spoon into the soup.

"You don't know what you're talking about, so I suggest you don't talk." Dering was not in the mood to have his younger brother tease him about any woman, let alone Felicity.

"I know what I saw. And I know that you were more than friends in the past."

Dering opened his mouth, but Eric put a hand up. "Correction," he said, his voice perfectly mild. "I know that you *wanted* to be more than friends in the past. Appears as though you may finally get your wish."

"Get your mind out of the gutter," Dering said, warning wrapped around every word. "Felicity is a lady, and she doesn't deserve to be spoken of as though she were some sort of paramour."

"Christ, Gavin, whose mind is in the gutter now? I only meant that I saw the interest and attraction between the two of you. Not that it matters. I'm not in the habit of gossiping to others."

Dering blew out a frustrated breath. He was overreacting, and he knew it, but damn if his brother didn't put his hackles up. He'd rather no one be privy to the details of his and Felicity's relationship. He wasn't going to marry her, for God's sake, and what the two of them engaged in as mature adults was nobody's business but their own. "Then drop it."

They ate their soup in silence for a few minutes. When he was done, Dering set down his spoon and settled his gaze on his brother. "How are things at the Kingsmen?"

Eric glanced up from the dregs of his soup, then finished the last spoonful before answering. "Excellent. You should come by sometime. We let dandies such as yourself in the ring if your pockets are full enough."

The comment made him crack a smile. "I think I'll stick with Gentleman Jackson's Saloon, but thank you. One scandalous Stark brother is good enough for now." His brother's boxing club drew some of the best fighters around, but there was nothing polished or civilized about the place. They enjoyed many a deep-pocketed patron from the upper echelons of society, but no gentleman would ever step in the ring.

They shared their first genuine grin since Eric's arrival. "We have the life-of-the-party heir, the academic, and the army officer. Of course it was my duty to be the black sheep."

"Not a black sheep. More . . . gray. Mother might not survive black."

Eric snorted. "Mother would survive the apocalypse."

As the footman whisked away the first course plates and set the second course in place, Dering's thoughts returned to the present. "I'm still rather shocked you'll be attending the festival. Anything in particular you'd like to see?"

Most people just thought that the once-sickly son of the Earl of Carlisle kept to himself. He wasn't quite outside of society, but he'd never chosen to attend the Season or any of its entertainments. Dering was less surprised by his brother's choice to visit their parents here than he was by Eric's comment that he was looking forward to the festival events.

"I'm not sure. I hear this is unlike any event out there. I like the idea of enjoying exceptional music while mingling with some interesting people."

Nodding, Dering cut into his broiled trout. "Very well. There's a performance of Handel's 'Music for the Royal Fireworks' in Sydney Park Wednesday night, complete with fireworks. I think that's the biggest event between now and the gala, and has the added benefit of taking place before our parents arrive."

"Music *and* explosions?" He made a sound of approval. "Who knew this rambling old city had it in her?"

"Does that mean you'll join us? The organizers decided against boxes, but I'm sure we can stake a claim." He'd already spoken with Radcliffe, who had agreed to meet up along with Lady Radcliffe. Sophie and Charity would both be coming without their respective spouses. Two of Dering's other friends, the Marquis of Gilcrest and Captain Andrews, would also be in attendance. He had asked Felicity earlier in the week, but she had declined, much to his dismay.

His brother hefted a forkful of the fish. "I think I will," he said before stuffing the food in his mouth.

Dering smiled. "Excellent." It would be a unique experience, spending a night in the society of not only his friends, but his reclusive brother as well.

His mind wandered back to Felicity, and the enjoyable afternoon they had spent. What would have happened if Eric hadn't come in when he had? Dering swallowed against the swell of exhilaration that washed through him at the thought. She had been so receptive to his touch. The feel of her pressed against his side had been pure heaven.

And he wanted more.

If she was comfortable with sharing the kind of contact they had already had, he felt confident that she would be receptive to a kiss. It was the simplest thing, but he ached with the desire to embrace her whenever she was near. He couldn't keep on with this, or he'd end up in the exact same position as he had a decade ago.

This was his opportunity to correct the mistakes of his past. No more allowing interruptions and excuses to get in the way. The next time they were together, he had to take a chance.

He might not have been risking his heart, as he had before, but he was still risking his pride, and possibly his friendship. It was a steep bet, but one that he felt could pay dividends.

It was time to make his move.

Chapter Eleven

Stepping out of the carriage and onto the pavement outside of the northernmost entrance to Sydney Gardens, Felicity drew a fortifying breath, attempting to quell the nerves that danced through her belly like autumn leaves in the wind.

She felt pretty—beautiful even—swathed in the gorgeous deep coral silk. Her hair was pulled up in the front with a cascade of curls draping down over one shoulder. Not wanting her jewelry to compete with the gown, she'd worn her mother's simple but lovely pearl necklace and earbobs along with a pair of ivory gloves that matched the color of the jewelry exactly.

The effect was striking, she knew, but that was precisely why her pulse was fluttering so fast. She felt pretty, yes, but more than anything, she felt *conspicuous*. She should have chosen the green gown. It was every bit as lovely, but not nearly as arresting. This one had drawn her like a month to a flame, and she hadn't stopped to consider that it might have a similar effect on others.

Already she could see heads turning and eyebrows lifting. A few of the passing gentlemen dipped their heads in acknowledgment when her eyes inadvertently met theirs. That was *not* something she was accustomed to. For the last year and a half, she had perfected the art of not calling attention to herself.

Looking down to avoid any more accidental eye contact, she adjusted her skirts, letting the silky fabric fall around her ankles. The setting sun was nearly the same color as the fabric, and when the light hit it just so, it shimmered like fire.

As Sophie stepped down, she glanced around at the bustle of people, her hands clasped in delight. "This is going to be so much fun. You'll be so glad you decided to join us after all," she said, her sweet face luminescent with excitement. Her dark curls had been tamed into several intertwining braids at her crown, which served as a perfect backdrop to the diamond tiara she wore. Her golden gown was elegant in its simplicity, with tiny crystal beads serving as the only embellishment.

Having taken in their surroundings, Sophie turned her attention back to Felicity. "You look as lovely as a Greek goddess in that gown, which I'm sad to say would never work with my coloring but which looks positively divine against yours, you lucky girl."

"Thank you," Felicity replied, offering her friend a grateful smile. Sophie always worked wonders at calming her nerves. There was nothing like the countess's easy confidence and happy chatter to help disperse her doubts.

Charity looked up from smoothing her skirts and offered Felicity a wide grin. "She's right, you know. Can you imagine if I attempted to wear that color? It would clash so violently with my hair, people would be forced to shield their eyes. More's the pity, because it is gorgeous, as are you."

Felicity wouldn't go as far as all that, but she appreciated the sentiment nonetheless. This was to be her rebirth, of sorts. This was her, stepping out from the dull grays and lilacs that she had hidden behind these last few months, and reasserting herself as something more than just a widow. She was a mother, friend, daughter, unique person, and yes, widow. Those things added up to so much more than just a woman whose husband was gone far too soon.

"You two are much too generous—with both your compliments and your gifts—but I thank you. I'm trying not to feel as though everyone is staring at me, so let us cease this talk of how I look and move on to what a lovely evening this is, and how very fine the flowers are."

"I do so love all the lilies," Sophie said, offering her elbow to Felicity. The three of them linked arms and joined the stream of people heading into the park. The smell of roasting nuts and fresh-baked breads fragranced the air as they passed the dozen or so street vendors lining the path. Felicity had been to several other events, but this seemed to be the most popular so far, which was saying something considering the popularity of the opening ball.

"Lady Cadgwith!"

They paused as Charity turned and looked for who had called her name. "Yes?"

Sir Anthony, a longtime friend of Felicity's cousins, the Potters, stepped back in surprise, his kind face turning the slightest shade of pink. "Oh, I do beg your pardon, my lady. I should have said the *Dowager* Lady Cadgwith. Though it is very nice to see you as well. And you, Lady Evansleigh."

Charity offered him a gracious smile. "Think nothing of it."

The baronet turned back to Felicity and offered a respectful dip of his head. "Mrs. Potter had mentioned that you were in town, and I merely wished to offer my welcome. You are looking quite, quite well, I'm glad to see," he said, his glance briefly dropping to her gown.

The compliment was meant in kindness, but Felicity couldn't help the blush that heated her cheeks. "Thank you, Sir Anthony. The same can be said of you. And please, call me Lady Felicity."

"As you wish, my lady." He smiled and gestured to the path before them. "May I escort you three ladies to the amphitheater? I just so happen to be meeting Mr. and Mrs. Potter tonight, and I'm sure they'd be delighted to see you all."

They agreed, and together they set off toward the dirt path that led to the park's center. Sir Anthony was exactly Felicity's height, so it was easy for them to converse as they strolled through the grounds. He was in his late fifties and had served for years as one of the king's advisors due to his extensive military background. With his short stature, mostly bald head, and kind smile, it was almost impossible to imagine him as the officer he had once been.

Patting her hand where it perched on his arm, he said, "It is so good to see you back in our fair city. Have you any plans to return to the fold?"

"Move back to Somerset, you mean?"

He nodded, mild curiosity lifting his gray eyebrows.

"No, not at all. I'm very happy in Cadgwith. It feels very much like home after all this time." She didn't point out that her immediate family no longer lived in the area.

"You don't miss having family around? Or the society of a bigger city?"

She tilted her head, her brow knitting. "But I do have family around. Lord and Lady Cadgwith are there, as is my daughter, and the villagers have quite accepted us into the fold. You have no idea what a feat that was," she added with a wry smile.

"As for the society," she continued, watching the path in front of them as they strolled forward, "I'm not one to attend these sorts of amusements, typically. Tea with friends and the Flora Day celebration are quite enough society for me."

"Yes, but I'm sure that makes it somewhat difficult to meet new people. It won't be long before you'll want to reenter the marriage mart, I imagine. You are still so very young, after all." He said it as though it was a foregone conclusion.

It was only good manners that kept her moving forward. It wasn't rude, per se, but her marital status, current or future, was none of his business. "That's not something that I've cared to think about, Sir Anthony. It's only been a little over a year and a half since my husband's passing."

He looked to her with some surprise. "Has it been that recently? I was somehow thinking it was two years ago." He shook his head. "Time does tend to get away from me these days. I hope you received my condolences, but let me just say again how sorry I am for your loss."

"Thank you. It is kind of you to say so," she murmured. It was her ready reply these days.

He pursed his lips as he kept his attention on the path. "It's so hard when tragedy strikes so young. My first wife was only two-and-twenty, and I twenty-seven when she died. I'm surprised by how often she still comes to mind."

Felicity cut a startled glance over to him. "You've been

widowed twice?" she asked, unable to keep the incredulity from her voice. She'd known him for two decades, at least. How had she not known that he'd had more than one wife?

He sighed and nodded. "I am not what I would call lucky in marriage. But," he added, sending her a rather devilish smile, "I imagine that, should I marry again, the odds are in my favor that she'll outlive me."

She probably shouldn't have laughed at such a morbid observation, but it was clear the statement was intended to amuse. "I have no idea how to respond to that, so I will refrain." She couldn't imagine risking her heart one more time, let alone twice. "I do admire your positive outlook."

He gave a dismissive shrug, as though it were of no consequence. "I don't believe that we are made to be solitary beings, my lady," he said matter-of-factly. "Moreover, I find that I quite like sharing my life. I've not had any great love match, so I know nothing about that. But a marriage based on respect, friendship, and mutual regard can be very fulfilling. Besides," he added, his eyes twinkling with a bit of mischief, "I've found that though my dogs are excellent companions, they are terrible conversationalists."

She smiled and shook her head. "They are that."

But she couldn't stop thinking about what he had just said. Every time she even considered the possibility of marrying again, a hard knot formed in her chest at the thought of going through this a second time. But, she hadn't considered the possibility of marriage for companionship. For the sharing of lives and conversation and intimacy without the all-consuming love that made such a loss so excruciating.

Perhaps the key to being happy sometime down the road was to simply find a man she could enjoy, but not fall in love with. Someone she truly admired, respected, and liked. Someone like Mr. Anthorp. She bit her lip as his name crossed her mind. She hadn't thought of him over-much since leaving Cadgwith, but he had been such a safe and comforting presence these last few months. He was an exceedingly kind and pleasant man, he adored Isabella, and he had certainly made his fondness for her known.

She shook her head and took a deep breath. Good-ness, she wasn't ready to think of such things yet. Right now, she wished only to focus on Isabella and herself, and figure out exactly who she was now. She looked down at her gown and smiled softly. Apparently, she was a woman who liked a little color back in her life.

"Ah, there they are," Sir Anthony said, nodding toward the far right side of the amphitheater.

Up ahead, she could see her cousin sitting on a wide blanket, her attention diverted as she spoke with her husband. When they approached, Mr. Potter tipped his head toward them and Martha turned, a wide grin already in place. In the space of a second, she went from jolly and welcoming to wide-eyed and openmouthed.

Scrambling to her feet with the help of her husband, she hurried to Felicity's side. "Good evening, Sir Anthony. Lady Cadgwith and Lady Evansleigh, so lovely to see you. Might I steal my cousin for a moment?"

As the others nodded, Martha pulled her aside, her apple cheeks bright with color. "My dear, whatever are you wearing?"

Felicity's heart dropped as she looked down at the beautiful gown. "Isn't it lovely?" she asked brightly. "Lady Cadgwith and her wonderful friends had it made for me."

Even as she said the words, a distinct sense of wrong-doing settled in her stomach. She hated that about herself. Whenever anyone criticized her, she immediately felt like a wayward child. It was always especially acute when it came from someone she loved.

Obviously trying to be tactful, Martha offered her a diplomatic smile. "It's lovely, dear, but it is a little shocking, isn't it? I thought you were still in half mourning."

Lifting her chin, Felicity said, "No, I'm not. I was still wearing my old gowns, but it's been over a year and a half. Long enough, I think." But was it? If it were, why would she suddenly feel as though she was flouting accepted convention?

"I see. Oh, I *see*," her cousin said again, her eyes widening.

Felicity's brow furrowed. "You see . . . what?"

Lowering her voice as she leaned in close, she said, "I hadn't realized you were already looking for a husband again. I mean, I can see why, what with the wee one and the new baron taking a wife, but I just—"

Cutting her off before she could go any further down that particular route, Felicity waved her hands. "No, no, I am not. I assure you I am not." For heaven's sake! She had barely thought two words about it until a minute ago, and now her cousin was acting as though she had specifically dressed to catch a husband.

Martha blinked, clearly at a loss of what to say. "I . . . I mean you . . . rather I should say that dress does rather sound the alarm, though, doesn't it? You can't help but be noticed, which is a good thing if you are looking—"

"I'm *not*," Felicity said again, starting to feel more and more mortified.

Her cousin shifted uncomfortably, her coffee-brown eyes clouded with confusion. "Very well, then. Forget

I said anything, dear. I just didn't think you wanted to give off the wrong impression, is all."

Somehow, she managed to feel both indignant and rightfully shamed all at once. "Well, I suppose I should be thankful for the setting sun. Hopefully I shan't shock anyone in the dark."

Even as she tried to hold her head high, all of her enthusiasm for the evening seemed to seep out of her like tea from a cracked cup. She had worn the dress to feel *better* about things, not worse.

"Felicity," Charity said, diverting her attention. "The orchestra is getting their instruments ready, so I imagine things will begin soon. Are you ready to join the rest of our party?"

"Yes, of course," she murmured. She offered her cousin an abbreviated smile before following her friends off toward wherever their agreed-upon meeting place with the others was.

Her heart thumped uncomfortably in her chest as she glanced around at the other attendees, suddenly afraid that people would be staring at her. Not everyone was, of course, but more eyes were turned their way than she would have liked. By the time they reached the surprisingly lavish setup where the others were, Felicity honestly just wanted to go home.

Among the luxurious blankets, brightly colored pillows, sumptuous displays of food, and trays full of drinks, the group laughed and chatted merrily. She knew May and the duke, Gavin, his brother Eric, and her own brother Thomas, plus there were two other men she didn't recognize and one woman who was vaguely familiar, but Felicity couldn't quite place her.

Gavin was the first to notice their approach and quickly stood to greet them. "Welcome, ladies, to our humble feast," he announced, gesturing grandly around him. He kissed Charity's cheek and Sophie's hand, then turned his full attention to Felicity.

Shaking his head with pure admiration in his dark gaze, he said, "God's knees, Felicity, but you look incredible this evening."

Something about the way he spoke made her stomach somersault. If even Gavin was taking notice, she really must be beyond the pale. More than ever, she wished she could go back in time and choose the green dress. There was being bold, and then there was being audacious.

Coming to her feet, May made haste to join them. Her gown was an unusual but lovely shade of blue that brought attention to her light eyes, making them seem almost turquoise. "Oh, Felicity, the gown is everything I hoped it would be for you. Please tell me you love it."

Guilt layered over her regret, making her feel worse than ever. Their gift had been so generous, Felicity didn't want to disappoint her with her reservations. "It is practically a work of art. Thank you so very much. The three of you really shouldn't have."

"Of course we should have," she replied, completely matter-of-fact. "That's precisely what friends are for. Particularly when said friend is in the textile business."

Gavin's lips slid into a pleased grin. "I should have known fabric as fine as this would come from our boat. It gives me confidence that my investment will continue to thrive."

Gavin's brother approached then, his half smile revealing the dimple in his cheek. "Lady Felicity, I didn't think to see you again so soon." He lifted her hand to his lips for a brief kiss. "Must be my lucky day."

"Good evening, Mr. Stark. I didn't expect to see you here." It was unfair, but her mind went right back to the day that he had been found half-dead in the garden. Was it wise for him to be here in the park?

He sighed and shook his head as though divining her thoughts. "I know that look. Trust me when I say I always have my own best interests at heart. I've come a long way since childhood."

She flushed and nodded quickly. "Of course you have. I can't help it, I'm afraid. As a mother, I'm always worried about everyone."

"Well," Gavin said, setting a hand to the small of her back, "perhaps someone should worry about you. Can I offer you something to eat? Or a drink, perhaps?"

She shook her head. Her appetite had fled the moment her cousin's eyes had widened in horror. And now she had managed to, if not insult Eric, certainly to cause some offense.

One of the men she didn't know came to join them, his sharp uniform easily marking him as a military man. "Dering, you must introduce me to your lovely friend here." He made no effort to hide the admiration in his eyes as he beamed at her.

Felicity smiled tightly, not at all in the mood to worry about the niceties of introduction.

"Must I?" Gavin quipped, offering her a teasing wink. "Captain John Andrews, allow me to introduce you to Lady Felicity, the Dowager Lady Cadgwith. I believe you're already acquainted with the current Lady Cadgwith," he said, nodding toward Charity.

The captain bowed over her hand, his eyes never

leaving hers. "A pleasure to meet you, my lady. I've known your brothers for a few years, and now I know where all the good looks went in the family."

Blessedly, the music started then, and after an abbreviated round of introductions, they all moved to take their places. As she sat in a spot beside her brother, he looked her up and down, his pale eyes bright with surprise and merriment. "Well, aren't we just a ray of orange sunshine in the gloom of twilight? I don't think I've ever seen Andrews fawn over someone like that."

"It is just a gown, Thomas," she murmured, quiet enough that the others wouldn't be able to hear her above the rising music. "It's not as though I've made some sort of great transformation."

He blinked, probably shocked by her sour response. She was never short with him. "I may have been teasing, but it was an honest compliment. And I beg to differ, actually. You look as though you transformed back into that which you once were: a sunny young woman with a light that shines from the inside out."

It was a sweet thing to say, but it didn't help the way she was feeling. "Well, according to Martha, I've inadvertently thrown myself back into the marriage market simply by wearing this gown. Who knew that coral was the color for desperate widows in search of husbands."

Her brother, who had just taken a sip of his wine, very nearly spit it out all over the gown in question. Swallowing, he coughed a few times, doing his best to stifle the noise with the sleeve his jacket. "For God's sake, give a bit of warning before saying something like that."

He coughed a bit more before looking back to her, his expression bordering on exasperated. "Our cousin is a sweet woman, but she's not one for subtlety, is she?

Given that she's from a different generation, I suppose we must give her the benefit of the doubt, but honestly I don't know what she was thinking."

"She was thinking I look like a woman on the prowl, so to speak."

He rolled his eyes. "Felicity, do you really care what she or anyone else says? You look beautiful, and coming from the moral authority of the family—me—I give you my official seal of approval. There. A man of God said it, so it cannot be countered."

That pulled a reluctant smile from her. "Still, my heart is really not in this evening any longer. I think I would rather just head home before it gets too late and enjoy a quiet evening."

He cocked his head, eyeing her carefully. "Are you feeling a bit . . . overwhelmed?"

Yes, that was it exactly. She nodded, the prickle of coming tears burning her eyes. She had finally experienced her first desire to be daring, to step outside of the confines that had cloistered her for so long, and now she felt as though she had stepped straight into criticism.

Guilt tugged at her. Even though it wasn't logical, she felt as though she'd let Ian down. She pressed her eyes closed for a moment. Perhaps she just wasn't as ready for this as she thought. As much as she longed to recapture the spirit of the carefree girl she might have once been, there was no way to get back to that place. Too much had happened, and she was a different person because of it.

Laying a comforting hand on her shoulder, her brother said, "Shall I take you home?" His voice was quiet. Respectful. Nothing like his normal lighthearted, teasing ways.

"No, I'd rather you didn't," she said as she successfully blinked back the tears. Swallowing, she added, "I'm more than capable of seeing myself home. I'll take the carriage and send it back for Sophie and Charity." The lump in her throat eased a bit with the plan. It was the right thing, even if it was the cowardly thing. "Will you tell them I wasn't feeling well and decided to leave?"

The music was in full swing now, holding the people crowded around the amphitheater in thrall. The last thing she wanted to do was interrupt their enjoyment. They likely would insist on coming with her.

Thomas quirked a golden brow. "You wish for me to lie? I do have to draw the line somewhere, you know."

"It's not a lie," she insisted. "I genuinely am not feeling well. Emotionally. Now promise you'll do as I say. You are still my younger brother, after all, and must listen to me."

"I don't answer to you, thank you very much," he said, only half teasing. "However, if you feel strongly about it, I will convey your message. Stay to the lighted path. Darkness always falls quicker than you expect." Already the sun had disappeared completely, and purple twilight was replacing the pinks and yellows of sunset.

Smiling, she leaned forward and kissed his cheek. "Thank you, Thomas. Enjoy the music, and I'm sure I'll see you this week."

As quietly as she could manage, she rose to her feet and weaved her way through the blankets to the path. They were close enough to the perimeter that she was able to quickly navigate away from the crowd, hopefully drawing a minimum of attention.

Already she felt better, getting away from the crush of people. Her heart was slowing to its normal rhythm, and the tight band that had settled around her chest seemed to be easing. She was a fool, really. Both for wearing the dress, and for letting the comments of others get under her skin.

Yes, she should have known that she'd be drawing attention to herself, which was never something that she enjoyed. But at the same time, why couldn't other people just mind their own business? Why should it matter to them what she wore, or whether she wished to remarry, or where she chose to live? Why should she be made to feel as though, by donning a gown, she was making some sort of definitive, irreversible decision to move on?

"Festivities are that way, love."

Felicity let out a little squeak of surprise at the unexpected intrusion, her hand flying to her throat. With her wandering thoughts, she had failed to notice a man in dark, formal clothing leaning against a nearby tree, a cheroot dangling from his lips.

"Yes, I know. Thank you." Her unease made her voice tight. Wary. She shifted to carry on again, but he pushed away from the trunk and walked toward her.

Flicking the cheroot to the ground, he angled his head, pushed out his bottom lip, and exhaled a stream of smoke. "I saw you at the opening ball last week," he said with that haughty, arrogant tone that only the most privileged can perfect. "Since we've a mutual friend in Lord Derington, why don't we fudge and consider that introduction enough. I'm Lord Bridgemont, heir of the Earl of Marks. And you are . . . ?"

The Earl of Marks. She knew that name. If she recalled correctly, her father rather disliked the man. She couldn't recall the details, but she was sure of the sentiment. Still, if he was a friend of Gavin's . . .

After a moment's hesitation, she said, "Lady Felicity Danby. My father is the Earl of Landowne."

Recognition flared in his pale, nearly colorless eyes. He really was handsome, in a cool, angled sort of way. Or perhaps *handsome* wasn't the right word. He had a beauty that bordered on feminine. "Ah yes. The elusive daughter who handily bypassed the marriage mart all those years ago. Always did wonder what we were missing."

She stiffened at the crassness of the statement. "Well, if you'll excuse me, I have somewhere I have to be."

"And I have someone else to meet, but that shouldn't preclude me from escorting you where you wish to go." His clipped, nasal tone grated on her nerves. Or perhaps it was the entitlement that he wore around him like a mantle. "It is getting rather dark, after all. One never knows what lurks just out of sight."

Pasting a cool smile to her lips, she shook her head. "I'll pass, but thank you. I wouldn't wish for your appointment to be delayed on my behalf."

She might as well have said nothing for all the impact it had. He gave a smile that made her shudder. "I'd miss it altogether for you, my lady." He held out his elbow. "As a gentleman, I must insist."

Blast. Pursing her lips together, she placed her fingers on the very edge of his sleeve. The sooner she allowed him to escort her, the sooner she could be done with him.

Chapter Twelve

Dering had sensed the moment Felicity had slipped away. He didn't know if it was the rustle of her skirts or the receding scent of gardenias, but by the time he turned his head, she was already making her escape.

He had raised a questioning brow to Thomas, who shrugged as he popped a handful of grapes in his mouth. Dering had not been pleased. Where would she be going just as the concert was beginning?

His first instinct had been to go after her immediately, but to do so would surely draw notice. Instead he had waited, counting down the seconds in his head. After three minutes had passed, he casually rolled to his feet and stepped off to the side, going a different direction than she had. As soon as he made it to the trees, he had broken out into a jog and skirted his way around, keeping an eye out all along for the shimmery orange gown that had knocked the breath from his lungs as surely as a well-placed punch to the sternum when he had seen it.

That feeling had been nothing compared to what he felt now, staring in absolute incredulity as Felicity laid her hand on Bridgemont's arm. *Bridgemont!* What the devil would she want with that snake of a man? His teeth clenched as he considered then immediately discarded the possibility of an assignation. She couldn't possibly have that bad of taste.

Still, that didn't negate the fact that she was walking away from the concert with the man, her orange skirts shimmering in the lantern light.

God, that gown.

It had been starkly different from any of the others he had seen her wear, all of which had plainly been in deference to her mourning. The question that had immediately assailed him at the sight of her was *why?* Was she shedding the restrictions of half mourning? Was she ready to move on to the next part of her life? His heart had surged with the possibility at the time, eagerly anticipating all that that could mean, but now a new thought came to mind: Did the dress have something to do with this cozy little meeting?

Setting his jaw, he stalked forward. When he was about fifteen paces behind them, he said, "There you are, Lady Felicity. Are you lost?"

She whirled around, her eyes wide in the dim light. "Gavin! I mean, Dering, what are you doing here?"

Bridgemont pressed his lips together in that way he liked to do when he was carefully observing potential gossip. "Derington," he said by way of acknowledgment. "Something we can do for you, old man?"

Dering's fists clenched at his sides. Punching the blackguard in the nose was *not* a good idea. Probably. Ignoring Bridgemont, he focused on Felicity. "I've come to escort you back. I know you must have gotten turned around in the darkness."

"Didn't Thomas tell you?" she asked "I've a headache and decided to go home."

Was she bloody mad? One did not go traipsing through parks at night looking like that. Or looking like anything, for that matter. His cheek muscles flexed as he gritted his teeth. "No, but I'm here now, so allow me to escort you to your carriage."

Bridgemont gave a dismissive flick of his hand. "Already taken care of. You can just go back to your little party. I'm sure everyone is missing your presence terribly."

Perhaps just the jaw. A hit to the jaw was much less painful than the nose. He glared at the man for a moment before turning his gaze to Felicity, infusing a healthy dose of warning into his expression. "Felicity?"

Her eyes narrowed just enough to tell him she wasn't pleased before she turned to her escort. "You do have that appointment, so I'll just go with Dering from here. It was nice to meet you."

Nodding, he reached for her hand and brought it to his lips. The kiss he pressed there lingered long enough for Dering to take an ominous step forward. Bridgemont finally straightened and smiled. "The pleasure was all mine, Lady Felicity. I look forward to seeing you again soon."

Dering stood still as he waited for the bastard to move far enough away that he wouldn't be able to properly hear what Dering had to say. Finally, he turned on Felicity, barely hanging on to his temper. "What in the hell was that all about? Have you lost your bloody mind?"

Instead of being contrite, she glared right back at him. "Have you lost *your* mind? You, sir, are not my keeper."

She turned and started stalking away, her footsteps soft on the dirt path despite her aggravation. Dumbfounded that she would walk away from him like that, he hesitated a moment before chasing after her.

"No, I am not your keeper," he said, annoyance thick on his tongue. "But this whole incident makes me wonder if you need one. Bridgemont? Seriously?"

She stopped abruptly in her retreat. "He's *your* friend, not mine. If you have any problem with my conversing with the man, that is your own problem."

Dering nearly choked on his disgust. "That man is no friend of mine. Acquaintance, yes, but I wouldn't trust him as far as I could throw him. Actually, I wouldn't trust him half that far." His chest burned with the anger he'd felt upon seeing them alone together in the darkness. "Did you plan to meet him?"

Sighing with exasperation, she shook her head. "No, I did not. I was telling the exact truth when I said I was on my way home. Lord Bridgemont waylaid me, enlightened me as to our mutual friend—*you*—and introduced himself. He insisted on escorting me, and frankly it just seemed easier than arguing."

She started walking again, forcing him to follow or be left behind. "If you would have just told me of your intent in the first place, I could have escorted you then. In that case, none of this would even be an issue."

He knew the feeling deep in his gut, even if he didn't want to admit it. *Jealousy.* He'd hated seeing her on another man's arm like that. She should be *his*, damn it.

"Dering, contrary to what you clearly believe, I am perfectly capable of seeing to myself. I've done so for a decade without having you to guide me."

Now she was well and truly aggravated. He scraped his hands through his hair, attempting to get a hold of his temper. "Yes, I am aware." If he had had his way, she wouldn't have ever left his side, but that was a ship that had sailed far too long ago to belabor the point.

"Felicity, what is going on here? Everything seemed fine when you arrived tonight. Brilliant, even. Why the sudden change of heart?"

She lifted her chin just a smidge, enough to let him know that there really was something wrong. "Please, Gavin, can we just let it go? I'd like to leave, and that's all you need to know."

There was his name again. He had told her not to use it, but the sound of it on her lips sent warmth rushing through him. "Was it Captain Andrews? I know he was a little obvious in his interest, but he really is a decent man."

"No, it wasn't him or anyone else. Like I said, I'm not feeling well."

He didn't believe that for a minute. "Don't be ridiculous. You've never looked more well in your life." The gown had an enticing sheen to it that showed her every breath and outlined her every move.

Her eyes narrowed as she shook her head. "No, Gavin, I'm not talking about how I look, or this silly dress, or what others see when they look at me. I'm talking about how I *feel*, and I don't. Feel. Well." She bit off each of the last three words.

Almost as much as her words, the way her breath hitched told him that she was not exaggerating. He instantly felt contrite. Stepping closer, he ran a hand lightly along the outside of her arm. "I'm sorry, Lissy. I didn't intend to upset you further."

She blew out a harsh breath, then shot him a frustrated look. "No, I'm in the wrong. I shouldn't have snapped at you like that. I'm just very tired, and I want to go home and lie down."

This wasn't like her at all. All of his anger from before evaporated to nothing as he glanced around, searching for a more private place where they could speak. A small copse of trees to their left concealed a little grassy knoll just on the other side that he knew about from his frequent visits to this park through the years.

"Here, come with me for just a moment."

"Dering, I don't want to. I simply wish to go home."

Dering again. He held out his hand, sending her a gently beseeching look. "Please, Felicity. Just for a few minutes, and then I will personally escort you to your carriage. Or mine, if you need it."

Blowing out a short breath, she reluctantly placed her hand in his. "I'm holding you to that."

He led her past the trees and to the small clearing beyond. Full darkness had finally fallen, and he could just make out the last strains of the piece the orchestra was playing. He knew that the main performance was about to begin, which meant the fireworks would start soon.

Turning to face her fully, he squeezed her hand. "Now, please, tell me what is the matter. I hate seeing you so upset and not having the first clue what to do to help."

"This isn't something for you to fix, Gavin. This is just me being foolish, and realizing that I'm being foolish but being unable to change it nonetheless."

He blinked at her, having no idea what the hell that meant. "I'm going to need more information."

She pressed her lips together for a moment, then exhaled a pent-up breath and grabbed a handful of her skirts. "I wore a dress that I thought I was ready to wear, but as it turns out, I am actually not. Not at all, in fact."

He did his best not to make a face. This was about *fashion*? "All right," he said uncertainly.

"No, it's not all right. Apparently by wearing this dress, I have set aside all thought or consideration for my dead husband, and I must now be on the search for a new husband. It isn't possible that I just wanted to wear something pretty for myself, and may still like to think of my husband on occasion. God forbid I be content with working through things in my own way, and wish to wear a pop of color because it makes me feel a spark of happiness."

She shook her head, her hands going to her chest. "I wasn't trying to make some sort of social statement. I'm just trying to heal *me* right now."

He gaped at her, astounded by the outpouring of emotion. God, but he felt like a proper arse. He himself had seen that dress and experienced a surge of optimism for what he thought was her signal that she was ready to move on.

He looked at her, really *looked* at her, and saw what he'd been missing since their reunion. She was not an old regret, or a missed opportunity. She wasn't a newly single woman in need of romance, and she wasn't a woman who deserved to be seduced. What she was, above all else, was his friend.

And in his selfish desire for her, he'd lost track of that.

Placing his hands on her shoulders, he looked her straight in the eye. "I'm sorry. Truly and honestly. You deserve to wear whatever the hell you want to wear. You deserve to be treated with respect. You deserve to live how you want, where you want, with whomever you want, on your own terms."

She closed her eyes and exhaled. Some of the tension

eased from her shoulders when she looked back up at him. "Thank you. I only wish the rest of society felt that way."

Releasing his hold, he tugged at the buttons of his jacket and pulled it off. Arranging it carefully on the ground, he sat down beside it and held out his hand. "Come, sit. Let's just . . . *be* for a moment."

Nodding, she gave him her hand and allowed him to help her down. He settled back, leaving an arm out for her, and after a moment's hesitation, she lowered herself down so she could use his arm as a sort of pillow to protect her hair from the grass.

They lay there quietly, listening to the muted sounds of Handel's masterpiece. When the first firework exploded, they saw the sizzling flash of light through the trees before they heard the boom a half second later. More followed, their brilliant bursts glittering through the sky as the music set the tone. Higher in the sky, infinitely far away, the hint of stars twinkled in the blackness of space.

He didn't think about kissing her. He didn't think about whether she would allow him more liberties or even want them. All he wished for as they shared the moment was her peace of mind.

He wanted to ease her pain. Soothe the anxiety and comfort her. He wanted the stillness and serenity to seep into her heart. And somehow, while doing absolutely nothing at all, he, too, found the peace he'd been missing for so long.

They lay there together for much longer than she had intended. It just felt so absolutely right. She hadn't even realized how much tension had built up between them until it wasn't there anymore.

She soaked in the calmness, allowing her mind to be still. No thinking, no worrying, no fruitless anxiety. Just . . . being.

Feeling the night air on her skin. The soothing heat of his arm beneath her neck. Listening to the distant perfection of the arrangement, played by the best musicians in the world. Staring at the stars in the heavens and the effervescent rockets closer to earth. Feeling the dull thump of the explosions in her chest between the steady rhythm of her own heart.

After a while, she turned to him, taking in the bold curve of his jaw and straight slash of his nose. She knew his features as well as her own, yet she felt as though she were looking at them for the first time. He turned his dark, fathomless eyes on her and she could see the sparkle of the distant fireworks reflected in his pupils.

He didn't say anything, didn't even move other than to blink. There was nothing about him that seemed to be rushing her. Tonight, something had changed in her. In him, too, though she couldn't say what it was. She realized now, lying in the dark with no words or expectations, that something really had shifted in her. The dress really had been an outward expression of the changes within her.

They weren't the changes that everyone seemed to think, though. It was more of the beginning of letting go. She wasn't done with mourning, not even close, but she was ready to start letting go of some of the things she had been holding so tightly to.

Her marriage had been wonderful, but it was time to move forward. She had to stop thinking of things in terms of what she would never do with Ian again, and start thinking of how grateful she was to have done them with him in the first place. By sharing those things with others, she wasn't dishonoring that. Those things were and always would be a part of her most treasured past.

She closed her eyes, listening to the music in the middle distance and the boom and crack of the fireworks. Life moved onward and forward. Moments like these were just that: moments. They were meant to be lived and enjoyed and hopefully set aside for memories that would later be cherished.

Opening her eyes, she met Gavin's silent gaze. Turning slightly onto her side, she lifted a finger and dragged it, feather soft, down the bridge of his nose, over his lips, and along the small dent in his chin. He didn't move an inch, didn't even tense. He just stared back at her, softly, somehow.

Tucking her hands beneath her chin, she wet her lips and whispered his name.

"Yes?"

"Will you please dance with me?"

He nodded, the gesture little more than a dip of his chin. Pushing up to a sitting position, she waited while he came to his feet and offered his hand. There was nothing hurried about his movements, nothing questioning in his gaze. He wasn't asking for reasons or making sure that this was what she really wanted.

He was simply trusting her to know.

She paused long enough to slip off her shoes and pull off her stockings. It was little more than a whim, but one she wanted to indulge. She wanted to feel the grass beneath her toes. She wanted to remember every moment of this dance, and dancing barefoot beneath the moon seemed just the way to do it.

Swallowing, she slipped her hand in his and allowed

him to pull her up. He moved one hand around to her back, while keeping the other firmly around her fingers. There was nothing possessive or pushy about the position. He was letting her make all the choices.

They stood there for a moment, completely still while they listened to the music. "Are you ready?" he asked, his voice whisper soft.

She closed her eyes and leaned her forehead against the firm wall of his chest. After this moment, she would never again be able to say that her last dance was with her husband. From this moment on, it would have to be good enough to say that she had shared many wonderful dances with him in her past.

But this was her present.

More than that, it was her future.

She drew a breath, looked up into his eyes, and nodded.

Chapter Thirteen

As gently as though she were made of glass, Gavin began to move with her in his arms. Felicity closed her eyes, trusting him to lead, trusting him to take care of her. He moved in time with the music, as graceful as reeds bending in the wind, each step so smooth they might as well have been floating.

It was nothing like any dance she had ever experienced. It was a pale, quiet interpretation of a waltz, just as the music was a distant echo of the orchestra. He held her much more closely than any public setting would ever allow, but there was nothing but sweetness in it.

The grass caressed her feet, the warm air embraced her, and the smell of roses and brandy comforted her. It was dreamlike, really. They glided together across the landscape, their bodies drifting closer and closer with each circuit. The music floated around them, the sky sparkled above them as they swayed back and forth in time with the music. Soon he released his hold on her hand and slipped his arm around her, embracing her as she rocked gently from side to side.

Tears spilled from her eyes then, falling down her cheeks and onto the fine lawn of his shirt. They came faster and faster as he held her close against his chest, saying nothing but everything all at once.

When the music faded, he didn't let her go. He held her, letting her soak his shirt as she cried for the last time for what had once been. For what could have been. For what never could be.

When she finally pulled back, he allowed his arms to fall away easily. The air was quiet now. In the wake of the explosions, tears, and music, there was peace. When he met her gaze, she saw the reflection of the moon in the damp trails down his cheeks. Whatever their relationship in the past, whatever it would be in the future, this moment, this single, fleeting moment in time, was exactly what it should be. Exactly what she needed it to be.

From this moment on, she was free.

Sitting in his study close to midnight, Dering stared into the amber depths of his brandy, contemplating the evening. He felt honored. More so than he ever had in his life. Felicity had trusted him with one of the most profound and moving moments he had ever been a part of or witness to, and for once he felt wholly worthy of that trust.

He had finally been the friend he should have been all these years.

Sitting back in his chair, he lifted the tumbler to the candlelight, idly swirling its contents around and around. If only he could go back and undo the way he had behaved. The way he *thought*. When she had come to play billiards with him, all he had thought about was how he could kiss her. How could he have stood there as she tried to recapture her joy, thinking only of how he could capture her?

What a bloody scoundrel he'd been.

From now on, their relationship would be about what was best for her. What she needed. Not to be lopsided, but just to be weighted toward which of them was most in need. If he was ever in such a position, then they could focus on him, but for now, he needed to be there for her.

The way he should have been all along.

Footsteps in the corridor pulled him from his introspection, and he glanced to the doorway just as his brother appeared, cravat untied and dark hair somewhat worse for the wear. "Do you make a habit of inviting people places and abandoning them?"

Setting down his drink, Dering shook his head and waved a hand toward a nearby chair. "My apologies. Something came up that required my attention." After what had happened between him and Felicity, he couldn't fathom returning to the party and making merry. He had taken her home and come back here, his emotions still too high from the experience.

Eric raised an eyebrow as he lowered himself into the overstuffed and oversized leather chair. "Yes, and would that something have been wearing an orange dress?"

"That something would be none of your business," Dering responded mildly.

"Tell that to the people you were supposed to be hosting. Do you think there was a single one of them who didn't notice the two of you had gone missing together?"

Dering shrugged, feeling absolutely no obligation to the others. They were friends, yes, but he didn't owe them anything. He servants took care of the food and cleanup, so all they had to do was enjoy themselves.

"She wasn't feeling well, so I escorted her home to make sure she arrived safely. By then it was late enough that it didn't really make sense to return."

Leaning back in his chair, Eric chuckled, the sound hollow. "If you say so, Gavin. I suppose you know much more about how the gossip in the *ton* works than I do. Especially since I don't particularly give a damn."

Dering wasn't going to let his brother ruin what he had shared with Felicity tonight. "Neither do I," he said curtly. Closing the subject, he stood and lifted the tumbler for a drink. The warm burn was as welcome as it was familiar. "I do, however, regret that you had to navigate your evening alone. I trust you enjoyed yourself?"

Accepting the change of subject, Eric nodded and came to his feet. "It was exceptional entertainment as concerts go. The company was decent enough, if a little civilized for my taste. Gilcrest invited me to a decent-stakes card game afterward, and I managed to win a few pounds."

Dering didn't comment on that last part. If he knew his brother, it was probably a few hundred pounds. "Glad you enjoyed it. And speaking of company, you'd best rest up. The family arrives tomorrow, and I imagine you'll need your wits about you."

Eric's smile was wry as he shook his head. "I'm not sure it's wits I'll need so much as armor. And I'm not the only one. Mother has taken to complaining even to me in her letters about her distinct lack of grandchildren. Gird your loins, dear brother, because I do believe she'll be on the warpath."

Light drizzle pattered at the nursery window as Felicity rocked Isabella in her lap, the pair of them reading her

ancient copy of *A Little Pretty Pocket-Book*. The book
had already yellowed by the time Felicity had received
it from her mother twenty-five years ago. It was so dear
to her that she loved sharing it with her daughter, despite its delicate condition.

"Bah!" Bella squealed, smacking the page with her
splayed hand.

"Yes, ball," she said with a smile. She ran her finger
along the words as she read, "The *Ball* once struck off,
Away flies the *Boy*, To the next destin'd Post, And then
Home with Joy."

The dull, colorless light of the morning might have
been dreary to some, but Felicity felt only peace this
morning. Last night had been so emotional for her, so
important, but it was obviously something she needed.
She hadn't realized just how anxious she still was until
that part of her that had been holding on so tight relaxed.

Most importantly, she could now say with authority
that the making of new memories didn't override the
old ones. They were still there, just as sweet, just as
beloved, and just as poignant as they had always been.
Of course, the memories weren't all happy. She remembered her and Ian's first fight—over landscaping, of all
things—and the times she could as happily have stran-
gled him as embraced him.

Theirs wasn't a storybook marriage, but in her eyes, that
was better than perfect. The fights led to makeups, the
struggles to triumphs. She dropped a kiss onto Bella's
head. The baby was proof of that.

Felicity didn't know what would happen next in her
life. She might marry someday; she might not. It was
possible she would move, although more likely that she
would stay. Whatever happened, she felt that she could

make her decisions from someplace other than a fear of losing her connection to the past.

And looking at Bella's sweet face and big blue eyes reminded her that, no matter what, part of Ian would always be with her.

"Good morning," Charity said from the doorway, a soft smile rounding her freckled cheeks. She was a bit pale, with faint purple smudges beneath her eyes, but still as lovely as ever. "Are you feeling better today?" She walked to the pretty little pink settee that was arranged at a right angle to Felicity's chair and more or less collapsed into the tufted velvet cushions.

Felicity returned her smile. Poor thing. She remembered those early days of her own pregnancy. "Much, much better, thank you. I hope you are."

"I'm alive," she said with a shake of her head. "I wish you would have told us you weren't feeling well yesterday. I would have been happy to bring you back."

Closing the book, Felicity set her daughter on the floor next to her blocks so she could play. "I know you would have, but there was no need. I didn't want to ruin such a lovely night when I could just as easily see to myself."

Charity ran her hands down the tops of her legs, smoothing out the pale peach muslin of her morning gown. "We couldn't help but notice Dering's departure as well." Her attempt at nonchalance fell short, but it only made Felicity smile. Charity didn't want to come right out and pry, but she was obviously curious.

"Yes, he caught up to me and offered to escort me back here. Apparently no one has faith in my ability to see myself home."

And she was so glad he had. She'd still be locked in her inner battle if it weren't for him. She felt as though she owed him a debt she could never repay, but she knew he wouldn't ever expect her to.

Charity bobbed her head up and down a few times in a slow nod, but it was clear there was more on her mind.

"You might as well say what you came to say," Felicity said, more amused than bothered. She knew Charity cared about her.

"All right," she said, scooting forward a few inches in her seat. "Is there something between the two of you that we should know about? I know he is an old friend, but, well, I've certainly never known Dering to leave a party like that."

Felicity paused in the act of reaching over to move more blocks to where Bella was playing. "He didn't return? That's a bit of a surprise."

"No, he didn't," she replied, a sly smile lifting one corner of her mouth. "And you completely skipped over my question."

Sitting back in her chair, Felicity met her curious gaze directly. "He's not just an old friend. He is the very best of friends to me—present tense—and I'm honored that he should think the same of me."

It was hard to tell whether or not her answer surprised her friend. "If you're sure. I'm not saying that there is anything wrong with that, because I truly am happy that he is such a good friend to you. But I just want to be sure that you realized that I'm not the only one noticing."

Yesterday, Felicity might have been bothered by that. In fact, she *knew* she would have been. But today? She gave a little shrug—not disrespectful, but just at peace with it. "People are free to think as they please. I don't intend to give them anything to gossip about, but I won't allow the curiosity or conclusion-jumping of others to affect me. Certainly not when I'm not doing anything that would warrant censure."

Charity raised her hands, "Your choice. I won't say another word about it. Except perhaps to say that I think that Dering is a very fine man. I hope that, whatever the nature of your friendship, that the two of you bring some happiness to each other's lives."

At this, Felicity almost laughed. "I'm glad to say that I think Gavin is not wanting for happiness in his life. A more affable, contented man I've never met."

Tilting her head, Charity nibbled her bottom lip. "I think he enjoys his life, but I'm not certain that he's quite found happiness. He always seems to be seeking, if that makes sense. Looking for happiness but falling short."

Felicity hadn't picked up on that at all. To her, he seemed to be perfectly happy with his life. "What do you mean?"

"It's hard to put into words. He's a seeker, going from one entertainment to the next, but I'm not really sure he's found what he's looking for. I think he's just filling the emptiness inside of him sometimes."

But . . . wouldn't Felicity have sensed that? Had she really been so wrapped up in her own struggles that she had missed the signs of this? She did agree that nothing really seemed to matter to him. There wasn't anything that he showed genuine passion for or real excitement about, save for perhaps his physical pursuits. But was his happiness really so hollow as Charity suggested?

What she needed to do was talk to him. Listen to him. Show him that she cared about and for him as much as he did her. "I hope that's not the case, but thank you for pointing it out. If I can be a better friend to him, I will."

"Do I hear you ladies scheming in here?" Hugh

asked as he stepped into the doorway, a smile lighting his face. He made his way across the room and settled onto the floor at Charity's feet, close enough to Isabella that he could play with her.

"Of course not," Charity said, leaning forward to wrap her arms around his neck. "Ladies don't scheme; they plan." She kissed the scarred skin at his temple as though to punctuate her point.

"Yes, the way the military plans battles," he quipped even as he reached up and covered her hand with his. "I'm convinced the war would have been won much sooner if the crown had used women to strategize."

Turning his attention to Felicity, he smiled. "I ran into Thomas this morning on the way home from the baths. Since the weather means the Strings by the Stream event will have to be canceled, he wondered if we might be interested in a friendly night of cards tonight. And by *friendly*, I'm certain he means *cutthroat*."

She chuckled. "You know him well. He may be even more competitive than I am. That sounds like great fun to me. Charity?"

Holding up her hands, Charity said, "Oh no, I learned my lesson when it comes to playing cards with any one of you. Three more merciless players I have yet to meet," she said with a wink. "Besides, I'm beyond exhausted today. I think I may just spend the day reading and napping."

Hugh craned his head so he could see her. "I didn't realize you were feeling so unwell. Why don't I bypass the evening and spend it with you instead? Felicity and her brother can battle it out together."

But Charity just shook her head. "I know that yesterday wasn't a good day for you, which I'm sure the coming rain didn't help. If you are feeling good today, I would love for you to have a little fun this evening, particularly since it will be a relatively quiet one."

He smiled. "Very well, then. Felicity, do you want to write him with our acceptance, while I take Charity to go lie down? And if you can think of a fourth whom you'd like to have join us, go ahead and issue an invitation."

Felicity brightened at that. There was exactly one person she would wish to have across from her when playing whist with Thomas and Hugh. As Hugh and Charity said their good-byes and headed down to their bedchamber, Felicity rang for the nursemaid so she could go write her notes.

Instead of playing against each other, Felicity was more than ready to play with Gavin on her team. And after last night, she suspected he would feel the same way.

Chapter Fourteen

"Good heavens, Gavin, how could you possibly look any larger than the last time I saw you?"

Suppressing the urge to roll his eyes, Dering smiled at his mother before bending to kiss her proffered cheek. "It's lovely to see you as well."

She patted his cheek fondly. "Darling, don't slouch. And I suppose you're fortunate that that handsome face of yours distracts from the brutish physique you insist on cultivating."

At this point in his life, he knew better than to argue with her. Holding out his arm to indicate for her to precede him into the drawing room, he said, "I do hope you had a comfortable journey."

She swept past him and went straight for the steaming pot of tea that had just been delivered moments earlier. Pouring herself a cup, she made a small noise of disgust as she glanced to Dering's father. "It would have been more comfortable if we had left yesterday as I suggested. My intuition told me it would rain, and just look at that mess out there."

She tipped her head toward the window, which showed nothing more than a misty, drizzly day. Hardly anything to bother an Englishman. Mother's "intu-ition" was little more than a feeling she claimed to get in her wrist, which she'd broken in childhood, whenever it was about to rain. He and his brothers had scoffed at her claims over the years, but in truth, it was accurate about half the time.

His father sighed before turning to greet Dering with an affectionate pat on his shoulder. "Good to see you, son. I appreciate your coming out to the house in such *atrocious* weather in order to greet us. Warms the heart, really."

At fifty-eight, the earl sported a headful of white hair and a belly that betrayed his fondness for sweets. Fortu-nately, with his height, the extra weight wasn't nearly as noticeable as it might have been on a shorter man.

"I heard that, George," Mother said from the sofa, her voice dry but with enough fondness to show that she wasn't truly offended by his mild sarcasm.

"I'm certain you did. Your excellent hearing is one of the things I admire most about you, my dear," he answered with a wink to Dering. "I will say, I rather pre-fer this sort of weather for shooting. Better than all that squinting in the sunshine. I hope you and your brothers will be up to a little hunting later this summer."

Nodding, Dering followed his father into the drawing room. "I imagine time can be made for such a thing. I do know how well you like to trounce the lot of us." He was only half kidding. His father had rather legendary aim, and was a welcome member of any shooting party during the fall.

Michael came stomping in behind them, still trying to shake the moisture from his clothing. "Please tell me there is some food prepared," he said, looking around the room.

"Cook sent word she'd have a tray to us presently," Dering said as he poured a glass of brandy for each of them. "Glad to see you, brother. How are things going with your studies?"

Michael, who was the youngest of them all at only two-and-twenty, offered Dering a raised eyebrow. "I'm assuming you wish for me to say *Very well, thank you*, and not go into any detail?"

Dering nodded as he handed him a glass. "You assume correctly. I'll leave the mathematical discourse to your colleagues and happily accept your generic response."

His brother smiled as he claimed one of the wing-back chairs and stretched out his legs. He might have been shorter than the rest of them, save Mother, but at six foot one, he was still taller than average. "And here is where I show polite interest in your latest endeavors. Anything to report?"

Dering gave a small shrug. "Things are well with my investments, my leisure pursuits, and my person. All in all, I'm pleased."

"Well," Mother said, setting her drink on the sofa table before pinning Dering with her dark blue gaze. It was the same piercing gaze that had kept her four over-grown sons in line during their childhood despite her petite frame. "It does my heart good to know that you are so settled in life. I wish I could say the same."

She was baiting him, and he knew it, but he wouldn't deny her the pleasure of being asked to expound on such a leading statement. "Oh? Are you unwell? I did wonder if you didn't look a little pale."

"Oh, hush, you thought no such thing," she said with a dismissive flick of her fingers, even as a wry grin tipped her lips. "I was referring to the fact that, in a matter of days, I shall have a thirty-year-old son, and nary a grandchild on the horizon. I am the last of my friends to become a grandmother, Gavin. The *last*."

"Hmm," he said, tapping his drink to his chin as though seriously considering her problem. "I'm certain if I apply myself, I may produce a grandchild by the end of the week or so. I am still a board member of the orphanage, after all."

Her glare somehow managed to be stern, exasperated, and amused all at once. "I'm also the last to be a mother-in-law, so let's work on that first, shall we?"

"I agree completely. I'm certain I can come up with a wife in three, maybe four years at the most."

Sighing greatly, she shook her head and retrieved her tea. "So cheeky, my firstborn. This will not do, Gavin. You've had your fun—and you may continue to have your fun—but I'm afraid I must insist that you apply yourself to procuring a wife. If I'm not planning a wedding by the end of this festival, you won't like the consequence."

"You're right. Going to bed without supper would be the worst of all fates."

She pressed her lips together, clearly trying not to betray her growing amusement. "Ungrateful boy. You'll feel terrible when your children are born when their grandmother is gone. Mark my words."

At that Dering rolled his eyes and grinned. "Yes, Mother, at the age of forty-nine, you clearly have one foot in the grave." She barely even had any gray hair yet. Just a few streaks at her temples that only made her look more regal.

Eric made an appearance then, his mouth set in a pale imitation of a smile. "Welcome, Mother, Father.

Good to see you, Michael." He bent down to kiss their mother's cheek before nodding to the earl.

As usual, Eric's presence took the scrutiny off Dering. Mother's gaze swept him up and down, doing her normal inspection to make sure he was still hearty and hale. Or, in absence of those, at least breathing. "Eric, I'm pleased to see that you are looking well. It would have put my mind at ease to know such a thing sooner, but I do know how very taxing it is to pay your parents a visit."

Eric didn't show any hint of annoyance at her chiding. All present knew that he was close enough to visit any time he wished when they were in residence at their London house, which they always were for the whole of the Season. "Rest assured, I'd send word if I were on my deathbed."

Her face paled, losing all the good humor with which she had bantered moments ago. "Please don't tease about that." Taking a visible breath, she regained her composure and said lightly, "Of course, if you had a wife, I feel certain she would keep me informed so I wouldn't have to worry."

"You feel certain?" Eric responded with a feigned surprise. "Because you yourself loved Grandmother *so* well when she decided to move out of the dowager's house and back in with the two of you last summer? You share everything with her, I'm sure."

One thinly arched eyebrow rose as she lifted her chin. "That's different. Your father's mother is a selfish old dragon who resented her son's wife. I would welcome my sons' wives with open arms."

"Serena!" Father exclaimed, shooting her a rebuking glance. "There's no need for that. You know Mother appreciates you in her own way."

Dering swallowed a smile. Grandmother would "appreciate" his mother right off a cliff, if she could. "Oh, look, the refreshments are here," he announced, silently praising Cook for her excellent timing. No one wanted to challenge Mother when it came to the dowager.

"Thank God. I'm starving," Michael said, pilfering a stack of sandwiches from the tray before the footman could even set it down.

"Don't be crass, Michael," Mother said, shaking her head at him in resignation. "And do try to show some decorum when inhaling those sandwiches."

"I believe giving thanks for one's meals is not only accepted, it's admired in most cultures," he replied before stuffing an entire sandwich into his mouth in one bite.

Sighing greatly, Mother glanced heavenward before reaching for a biscuit. "You boys will surely be the death of me. Which is why I need grandchildren sooner rather than later."

Dering pretended to consider this as he popped a tiny square of cake in his mouth. "Do you know, with Birch off with his unit on the continent, who's to say that he hasn't a wife and child already?"

Father nearly choked on his ham sandwich. "Gavin, do try to refrain from giving your mother heart failure." The humor in his voice was unmistakable as he reached for his glass.

Narrowing her eyes on Dering, his mother said, "I'll have you know that Birch is a very regular correspondent. I receive letters from him weekly, unlike the rest of you. Furthermore, he is still only three-and-twenty, so I wouldn't expect such a thing of him yet."

"So what is the invisible line, I wonder," Eric mused,

his watercress sandwich untouched on his plate. "Twenty-five? Twenty-six? At what point do we go from blameless young men to hopeless bachelors in need of haranguing?"

Mother dabbed daintily at the corner of her mouth, her rings flashing in the dull light. "Your father was seven-and-twenty when we married. A finer example of a man I cannot envision, so he shall always be the standard by which you boys are measured."

His father sent her a rather pleased grin, which she returned with the subtlest of winks.

"Ah," Dering said, leaning toward her a bit, "but he had found *you*. Were any of us to find such a paragon of femininity, I'm certain our bachelorhood would be gleefully forfeited, posthaste."

The over-the-top encomium made her laugh, just as he had intended. "And if you'd apply your handsomely developed skills of flattery among the females of the *ton*, I've no doubt it would have the same effect."

"You should be pleased to know that I am thoroughly dedicated to exploring each and every candidate the beau monde can produce. Nary a day goes by that I don't find myself at some function or another, carefully considering any prospective females." He waggled his eyebrows, earning a much-sought-after but rarely elicited eye roll from his mother.

Picking at a nonexistent piece of lint on her skirts, she said, "I can speed up the process by hosting a house party here at the end of the summer. I'll invite all of the prospective women I have on my list of suitable wives for the future Earl of Carlisle."

He shouldn't have been surprised, but he nearly spit his drink out at her words. "You have a *list*?"

"Don't be silly, darling. I've had a list since you were eight." She turned to Eric and smiled. "For all of you, in fact. As a loving mother, I realize those females who are compatible for one may not be compatible for another. See? I have your happiness at heart."

Dering gave a little snort, marveling that he didn't know this before now. "As curious as I am to see whom you believe would suit my brothers, I can tell you with complete sincerity that I have no need of your interference."

"I am your mother," she replied, her chin lifting a notch. "Mothers cannot interfere; they can only love."

The earl gave a solemn nod, his eyes showing only the slightest hint of mischief. "So true. In fact, my mother feels precisely the same way."

Dering and his brothers laughed aloud at the look on her face. He really did enjoy his family, interference and all. He was well aware of how many of his peers held no love or even care for their own families. Shaking his head, he laid a hand over his mother's and smiled with genuine regard. "Rest assured, Mother, I do intend to give you your grandchildren. Trust me to know my own mind and heart, and I promise I will not disappoint you."

She softened as she smiled back at him, her blue eyes full of affection. "You never have, and you never will. I'm proud of the men I raised. However," she said, the smile turning the slightest bit devilish, "I cannot promise that I won't provide *encouragement*."

His father's snort drew Mother's scowl and made Dering grin. It was too much to hope he could get off that easily.

As they moved on to how things were with the northern

estate, his parents' longtime butler strolled into the room, one hand behind his back and the other holding a silver salver with a note. "Pardon me, Lord Derington," he said quietly with a deferential bow. "One of your footmen just delivered this for you."

"Thank you, Picksworth," Dering said as he accepted the folded piece of foolscap. He slid a finger beneath the thin wax seal and unfolded it. He immediately recognized Felicity's handwriting. He frowned, concerned for what would have prompted her to write him. Was she faring poorly today after such an emotional evening? He had wanted to visit her, but didn't want to intrude.

"Everything all right, darling?"

He glanced up to find the others watching him. Offering a brisk nod, he said, "Just something with one of my interests. Pardon me for a moment, if you don't mind."

At their nods, he headed to the library where he could read the note in peace. Closing the door, he sat on the nearest chair and scanned her words.

What a wonderful day it is. Thank you, from the deepest part of my heart, for being exactly the person you are. Today, I feel ready to take on the world. I wonder, since we've competed against each other twice, can I tempt you to compete with me? Just a quiet game of cards tonight with Thomas and Hugh, not at all your normal speed, so feel free to decline, but I would be honored to be your partner should you choose to join us. Hopefully the only tears that will be shed tonight will be the tears of defeat from my brother and brother-in-law. Awaiting your reply,

—F

She was right. It wasn't normally the manner in which he would spend an evening. He preferred bustle and conversation and music to a quiet night every time.

At least he used to.

When he was with her, that part of him that craved noise and distraction calmed. If it would please her, he would happily spend the evening at her side, enjoying a simple game of cards and the company of her family.

It would be a bit tricky, abandoning his own family the first night they arrived, but Felicity was worth it.

Chapter Fifteen

"Dering, old man!" Thomas clapped him on the shoulder as he welcomed him to the townhouse his father had rented for the summer. The place was enormous, one of the city's largest, and his voice echoed through the ostentatiously large foyer. "Excellent of you to join us, especially in this damnable rain."

"My pleasure," he replied, shaking the water from his coat before slipping it off. The drizzle had turned to steady rain by late afternoon and had yet to let up. With no servants to be seen, he said, "What should I do with this? And why the devil are you answering the door?"

Thomas grinned as he took the coat and hung it from a stand nearby. "Father rented the house for the summer, but he'll bring his own servants when he comes. I'm used to a simpler life these days, so I'm faring just fine with Mrs. Thorn, who serves as a maid of all work, and her son, whom I suppose could be called a manservant for the time being."

Dering nodded, more than a little surprised that Thomas would be rattling around in this huge old place by himself. "Did Felicity not wish to join you here?"

The vicar chuckled and shook his head. "Apparently she can't bring herself to separate Lady Effington from Isabella. That, and I suspect she likes having a cook and whatnot," he said with a wink.

He led them past the front drawing room to a handsome room at the back of the house, which was rustically decorated in deep greens and golds, almost like a refined hunting lodge. A baize-topped card table dominated the center of the room, with four chairs, a stack of whist tokens, and several packs of new playing cards at the ready.

"Lady Effington? I wasn't aware there was a connection." He knew that the dowager viscountess had moved down to Cadgwith with Charity, but he hadn't considered that there would be some sort of bond between her and the baby. Children spent most of their time in their nurseries, didn't they?

"That's putting it mildly. Lady Effington is the grandmother Isabella never had, and the two adore each other. I declare that the dowager's recent improved health has as much to do with the baby as it does the sea air down there."

"Well, I suppose that's nice for both of them." The girl had obviously started life at a disadvantage, so it was good that she had a surrogate grandmother.

"Whiskey?" Thomas asked, motioning to a table holding a handful of crystal bottles. At Dering's nod, he poured two glasses. "Since you're here first, I suppose it's a good time to ask what exactly happened between you and my sister last night."

The question actually surprised Dering. A more affable and easygoing man he'd be hard-pressed to find than

Felicity's young brother, but there was an edge to his voice
that was unmistakable. Accepting the glass, he gave a
light shrug, purposely appearing unconcerned. "I simply
wished to see her home safely. Bath can be a different
place from the quiet streets of Cadgwith."

"Indeed. Though I'm certain there are gossips
aplenty in both places."

The sound of the front door closing and the clatter
of footsteps saved Dering from having to go through a
conversation he rather wouldn't, especially with one so
much younger than himself. "I'm aware, I assure you.
I value Felicity's friendship and have no intention of
allowing harm to come to her, particularly by any of
my own actions."

Thomas nodded, his carefree grin back in place. "I
am glad to hear it. As a man of the cloth, I'm confident
I could gain forgiveness from the Lord should I sin by,
oh, let's say murdering, but I'd rather not test it." He
gave an easy wink before going to greet the others.

Dering blinked, surprised by the statement. He'd
best be more careful in the future with how he inter-
acted with Felicity if Thomas was taking notice.

He turned then, just as Felicity walked through the
arched doorway into the room. Her smile was luminous
in the shimmering candlelight, free of reservation or worry.
She walked straight to him, her eyes bright with welcome.
"You, sir, are my hero. I'm so glad you could come."

He wasn't sure what he was expecting, but seeing her
so perfectly happy and at peace loosened something inside
of him. Some residual part of him that he wasn't even
aware of that had worried that, perhaps, she might have
had second thoughts about the outcome of the evening
last night. That dancing with him had been a mistake, and

she was worse off than she had been to begin with. He was beyond relieved that that was not the case.

His smile was wide and unreserved as he bent forward in a lighthearted little bow. "I am at your service, madam."

"For the record," Cadgwith said, "Felicity and Charity lost spectacularly last time we all played. She's hoping she can redeem herself, but I have some very serious doubts. We played six games, and Thomas and I won all but one." He shook his head in mock disgust. "My wife is the most amazing woman I have ever met, but she is rubbish at cards."

"Precisely," Felicity said, turning her golden brown eyes back to Dering. "It was all Charity, I swear to it. If I'd a better partner, I would have handily prevailed."

Cadgwith snorted with a short laugh. "Remind me to warn Charity not to walk beside you on a busy street. You are liable to toss her beneath a speeding carriage at any moment."

Thomas lifted his drink. "I must point out that when we eventually switched partners, you and I crashed upon the rocks as well."

"I will swear to my dying day that you sabotaged that game to make me look bad. Don't you dare deny it," she said, laughing at his look of appalled innocence.

"Me?" he said, setting an aggrieved hand to his chest in an act of drama worthy of the stage. "Sabotage my own good name in order to make you look bad? That is a pack of lies, and I demand that you repent immediately."

She scrunched up her nose at him, her hands going to her hips. "I most certainly will not. Under no circumstances should Charity have won that game, even with Hugh as her partner."

"I don't know, Felicity," Dering said, keeping a perfectly straight face. "I feel as though I've agreed to this under false pretenses. If partnering with you means certain loss, I may have to take a pass and find a party after all."

It felt good to laugh and tease with them, without any worry for the normal social niceties. These were the friends he had known for years, the ones that he didn't have to be witty and charming and sophisticated around.

"Oh no," Thomas said, shaking his head. "I won't be denied my win. Let us retire to the table, my friends." He waved a hand toward the table, wolfish grin already in place.

"What shall we stake?" Dering asked as he took the seat directly across from Felicity.

Cadgwith shook his head, holding up a finger as he swallowed the mouthful of whiskey he had just taken. "No stakes. I play for eternal bragging rights when it comes to these two. Wouldn't want to be accused of swindling a helpless widow and her poor vicar brother."

Felicity rolled her eyes as Thomas threw a whist chip across the table at him, both of them laughing.

"Hm, I see your point," Dering said, earning a scowl from the siblings. "In that case, I suggest a nonmonetary bet."

"Such as . . . ?" Cadgwith said, his scarred eyebrow lifted in question.

Dering thought for a moment. The only time he'd done nonmonetary bets in the past, there had been females and a forfeiture of clothing involved. Not the sort of thing one suggested in polite company. "Well, if Felicity and I win, the two of you must compose a sonnet for the occasion, praising our exceptional skills and unrivaled beauty, to be published in the newspaper next week. Fortunately, I am friends with the editor."

Both men made faces, just as Dering had expected. Thomas shook his head. "That is diabolical, old man."

Felicity grinned. "I think it's absolutely perfect. And what do you suggest if they win?"

"A heartfelt pat on the back?"

"I like it!" she announced at the same time the baron and Thomas groaned.

"Not on your life," Thomas said, rubbing his hands together as he narrowed his eyes in thought. "Let's see . . . something that is quiet and introspective for Dering, and something that is the exact opposite for Felicity."

"Oh yes," Cadgwith said, crossing his arms. "Felicity would hate it if we made her give a speech."

Thomas lifted both hands, "I've got it! I'm giving a guest sermon at the Octagon Chapel this Sunday. Felicity can do a reading, and Dering can sit quietly through the entire service, attempting not to be struck by lightning."

Felicity blanched a little. "That is a horrid suggestion, Thomas. I'm a woman—they'd never allow me to be part of the service."

"Who's *they*?" he asked with a lift of one of his blond eyebrows. "I shall preside, so I may choose the participants."

"No, please, I won't thumb my nose at the convention of the church, and I won't have you do it, either."

Her brother sighed. "Fine, fine, if you're going to make a fuss over it." He brightened, smacking the padded table with his left palm. "I have it! Samuel Wesley himself will be there. I'll have him direct one of his hymns, and *you* may sing the lead."

Cadgwith nodded slowly, clearly impressed. "Now, *that* is diabolical. I say that it stands. In fact, I say Dering must sing as well."

Thomas grinned and looked to Dering. "Is this for the rubber, or for the whole night?"

"I propose for the rubber, unless you wish to decide now exactly how many games we'll play. If we just do the bet for the best of three games, then later you may very well enjoy switching to penny stakes, where not near as much is on the line."

Cadgwith nodded. "Good plan. I say we play to rubber for the pot."

Dering raised his eyebrows toward Felicity, who watched him through narrowed eyes. "Oh, very well," she said at last, looking more than a little concerned that she may actually have to make good on the bet. "You had better carry us to victory, Gavin Stark. If we lose, I assure you that I have an exceptionally long memory and will not soon forgive you."

Leaning back, he opened a new deck and expertly shuffled, the whirl of the cards music to his ears as they fanned into a neat bridge. "Fear not, Lady Felicity. I may be a viscount, but for tonight I'll happily play your knight in shining armor."

Felicity knew she had made the right decision by calling on Gavin to be her partner. As Thomas dealt the cards for the second round, she grinned hugely at her friend, so glad he had decided to come join them. And not just because they had run away with the first game, winning nine of the thirteen tricks.

If she had harbored any worry that things might somehow be awkward between them after their time together last night, she need not have worried. He was as easygoing as ever, with no hint that anything had changed between them.

Actually, that wasn't true. There was a certain warmth with which he regarded her now that hadn't quite been there before. An understanding and acceptance between two people who shared something important.

And fortunately, that bond so far had translated to an excellent partnership in the game. There was a connection there, something that passed between them when she looked into his eyes to try to divine his next move. She had just seemed to know when to toss in her low cards and when it was best to use her highs. He had started the round with the ace of clubs—the trump suit—and things had only improved from there.

"All right," Thomas said with quite a bit less humor than he'd had ten minutes earlier. "Spades are trump suit. Felicity, you're up."

She glanced down at her cards, up at Gavin, then smiled as she laid down the seven of hearts. Honestly, she couldn't seem to *not* smile when she looked at him. This whole day had been so lovely, so free from heaviness, she could just kiss him for having freed her. A knight, indeed. As far as she was concerned, he had earned the distinction permanently in her mind.

Hugh played the jack of hearts, Gavin the queen, and Thomas the king. Her brother let out a whoop of joy as he raked the cards toward him. "Starting this one off on the right foot."

Moving on to the next trick, he threw down the ace

of clubs and grinned. "You might as well just toss me your cards, since I know none of you could have played out all your clubs yet."

"That's one way to waste an ace," she said as she tossed out her three of clubs. She grinned at Thomas as he scowled at her. "This is why you two are going to lose. You need a better strategy, my friend."

Hugh played the two of clubs, and Gavin offered up the six.

"At this rate," Gavin said dryly as he lifted his drink, "you'll wring all our low cards out of us in no time."

"It will all make sense when you two lose this round," her brother retorted with an excess of false bravado.

They won the next two tricks, while Felicity and Gavin took the next three. As the round played out, they were left dead even, each having taken six tricks, with only one trick left to go. Felicity's heart began to pound with excitement. This was where that competitive nature of hers always reared its head. She could practically taste the victory, especially with the king of diamonds as her last card. She'd lost track of the trump cards somewhere around the tenth trick, so she had no idea if there was one left. The only thing she knew for sure was that the ace of hearts was out of play.

Hugh pursed his lips, looking to Thomas with something akin to dread drawing his features. Oh yes, this could definitely spell sweet, sweet victory. She could hardly wait to tell Charity what the men would be doing for their forfeit. She almost snorted. She could not for anything imagine a sonnet coming out of Hugh.

With a decidedly evil grin in place, she laid down her king. Hugh groaned as he tossed out his ten of hearts. Gavin didn't look nearly so happy as he flicked his jack of clubs out. Didn't he realize that they were about to win? She turned to her brother, who stared at his card with his lips pursed.

Looking straight at Felicity, he winked as he tossed his card on the table. "I told you it would all make sense." His grin was one of pure, devilish delight, making her heart plunge as she glanced to the card on the top of the pile.

Blast it all, there was a trump card left after all. He crowed with glee, reaching across the table to smack Hugh's outstretched hand. "Oh, Lissy, if you could have just seen your face. You were so sure you had that one. Well, looks like your formidable opponents aren't rolling over as easily as that."

Groaning, she leaned back in her chair. *So close.*

Thomas came to his feet, still grinning with his win. "I say we pause for sustenance before the tiebreaking game. Nothing builds up an appetite quite like trouncing one's sister," he said, patting his flat belly. "I've some cake in the larder, and a tray of cheese and fruit if you like. Let me go get that while the two of you," he said, pointing to Felicity and Gavin, "think about what you want to wear to my sermon on Sunday. And song choice, of course. Song choice is key to a good performance, especially when making a joyful noise unto the Lord."

Rising from his chair, Hugh rolled his head to stretch out his neck. "I'll help you with the tray. I've been sitting still too long, anyhow."

She smiled at Gavin while they retreated toward the kitchen, shaking her head all the while. "And here I thought you were going to save the day."

One side of his mouth tipped up as he looked around him as though searching for something.

Felicity frowned. "What are you looking for?"

"That runaway carriage you are trying to toss me under." He laughed when she kicked his shin lightly with her slippered foot beneath the table.

"What?" he said, crossing his arms. "You're the one who didn't even realize that the last trump card was still in play."

"And you did?" She pushed back from the table and stood, stretching a bit.

"I did. Always count the trump cards as they're used. You may lose track of other things—though I don't recommend that, either—but the trump cards will tell you more about the game and your chances than anything else."

"Mmm. I suppose that's good enough advice."

"Yes, well, I didn't leave my family behind tonight so I could lose."

She straightened, realization assailing her. How could she have forgotten that they'd be getting in today? "Your family is here? And you left them?"

Well, now she felt awful. She couldn't keep allowing him to give up things that were important to him in order to fulfill her whims. She was well aware that, after last night, he might think her to still be fragile, but he needed to realize that he shouldn't be sacrificing for her.

"They are, and I did. I have my priorities," he said with a wink.

"Don't tease. I feel terrible. You should have stayed with them tonight instead of wasting the evening with the three of us jokers."

He rose and came to stand beside her, leaning a hip on the edge of the table. "Have you met my parents?

They are like dessert: delightful to partake in but tolerable for only so large a portion. They've been here less than twelve hours and I have already had the grandchildren guilt heaped upon my sorry bachelor head."

Felicity drew in a surprised breath. Grandchildren? She had never thought to picture him as a father. It was an odd but lovely thought. "I should have realized how anxious your parents would be to see their sons marry and procreate. Most everyone else of their age has at least seen their children marry."

He made a low sound deep in his chest as he shook his head. "Devil take it, Felicity, don't tell me you're on their side."

"Are there sides?" she asked, tilting her head with an affectionate but challenging grin. "You did say you wished to marry. And moreover, I know you'd be a wonderful father."

The very thought of it made her chest bloom with warmth. She could just see him, big, strong man that he was, cradling a tiny infant in his arms. It was something she had dreamed of seeing with her own daughter when she was born, being held safe and sound in her father's arms, but of course it wasn't to be.

He shrugged off her compliment as he glanced to the coffered ceiling. "I imagine I'm as capable of hiring excellent nursemaids and governesses as the next man."

She wasn't about to let him get away with that. Any man as caring and compassionate as he could be nothing but loving and involved with his own children. "You're putting me on, and you don't even know it. You are one of the finest men I know, Gavin. Your children will be blessed a thousand times over to have a father like you."

Amusement chased across his features as he glanced

back to her. "Why, thank you. I'm gratified to know that my nonexistent offspring will be so very fortunate."

He was being facetious, but she smiled anyway. "Very well, I shall drop the topic. That does, however, lead me to your nonexistent social life."

He gave a short bark of incredulous laughter. "What? Surely you jest."

"I jest not at all. You, sir, have sacrificed far too many of your enjoyments for me since the festival began. I wouldn't be any sort of friend at all if I allowed that to continue."

He pursed his lips and crossed his arms, adopting as belligerent a stance as she had seen out of him. "I have done exactly as I've pleased this summer. Whether that be with multiple people or just one, it is as it should be."

"I don't believe you." Setting her hand against his sleeve, she waited until he met her gaze. "This has been a difficult but cathartic visit for me. You saw that, and you did so much to help me let go and move on. I'm most grateful, but in the process, you have stepped away from the things that you enjoy. Now allow me to be a proper friend and worry about *your* happiness for a change."

"Felicity—"

"No, I insist. You are the most social person I know, and I have done nothing but pull you—"

"Felicity," he said again, the insistence in his voice effectively cutting her off this time.

She closed her mouth and looked up at him, her eyes wide. He settled his hands around her upper arms and bent his head down so he could look her directly in the eye. "Let me say this clearly so there is no misunderstanding." His gaze was soft yet compelling as his roughened hands gripped the bare skin beneath her short puff sleeve. "I am *exactly* where I want to be, with *exactly* the person I wish to be with."

Oh. She swallowed, absolutely no words coming to her mind at that moment. Her heart gave a little leap as she looked back and forth between his dark velvet eyes. No one could possibly make her feel as wanted, as cared for, as he did.

He lifted a brow. "Understood?"

She wet her lips and nodded, trying to remember what it was she was even going to say before. When he released his gentle hold, she exhaled and stepped back. *Good heavens.* She couldn't deny the honesty in his eyes when he'd spoken, but she still couldn't help but feel as though she was holding him back. However, if she were to get around his stubbornness, she had to use his gallantry against him.

When he started to move away, she put a staying hand to his elbow and said, "Except it's not just for you, you know. It will make me feel better to focus on somebody else for a while. I think I've had enough introspection to last a lifetime."

He narrowed his eyes as he peered at her as though trying to divine her innermost thoughts. "Mmhmm." Clearly he wasn't convinced.

"Honestly! I've fled every party I have been to since I arrived. I'd like to properly attend one. Since I know you enjoy them, I imagine you would be the perfect person to direct me to the best events."

Dragging a hand over his slightly stubbled cheek, he said, "I have it on good authority that you and your family will be invited to the ball my parents are throwing for my birthday next Saturday. You know the Starks—any excuse for a party. I know our outing to the ruins is on Thursday, but would you wish to join me as my special guest and fellow birthday celebrator?"

She didn't hesitate as she nodded decisively. Balls might not have been something she enjoyed, but if it would make him happy, she would gladly attend. "I would be honored. And I'm certain Charity and May can even help me to procure a proper ball gown this time." She cringed to think of the one she had worn to the opening ball.

"Enough with the scheming, you two," Thomas scolded as he and Hugh returned with the food. "If I see either of you using hand signals or eyelash fluttering during this last game, I will personally toss you out in the rain like so much baggage."

Dering laughed as he moved to stand beside her brother, towering over him. "Indeed? I'd like to see you try."

Thomas threw him a smug grin. "Ah, but you forget how very faithful I am. 'If ye have faith as a grain of mustard seed, ye shall say unto this mountain, Remove hence to yonder place; and it shall remove.'" He paused and lifted a challenging brow. "Therefore, mountain, I don't suggest you test me, or you may be removing *yourself* to my rain-soaked stoop."

Chuckling, Hugh set the small platter of cheeses and sliced fruit on the table. "Don't go removing him yet. I can't wait to hear the sound of their angelic voices lifted in song at church this Sunday."

"You do realize," Felicity said as she chose a strawberry from the plate, "that witnessing such a thing, on the off chance it were actually to occur, would require attending the service yourself."

He pointed a finger back at her. "Completely. Worth it." With a wink, Hugh took his seat, grinning as he popped a piece of cheese in his mouth.

Rubbing his hands together, Gavin strode to his own seat. "Enough bluster. It is time to lay our cards on the table."

Felicity hurried to her own seat, the competitiveness roaring back to the forefront. This would be the tie-breaker, and by the end of the game, she and Gavin would damn well be the victors.

Chapter Sixteen

Dering stared at the two cards left in his hand, carefully counting back in his head what cards had already been used. He had the eight of hearts—the trump suit—and a jack of spades. His spade card was the highest left in play, but it was useless if one of the other two men held the queen or four of hearts.

He looked up at Felicity, attempting to read her expression. Did she have one of the hearts? Currently, the game was at six to five, with their team holding the advantage. They needed to win only one of the two tricks to take the round.

Cadgwith narrowed his eyes as he looked around the table, then set down the first card of the trick. The nine of spades. Dering breathed out a sigh of relief, hoping like hell Thomas wouldn't play one of the remaining hearts. He tossed out his jack, then flicked his glance to Thomas, who was chewing the inside of his lip. After a moment's hesitation, he laid down the four of hearts.

Dering silently cursed. Unless Felicity had the queen, they were going to the final trick. The queen would win this round, thus the game, so if she didn't lay it down, there was no doubt that either Cadgwith or Thomas held it, ensuring that the game would be theirs. *Not* that either of them would realize it. It was clear from the onset that, though they were good strategists, they weren't keeping as close track of the cards as they should.

He watched, breath held, as she glanced up at him, back down at her cards, then tossed out . . . a bloody ten of diamonds.

Dering groaned aloud as Cadgwith pumped a very undignified fist in the air.

"Neck and neck," Thomas said as he gleefully pulled the cards toward him. "I can practically hear the choir music now."

Felicity made a face at him. "Feeling cocky, are we? Well, let us see who's singing what after this trick."

Cracking his knuckles, Thomas laid down his last card with a flourish: the jack of clubs. Oh, but the man would be miserable to lose to. Dering could practically hear the celebration, the cackles of victory, and the teasing of the defeated. Merciless teasing that would likely persist for the rest of the summer. Dering knew it because he himself would do that exact same thing. That was half the fun of playing with true friends: none of that pesky good sportsmanship required.

Felicity held out her card then, looked around to each of them at the table, and released her hold. It fluttered to the table, faceup, and for a moment, Dering didn't even look at it. He was too busy watching her, trying to figure out the look on her face. She looked utterly, beautifully triumphant.

His gaze shot to the cards then, and he blinked as the queen of bloody hearts stared back up at him. She'd just fooled them all. His mouth fell open at the same time Cadgwith dropped his forehead to his arms on the table and groaned.

"Felicity Faith Wright Danby, you sly vixen, you," Thomas said, his green eyes nearly bulging with the shock. "You purposely let us believe we had a chance! You could have played that card the last trick!"

She laughed, the sound nothing but pure, unadulterated joy. "Indeed I could have, dear brother. But what would have been the fun in that? From the moment Hugh laid down his card, I knew I had you all."

Dering sat there, shaking his head back and forth like an idiot. "You clever, clever girl," he said at last, absolutely in awe of her. "You had me fooled as well."

She gave him a cheeky wink. "Yes, I did. I knew that the victory would be that much more sweet if you thought you had lost."

Settling back in his chair, Cadgwith scrubbed both hands over his face. "God above, but Charity will never let me live this down. Neither of you will," he added, tipping his chin in Felicity's direction. Still, good humor lifted his cheeks as he shook his head. "That was rather brilliant, Felicity. I said it before and I'll say it again, women should *definitely* have been in charge of the war."

Dering was beginning to agree with him. His chest expanded with pride for her as he looked back down at the winning card. "This calls for a toast," he said, picking up his nearly empty glass of whiskey and holding it aloft.

Thomas snorted and came to his feet. "Oh no. I refuse to toast the enemy. Cadgwith, let us go find some paper on which to pour out our sorrowful sonnets while these two celebrate their victory. The sooner we can be done with it, the better."

Patting Felicity on the shoulder, Cadgwith said, "Good job, truly. Enjoy your moment, no matter how much we bitterly begrudge you."

She flashed a smile to him before he went to join Thomas at the stout writing table at the far end of the room. When she looked back to Dering, he held out his glass to her. "To the cleverest player here tonight. I couldn't have asked for a better partner." He paused, meeting her sparkling gaze. "And even if there was a better one to be had, I would still wish to be by your side."

She chuckled, holding out her own glass of sherry but not quite touching his yet. "Even if it meant singing from the altar in front of half of Bath?"

His heart beat strong and steady as he smiled at her, contentment warming every ounce of his blood. "Even if it meant singing in front of the *whole* of Bath."

Her smile relaxed a bit, but even so her eyes seemed to shine even brighter. "Cheers," she said, clinking her glass to his.

He brought the tumbler to his lips but stopped just short of taking a drink. "For the record," he said, leaning forward a few inches, "I'm exceedingly glad I don't have to."

At that she laughed fully, her whole countenance alight with happiness. "You and me both, my friend."

It was hard to describe the way Felicity felt when Gavin looked at her the way he had last night. *Admiration.* That was what she had glimpsed in those warm brown eyes of his. It wasn't something she was used to seeing from others.

And it was incredibly heady.

When was the last time someone had thought of her

in any other way than Felicity the widow, or Felicity the friend? Or even Felicity the good-natured soul who hadn't deserved her fate? To see something like that in his regard made her feel clever and happy and warm in a way that had nothing to do with the weather.

It was a feeling she was determined to simply enjoy. She was in no mood for analysis or introspection. She felt wonderful, and that was enough for her.

As the carriage slowed to a stop outside of Gavin's parents' estate, she sighed with contentment, fondly remembering the day they had played billiards here. She'd been rather surprised to receive a missive from Lady Carlisle this afternoon. Normally, Felicity would have waited a few days for the family to get settled before dropping by her card, or perhaps an invitation for tea. But the countess's note had been short and pleasant, begging her indulgence in a visit.

Stepping from the carriage, she smiled at the footman before allowing the waiting butler to lead her inside. Clearly they had seen her coming. He took her straight to the well-appointed drawing room at the front of the house, a pleasant space with ivory-and-rose wallpaper and tasteful floral fabrics. As lovely as it was, however, it was almost impossible to imagine Gavin and his brothers being comfortable here. The wing chairs were substantial enough, but the sofa and Windsor chairs looked as though they couldn't stand up to a strong wind.

Lady Carlisle sat perched in the center of the sofa, for all the world a queen awaiting her subjects. Her silver-streaked hair was smoothed back from her face and artfully arranged in a glossy cloud of curls atop her head. Her blush-colored gown lent color to her cheeks and accentuated her bright blue eyes—a color that only one of her children, Birch, had inherited. In fact, the two younger boys had looked so much alike as children, their eye color was the only way Felicity could tell them apart.

As Picksworth showed Felicity into the room, the countess smiled regally and nodded toward one of the Windsor chairs. "My dear Lady Cadgwith. It is so very lovely to see you again."

Felicity obediently settled into the narrow wooden chair. "And you, Lady Carlisle. Though, please, I generally go by Lady Felicity these days. As an old friend of the family, do please feel free to call me Felicity."

"As you wish," the older woman said with a nod of acknowledgment, though she didn't reciprocate the offer. "May I offer you some tea?"

Nodding, Felicity said, "Yes, thank you. Just one lump of sugar, if you please."

"Of course. I wish for you to be comfortable, my dear. After all, I have no idea what sort of manners you were shown when you were here last week."

Felicity blinked, not at all certain that she didn't detect one of the countess's legendary underhanded comments. She and Gavin hadn't been hiding the fact that they had been here together, but now that she was faced with the countess's sugary-sweet smile as she handed over the tea, Felicity suddenly wished they had found somewhere else to play.

"I've never been treated with anything but the utmost respect and kindness in your home." It was the most diplomatic answer she could think of.

"That is a relief to hear. Now then, I'm sure you are curious why I invited you out here like this, and the reasons are twofold."

Felicity waited expectantly as she lightly blew on the steaming cup of tea.

"First of all, I hope you realize how very saddened we were to hear of your husband's passing. I cannot begin to pretend I understand how you feel, but suffice it to say that I'm devastated on your behalf."

"Thank you," Felicity murmured with a nod before taking a quick sip of her tea. It was still too hot and burned her tongue, but she smiled anyway. The countess was not a woman to whom one showed weakness. She was in no way cruel, but one knew better than to give her ammunition.

"Conversely," Lady Carlisle continued, her back ramrod straight as she finished pouring her own tea, "I wish you the greatest of felicitations on your daughter. I know exactly how precious a child is to his or her mother. There is nothing we won't do in the best interest of our children, yes?" She lifted her cup for a dainty sip.

Again, Felicity nodded. "Yes, of course. Isabella is the light of my life, and I am so very happy to have her."

"Now then, that brings us neatly back to my own child. My firstborn, in fact."

There was no way to tell where this particular statement was leading, but Felicity was very much on her guard. The countess was up to something; she was sure of it now.

"As you know, Gavin's birthday is next week, and we are throwing him a ball to celebrate. He's informed me that you shall be in attendance, which is wonderful."

It was? Felicity took another sip of tea rather than respond, waiting to hear where this was going.

"I've heard quite a bit about how close the two of you have become this summer. Gavin proclaims you to

be a great friend, in fact, which I think is excellent."
Setting down her teacup, she scooted the tiniest bit forward in her seat, her sharp blue eyes leveled directly on Felicity. "It would be my greatest desire if you could help me find him a suitable wife."

A *what*? Felicity worked not to show her shock, but she wasn't at all certain she succeeded. Gavin had already told her about his mother's desire for him to wed and produce an heir, but for some reason, the request left her breathless. Swallowing, she tilted her head and said, "Oh?"

"Indeed. Someone young, from an exceptional family, and virginal as the driven snow. I only say that between us, matrons that we are, because you and I both know some of the loose women he enjoys sometimes." Lady Carlisle cast her gaze heavenward for a moment as she shook her head. "Such a thing is forgivable—wild oats, as they say—but when it comes to his wife, we of course must have the highest of standards."

Felicity's ears began to ring, but she forced herself to nod. Her head might as well have been on a wobbling spring for all the bobbing it was doing.

"I knew you'd understand. We mothers must stick together, after all. And with your friendship, I know you will be just as devoted as I to finding the exact right wife for him. As the future Earl of Carlisle, nothing but the best will do for him."

Why was the countess putting her through this little charade? It was obvious she felt threatened by Felicity's presence in his life, and wished to make abundantly clear that she was nowhere near good enough for her son. As though Felicity had ever even considered it! She had never been so insulted in her life, but a lifetime of good manners—not to mention her desire to maintain that friendship with Gavin—prevented her from saying what she truly wished to.

Instead, she offered a bland, unconcerned smile and said, "Yes, of course. Now please, you must tell me, whom did you hire to undertake the renovations of this place? Whoever it was, he did an outstanding job."

The countess allowed the change of subject, waxing on about the Parisian designer she had hired right out from under the Marchioness of Kenwick. The whole time, Felicity's head continued to bob, counting down the seconds until she could leave this place and the unfair judgment that the woman before her had laid at Felicity's feet.

By the time she was able to make her excuses, the countess was all smiles. "Thank you so much for coming out to see me, Felicity. It's so nice to have an ally. I look forward to seeing you at the ball next Saturday, and in the meantime I'll send you a list of debutantes whom I feel would be suitable matches for Gavin. That way, you can see just the sort of young woman I have in mind for him. Hopefully, you'll be able to point him in the right direction when the time comes."

Felicity's smile felt as brittle as dry grass as she nodded. "I'll see what I can do, my lady. Do have a lovely stay this summer." With that, she fled to her waiting carriage, her hands fisted into her skirts as she walked as quickly as decorum would allow.

It was the first time in her life she'd ever been made to feel like she was somehow damaged goods. God willing, Gavin wouldn't hear of this humiliating little talk. It was not as though she'd wish herself upon him, for heaven's sake. He deserved a fresh start with a sweet young debutante who didn't come with heartbreak and another man's child. She'd not once even considered such a match. The very thought . . .

She swallowed, unsure how she felt about that thought.

Obviously she was more suited to a widower who didn't have the task of producing the heir of a great peerage. A man like Mr. Anthorp, who had two beloved sons but no daughters, much to his dismay. Someone who lived where she lived, so she wouldn't be uprooted from the village and people she loved. She knew how well they were suited, and should she look to marriage again, he was exactly where that search would likely start.

There was no need for Lady Carlisle to speak to her as though she were some sort of marriage-minded schemer who needed to be curtailed. Gavin would certainly be an incredible husband for someone. But Felicity knew full well that someone was *not* her.

And if that thought made something inside of her rebel, well, she had no intention of examining it. She pressed a hand to her lightly pounding heart and exhaled. Some things were better left alone.

Chapter Seventeen

The sound of a squalling baby was not one Dering was sympathetic toward as he stalked down the street, heading for Felicity's house on Sunday. He was still stewing, having learned from Eric—rather belatedly, damn him—that Mother had invited Felicity to tea the day before yesterday, and presumably things had not gone well. That was Eric's inference, anyway, based on the set of her shoulders as she had hurried to the carriage afterward.

Dering hadn't heard from or seen Felicity since their card game Thursday night, but since it was only Sunday morning, he hadn't been particularly worried, especially since he knew that she planned to visit family on Saturday.

He clenched his jaw. Well, now he was definitely worried. He hadn't confronted Mother yet, since she had gone to church this morning with his father and Michael. He wasn't even sure he should. First of all, he suspected she would neatly sidestep any of his questions. She could be exceedingly cunning when she set her mind to it. Second, if she was up to something, he wasn't certain he wanted to tip her off just yet that he was aware of her machinations.

But Felicity? He felt confident he could learn the truth from her. They had progressed to a place of openness and honesty, and he doubted she would hide anything from him if he asked directly.

Already in a devil of a mood, he glared toward the racket, which was originating from the crossroad down the street. A woman in a pale yellow gown was struggling to keep hold of her flailing child, whose screams could surely rival those of the damned.

When the woman turned, he came up short. *Felicity? Bloody hell*—it sometimes slipped his mind that she was a mother at all. Where the devil was the nursemaid, anyway? Weren't those sorts of servants always supposed to be at the ready in case of moments like this?

Sighing, he strode the forty paces or so down to the cross street. Sympathy propelled him along faster, especially seeing how upset she was. "Felicity," he said loudly, a necessity thanks to the crying.

She jerked around, her brow wrinkled in consternation as she fought to maintain her hold on the baby, who seemed to have doubled the number of appendages she possessed. She could easily have been likened to an octopus trying to escape a fisherman's net.

"Gavin, what on earth are you doing here?"

He winced as the baby let out a high-pitched wail. Lord, but the child had a set of lungs. Felicity shook her head, turning her attention back to the girl. "I'm sorry, but I can't talk. She's having a bit of a fit."

A bit? Dering would have described it as a full tantrum, but what did he and his eardrums know?

Still, he couldn't very well just let her struggle. People were giving them a wide berth, but there was plenty of staring going on. He was tempted to scowl back at them to encourage them to mind their own damn business, but it wouldn't accomplish anything.

"Can I help?"

When she finally was able to get a good hold on the girl, she tucked her firmly against her hip and wrapped her arms around her. She was the very definition of harried, with her shoulders tensed, her lips pressed together in a frown, and the hair beneath her bonnet quite a bit worse for the wear.

Taking a deep breath, she offered him a perfunctory smile. "No, but thank you. I can manage well enough on my own."

The screaming had decreased in volume, thank God, but now the girl was bawling her little eyes out, as though the world itself was about to come to an end. Felicity started to walk toward the house, but Isabella began to kick and struggle again, attempting to throw herself backward.

Dering cringed on Felicity's behalf. It had to be humiliating for her. Hell, it wasn't even his child, and he was feeling the censure from those around them. Coming around to stand in front of her, he said, "I never said you couldn't. But I'm here, so please let me help you."

He held his hands out, encouraging her to let him handle things.

She scowled as she struggled to maintain her hold, all the while shushing the baby. "Have you ever even held a child in your life?"

Shrugging, he said, "No. But it seems like a good day for a first time."

At least he hoped it was. For all he knew, the child could be terrified of someone as large as he, which wouldn't bode well for his eardrums. However, he at least felt certain that he could keep a hold of her, no matter how much she might flail. He could get them back to the house in no time.

Blowing out a short breath, she nodded. "Very well. Just . . . be careful, please." She shifted her position and lifted her daughter out toward him. The girl's blue eyes went huge, and she momentarily stopped her wailing as she stared at him, seemingly stunned that her mother would offer her up to him.

He relaxed his lips into as nonthreatening a smile as he could manage. "Good morning, Isabella. What seems to be the problem?"

Her little body jerked as she sucked in a few unsteady breaths, blinking all the while at him. Her uncertainty was almost comical, especially when she turned her wide eyes to her mother, a thousand questions ripe in their brilliant blue depths.

"It's all right, baby," Felicity crooned, setting a hand to her back. "You remember Gavin?"

He waited, holding perfectly still, willing the girl not to squall again. He couldn't believe how *light* she was. So tiny. He had been eight when his last brother was born, so the size difference hadn't seemed so very great. Now it was like holding a little cotton doll.

Unfortunately, the peace wasn't to last. Apparently deciding that he was no friend of hers after all, she sucked in a huge breath and let out a wail that could surely be heard all the way back in Cadgwith. Gritting his teeth against the noise, he strode back toward their house, using every inch of his long legs to move them as quickly as possible without actually running.

Felicity hurried along beside him, her skirts swinging with her effort to keep up. When they reached the front door, it blessedly opened from the inside and they were able to go straight in.

"Up the stairs, to the nursery," Felicity said, her voice breathy from the exertion. Dering followed her instructions, wincing when the girl tried to scream over their words. The nursemaid appeared at the top of the stairs, her eyes wide.

"Is everything all right, my lady? She isn't hurt, is she?"

Felicity blew a clump of fallen hair from her forehead and shook her head. "No, Hedley, nothing like that. She's just cross that I wouldn't let her walk into the street."

Dering did his best not to make a face as he set the girl down on her cot. All this, just because she didn't get her way? He vaguely remembered his brothers going through a similar stage, but he supposed the lens of time had blessedly dulled the memories.

"Thank you, Gavin," Felicity said distractedly. "You can go wait for me downstairs, or be on your way if you hadn't intended to visit."

Not needing to be told twice, he nodded and headed downstairs, where he went straight to the place he had seen the liquor bottles last time he was there. He poured a half glass of whatever the first bottle held and tossed it back. It was halfway-decent scotch, burning its way down his throat. Truly, as cute as children could be, it was moments like that one that made him marvel at the fact the human race had survived as long as it had.

Blowing out a long breath, he settled onto the sofa and waited for Felicity to join him. He tilted his head and listened, but he didn't hear anything. Thank God. Hopefully that meant the women had managed to calm Isabella down. Five minutes later, Felicity came into the room and plopped down on the couch beside him, completely devoid of her normal decorum.

"I'm sorry you had to witness that, let alone be a part of it."

She looked utterly exhausted. Not that he was surprised. Who knew how long that had been going on before he'd arrived? "Nothing I can't handle. Are you all right?"

"I'll be fine. I just hate seeing her so upset like that. As a mother, there is nothing worse than not being able to console your child."

"That's the worst thing? I would have thought the tantrum itself would have been more distressing." The noise, the attention, the scowls from others—the whole thing had been a disaster in his eyes.

She rolled her head sideways to meet his gaze with a soft smile. "It's not logical to you, I'm sure, but I love her so much, it hurts my heart to see her so upset. She's still just a baby, and at her age it's impossible to understand that Mama won't let her do what she wants because I don't want her to get run over by a carriage."

"I suppose that is rather advanced logic for a one-year-old," he conceded, returning her smile. She was right, though—it was impossible to understand not being angry or cross at the girl when she'd acted so atrociously. "Why wasn't one of the servants there to help you, anyway?"

Sitting up to a more dignified position, she gave a little shrug. "I like having time alone with her. We were just going on a short walk in the sunshine. In Cadgwith, we take frequent walks to the beach, so she's used to having our special time together. Of course, on those walks, there's nary a single vehicle, let alone a whole city full of traffic."

Setting her hands to her knees, she pasted a determined smile on her lips. "Now then, were you intending to come see me, or was that just a serendipitous crossing of paths?"

The question caused the burn of anger to reignite in his gut. "I was coming to see you. I heard an interesting bit of gossip from my brother this morning involving a certain countess and a certain dowager baroness who may or may not have had a very interesting conversation."

She wrinkled her nose and sighed, leaning back onto the sofa. "I really am too tired for this."

Aha! So it was true, then. "Excellent. In that case, I can expect the truth of the matter from you about what, exactly, occurred during the visit."

Shaking her head, she pushed to her feet and walked to the window. Just beyond the glass, the cozy little private garden offered a fountain, benches, and several small trees, all enclosed by a high hedge that looked to be as tall as he was. "It was nothing. Your mother wished to have a little chin-wag, and I indulged her."

Right. He abandoned the comfortable cushions and came to stand behind her. Taking her by the shoulders, he gently turned her around to face him. "Try again."

He could see the reluctance in her warm brown eyes as she lifted her shoulders in a tired shrug. "Mothers care more deeply for their children than anyone else can possibly understand. She just wants what's best for you, Gavin. As do I."

What was *best* for him? Struggling to contain a scowl, he tilted his head and said, "Do you know who gets to choose what is best for me?" He waited, making it clear the question wasn't rhetorical.

A faint blush came to her cheeks as her eyes dropped to his cravat. "I suspect you will say that you do."

"And you suspect that because . . . ?"

She allowed her gaze to flick back up to his. "Because it is true, of course. But that doesn't mean that others can't care about you."

"We are in agreement on that. Now tell me what it is that she said to you."

"She . . . wished for my help. That is all I'm saying."

He crossed his arms and gave her a stern look. "I don't do well when I'm in the dark. Would you rather I go to her and tell her exactly how pleased I am that she is interfering?"

Felicity's hand settled over his forearm as she shook her head. "Please don't do that. It's really no matter. She merely wished for me to help you find a proper match."

Dering's teeth ground together as he imagined exactly how his mother must have phrased such a request. "And what, in her opinion, constitutes a proper match?"

He could practically see her disengage from him as she gave a light shrug. "The same thing that constitutes a proper match in everyone's eyes. A lovely young debutante with enviable beauty, impeccable breeding, and palpable innocence."

His mother was a master of her game, no doubt. With absolutely no justification in doing so, she'd managed to preemptively attack and insult Felicity all on the pretense of uniting them in what's *best* for him.

"You do realize," he said mildly, working to hold back the anger that simmered in his gut, "that I stopped allowing my mother to pick out my clothes decades ago.

I can *assure* you I have no intention of allowing her to choose my wife."

Her cheeks blossomed fully with color. "It really is none of my business. I cannot imagine why she even thought to involve me."

"She involved you because she clearly understands how partial I am to you. You don't fit the mold she has in her mind, so she thought to be preemptive."

"She mistakes friendship for something more."

Dering looked down at her, taking in the soft curve of her jaw, the supple fullness of her cheeks, the slight tilt of her eyes. Features that he knew as well as he knew his own. The line between friendship and "something more" seemed to blur by the day. Why did there have to even be a line?

Exhaling, he allowed his fingers to glide, feather-light, down the back of her arm. "It doesn't matter what she thinks. As far as I'm concerned, young, blushing, vapid debutantes are highly overrated.

"Whether for friendship or 'something more,' I prefer a woman who knows her heart and mind, who has experienced love and loss, triumph and failure—just as I have—and has come out stronger because of it. In my mind, *that's* what a proper match looks like."

He hadn't even realized how true the words were until he spoke them. He had always assumed he would merely choose a nice, pleasing debutante from the latest crop with whom he felt he could get along with reasonably well. After all, he couldn't lose his heart to somebody like that, and that had always been his ultimate goal. Protecting himself from the devastation that he'd gone through once before.

But, at that moment, the thought of cleaving himself to a girl like that made everything in him rebel.

When she looked up to meet his gaze, there was a flicker of genuine pleasure in her eyes. "I appreciate the sentiment more than you know. Regardless of what happens or what direction you go in life, I truly do care deeply for your happiness. I care for you, period."

Despite the inauspicious start to his visit and the unpleasantness of learning of his mother's tactics, something inside him warmed at her words. He cared about her tremendously, more so now than ever before. Yes, he fancied himself desperately in love with her when they were young, but his feelings for her now were so much richer. More honest. His feelings weren't based on a randy young man's enamorment with the prettiest, most clever girl he knew.

They were based on him deeply appreciating the woman she really was. The good, the bad, the difficult; all of it came together to form exactly who she was today. But did she truly care for him, too? In the same way, with the same intensity? The warmth licked down his back, trickling down his spine like a bead of bathwater. One corner of his mouth lifted the slightest bit as he held her gaze.

"Do you truly? I should count myself very fortunate were that the case."

"Of course I do. You know that, Gavin. Your friendship is invaluable to me."

Friendship. Yes, that. Only, that word simply couldn't encompass the way he felt about her. "Good. Then can you please purge from your mind the ridiculous things my mother said to you?"

She allowed her eyes to slide away from his as she brushed that fallen lock of golden hair from her forehead again. "Truly, it was nothing to worry about."

Without even thinking about it, he reached up and slipped his fingertips beneath her chin. Tipping her face up so that she would meet his gaze, he said, "If it upset you, then I can't help but worry about it."

He should have broken the touch, but he didn't. He kept his fingers where they were, even though his heart kicked up at the feel of her soft skin beneath his touch.

This was different from before. This wasn't the single-minded pursuit of a stolen kiss or touch. This was him, connecting with her in a true and honest way. No matter how much he tried to keep himself from reacting this way to her, it was just so natural to him. It was like breathing—just part of who he was.

"Gavin," she breathed, the word pleading and chiding at once. "You must stop worrying about me."

"Must I?" He savored the soft scent of gardenia and sunshine, wondering all the while what spell she held over him. Whatever it was, he didn't want it to go away. "What if I don't wish to?"

She watched him through half-lidded eyes, her chest rising and falling with each shallow breath she took. The moment stretched taut between them as he battled against his need to lower his lips to hers. To give physical manifestation to the closeness he had shared with her for so long. An eternity, really.

But he couldn't simply take what he wanted. He had to know what she wanted, what she desired. He had to know if she felt the incredible pull between them that he did, every blasted time they were together. After all she had been through, after all she was going through now, she deserved to do things on her own terms.

Exhaling softly, he pressed his eyelids closed for a moment to gather himself before meeting her eyes. They were as clear and rich as brandy, and certainly every bit as intoxicating.

But he was stronger than this. He was stronger than the heart-pounding, air-stealing addiction that he seemed to have to her. He had to be, because her happiness was paramount to everything else.

Swallowing, he let his arm slip away, breaking the contact between them.

"Wait," she whispered, reaching up to clasp his fingers between her hands. Heat sluiced through him at the feel of her touch. Her *purposeful* touch. She pressed his fingers between her palms, lacing her own fingers together tightly.

He waited, holding himself utterly still, not daring to move even a single muscle. She dropped her chin and pressed her lips to her fingers, lingering for the space of two seconds. When she finally lifted her head, she looked straight up into his eyes, purposefully holding his gaze.

"Close your eyes," she said, her voice barely more than a whisper.

He sucked in a surprised breath. With his heart pounding thunderously in his chest, he hesitated for little more than a moment, exhaled, and did as she commanded.

Chapter Eighteen

Felicity stood there, pulse hammering, staring up at one of the most beautiful men—inside and out—she had ever met. That hint of *something* that she'd sensed between them over and over again had suddenly broken free inside of her.

Attraction.

On the deepest, most elemental level. All at once, she recognized the sizzle that seemed to pass between them every time they stood too close or allowed those stolen touches to linger a little too long.

More than that, she recognized the look he had given her again and again. She hadn't seen it before. Hadn't *let* herself see it. He desired her but had held himself in check for her. He had been giving her the time she needed to come to this moment of her own volition.

She allowed her gaze to take in every inch of his face, from his dark, disheveled hair to his parted lips, down to the bold curve of his chin and the broad expanse of his chest. This was a man who could have anything he wanted. Yet over and over again he had told her, whether by words or actions, all he wanted . . . was her.

With butterflies dancing deep within her, with her heart pounding and her mind racing, she opened her laced fingers to reveal his captured hand. Slowly, deliberately, she lifted it to her mouth and pressed a soft, lingering kiss to his palm, allowing his fingers to splay fully across her cheek.

She waited, holding her breath for fear that guilt or worry or self-reproach would set in, but there was nothing but the flutter of hope and happiness. Lowering his hand, she moistened her lips and said, "Open your eyes."

He did as she directed, immediately seeking out her gaze. His only movement was the rise and fall of his wide chest as he watched her, his lips still parted. He was wound tight as a spring, but still he waited for her.

She smiled then, showing him exactly how present she was in the moment, and exactly how sure she was of what she was about to do. With the barest of touches, she gripped his chin between her thumb and forefinger, lifted onto her toes, and pulled him down for a kiss.

The moment his lips touched hers, something inside her gave way. All of the longing she hadn't even realized she'd been denying came flooding through her, heating her blood and soothing her heart. She groaned softly against his mouth, unable to contain the pleasure of the sensation.

It was all the encouragement he needed. He came to life, wrapping his arms around her back and pulling her solidly against him even as he slanted his lips more fully over hers. It was possessive but undemanding, wide-open but still somehow contained.

No, not contained: *concentrated*. Every fiber of his being was focused completely on her and nothing else.

She could feel the rush of energy between them, the intoxicating whoosh of exhilaration that seemed to consume them both.

The kiss went on for several long, glorious heartbeats, stealing her breath even as it seemed to breathe new life into her. At once she felt as light as air and as liquid as honey, conforming her body to his.

It was Gavin who finally pulled away. With palpable reluctance, he allowed his arms to loosen from around her back and ended the kiss with one last, lingering press of his lips to her mouth. As he straightened, he kissed her cheek, her temple, and her forehead before pulling her into his embrace, tucking her head beneath his chin, and wrapping his arms around her shoulders.

After a moment, he pulled back and met her gaze. There was elation and joy and pure pleasure—echoes of all the things she felt—but also the unmistakable undertones of worry in his deep brown gaze.

"Too much?" he asked, even as his hands tightened on her arms.

She shook her head, still trying to remember how to breathe again. "No, not too much. It was exactly right."

He closed his eyes and exhaled, and when he looked at her again, all she saw was contentment. "I couldn't agree more."

She didn't try to analyze things. She didn't worry about what it meant for their friendship or their futures. She simply soaked in the perfection of the moment, allowing herself to be blissful in the knowledge that she was safe with him in every way.

It wasn't until the swift clip of approaching footsteps echoed from the corridor that they pulled apart. "Richardson," she said with a smile in answer to Gavin's furtive glance to the door as he raked his hands over his hair and leaned against the window frame. She knew the butler's distinctive footsteps anywhere.

He sailed into the room a moment later, a silver salver in hand. His expression spoke volumes about his thoughts on Felicity entertaining alone. She suppressed a sigh. Sometimes she wondered if he would ever stop thinking of her as the master's wife.

"A letter, my lady. A footman awaits your response."

"Thank you, Richardson," she murmured as she accepted the note. The thick ivory card stock was folded in thirds and sealed with wax. She immediately recognized her father's seal. Her eyebrows inched up. Was he already in town? She quickly popped open the seal and unfolded the paper.

Dear Daughter,

Your brother and I have arrived in Bath. The lodgings are adequate and our staff complete. Your presence is requested for dinner this evening at seven o'clock. My footman has been instructed to await your response.

The note was signed formally, as he always did, with *Your Father, the Earl of Landowne,* as though she might somehow forget who he was. She gave a small shake of her head at the thought.

"Shall I leave you to your correspondence?" Dering asked, his voice quiet as he pushed away from the window.

She looked up and offered a reluctant smile. The last thing she wanted was to part ways, but it would take a few hours to get both her and Isabella ready for the evening. "It appears my father and brother have arrived. My presence is formally requested for a family dinner tonight. I'm sure you know how thrilling that prospect is."

Any evening with Thomas, Percy, and her father inevitably ended in stony silence, at minimum, or outright arguing at worst. It had been years since she'd sat down at a table with all of them, but she doubted much had changed.

She sighed and looked to Richardson. "Please convey to the footman that I shall be present as requested."

When the butler left to do her bidding, she turned and met Gavin's gaze. She smiled at the warmth she saw there, feeling it as tangibly as if he'd touched her. "I should probably prepare for the evening." She batted at the rogue lock of hair that her struggles with Isabella had dislodged. A bath for both her and Isabella was probably in order. "I do hope I can see you again soon."

"*Very* soon," he said, his expression so sweet and promising she wanted to wrap her arms around him all over again. "I hope you enjoy your visit. When you are ready to see me again," he said, pausing at her side and squeezing her hand, "please don't hesitate to send word. I am ever your servant."

She held her breath as he brushed a kiss across her lips. Her stomach danced all over again at the contact. It'd been so long since she'd experienced that feeling, and it was all she could do not to draw him closer and savor the sensation. When he left, she wrapped her arms around her waist and exhaled.

She had no idea what would happen next, but she knew one thing for certain: She couldn't wait to see him again.

* * *

"What the devil are you doing here?" Dering grinned as he welcomed the Duke of Radcliffe into his study. Dering hadn't been home but twenty minutes and was still reeling from his afternoon with Felicity.

God Almighty, he had finally kissed her.

And not just a chaste peck or simple brush of their lips. They had fallen into each other like old lovers, like *new* lovers, with a kiss so charged his heart still pounded. It had been utter perfection. Better than he had even imagined it would be, all those years ago when he had dreamed of just such a thing.

His friend smiled as he took a seat in one of the leather chairs. He looked exactly opposite of the way Dering felt, with every hair in place and every stitch of clothing neat and tidy. "I spent the morning looking over the ledgers from the *Anna Britannia*'s latest voyage, and thought you'd be pleased to know that things went even better than anticipated."

The ship, a joint venture of theirs, was currently at dock while the captain, Radcliffe's father-in-law, spent a few weeks with them here in Bath. Captain Bradford had been present at May, Sophie, and Charity's trio concert, in fact, and his pride and delight had been palpable.

Nodding, Dering said, "That's good. Glad to hear it." At that moment, he didn't care a fig about whether the ship had doubled their estimates. His mind was thoroughly, delightfully engaged elsewhere.

Radcliffe's brow furrowed as he tilted his head. "Is all well, old man? You look, I don't know. Agitated? Distracted? You tell me."

"Neither," he said, unable to keep a grin from surfacing. "Happy. Exuberant, perhaps."

Giving a short laugh, Radcliffe shook his head. "How many drinks have you had this afternoon?"

Dering shook his head resolutely. "Nary a one."

He didn't want anything to wash away the taste of the kiss. Of Felicity. He exhaled and dragged a hand through his hair, not even sure what the hell to do with himself. He needed to keep his emotions from getting too out of hand. It wasn't as though he was looking to sweep Felicity off her feet and hie to Gretna Green. It was simply one glorious afternoon, where they could come together in the best possible way.

"Really," the duke said, peering at him with renewed interest. His old friend knew him well enough to know he was acting strange. "The last we spoke at length, you were rather decidedly *unhappy*. After that, things were 'fine,' so I am left to wonder what has you so exuberant."

After that first rather undignified conversation the night of Dering's party, Radcliffe had inquired a few times if all was well regarding Felicity, and he had dismissively assured him it was. Dering had even said something about how *glad* he was that she had come, so he could realize how ridiculous he had been about the whole matter. He was grateful for the opportunity to put the whole thing behind him and simply be friends with her again.

And he hadn't necessarily been lying. He really had been glad for the chance to redefine their old friendship into something so much better. He met the duke's curious gaze, not wanting to betray Felicity's confidence, but wanting to share part of the excitement that made him feel as though he were soaring.

He shook his head and expelled a huge breath. "Let's just say that I've made quite a bit of progress in my relationship with a certain former friend of mine."

Radcliffe's brow lifted. "The baroness?" He seemed more surprised than Dering would have suspected.

"Yes, the *former* baroness," Dering replied, stressing the word. "She and I have enjoyed a rebirth, of sorts, of our old acquaintanceship." That was putting it mildly, but the wariness of Radcliffe's expression had him rethinking his decision to discuss the topic with him.

"Is that really a relationship that needs a rebirth? You do remember the aftermath of the death of it, yes? Because if you don't, I'd be happy to remind you of just how bad it was."

"What the hell, Will?" Dering said, scowling at the man, who was supposed to be one of his closest friends. "I tell you I'm happy and you try to put me in my place? I was there; I know exactly what I went through."

But Radcliffe didn't back down. Crossing his arms across his chest, he angled his head and said, "Your happiness is exactly why I am bringing this up. I'm delighted at the prospect of you and Lady Felicity forming an amicable relationship. But I know the look of a man in serious danger of falling for a woman when I see one, and you, sir, have one foot over the edge."

"You know the look because you've been there, and it seems to me that it turned out bloody brilliantly for you."

Radcliffe's eyes rounded in astonishment "Are you saying you wish to marry her? That you *want* to fall in love?"

The question was a solid punch to Dering's chest. Marriage? Did he want to marry her? He dragged a hand over his face, suddenly unsure of what the hell he wanted. "I don't know," he replied guardedly, wishing he'd kept his mouth shut.

"Her husband has been gone barely a year and a half.

She only just came out of half mourning. Don't you think she deserves a little time to sort things out? More than that, don't you think you deserve a woman who can give you her whole heart?"

Another punch, this one to the gut. Of course he knew she still loved her husband. He wouldn't want or expect her to give that up, but, if he was honest, there were still lingering fragments of jealously tied up deep inside of him. He didn't want it to be there, and he sure as hell didn't want to admit it, but there was still a part of him that resented the man who had stolen her from him. The man who had fathered her child and given her a life she cherished. *He* had wanted to be the man to do that.

He gritted his teeth, hating that the sentiment existed inside of him at all. Was he falling in love with her again? It was possible, even as he tried to refrain from labeling the way she made him feel. Up until that moment, he had been satisfied just to call it happiness.

Raking a hand through his hair, he said, "For the time being, I just want to enjoy her company. It's easy to remember why we had been such good friends for so long. I feel at home when I'm with her, and I know that she feels the same way."

Radcliffe nodded slowly, his mouth still pressed together with uncertainty. "Just . . . be aware, my friend. If your goals are different from hers, I fear one of you may be hurt, if not both of you."

One thing was absolutely certain: Dering sure as hell didn't want to hurt her. He didn't wish for either of them to be hurt, but after all she'd been through, he just wanted her to be happy.

Giving a perfunctory dip of his head, he said, "Right now, I merely wish to enjoy the present."

A hint of a smile worked the edges of the duke's mouth up. "I suppose I can trust you with that," he replied with a wry grin. "You are, after all, the most accomplished seeker of enjoyment I have met to date. Are you certain she is aware of your intentions?"

Dering thought of the beautiful smile she had given him right before pulling him down for a kiss. "Definitely."

"In that case, you are both adults, and I have said my piece, and so we shall leave it at that."

Dering smiled, throwing him a suspicious glance. "That sounded surprisingly reasonable. Just how much has the lovely duchess mellowed you, anyway? Or is that old age?"

His friend chuckled and shook his head. "I cannot wait until Thursday, when you finally turn thirty. For a few weeks, you and I will be the same age again, and you can shut the hell up."

"Won't matter, old man. You'll still be a year older and that much closer to the grave."

Coming to his feet, the duke paused and met his gaze. "I hope you know that I do wish for your happiness. I wasn't attempting to tear you down, but merely making sure you were keeping a good head about those massive shoulders of yours. I assure you I have only your best interests at heart."

Dering groaned. "You and my mother are conspiring against me, I swear. Suffice it to say that I have my own best interests at heart as well. But thank you, I suppose. I do recall having your best interests at heart, not too long ago."

Radcliffe laughed outright at that. "Actually, I believe it was May's best interests that you were concerned with.

But since you were looking out for her, I'll let that one go. Her interests are mine, after all."

Yes, that was exactly the way he felt about Felicity. Whatever the summer brought for them, he always wanted the best for her. At that moment, he was absolutely certain that their being together, in whatever form that took, was the best thing for them both.

After all, anything that felt this right couldn't possibly be wrong.

Chapter Nineteen

"Good afternoon, Papa. I hope you are well."
Felicity offered a small curtsy to her father as he looked up from his newspaper. She was a little early, so she wasn't surprised to find him alone in the drawing room reading.

Coming to his feet, he accepted her kiss to his cheek and offered a perfunctory smile. "I am, as I trust you are."

His hair was threaded with even more gray than it had sported the last time she had seen him, but he looked much the same otherwise. She had inherited her eye color from him, and his one vanity seemed to be wearing clothes in tones of gold and brown to match. Tonight he wore a handsome mahogany jacket, the solid gold buttons of which strained against the rounded paunch of his stomach.

Though he wasn't a handsome man, he had pleasant features that looked particularly well on the rare occasions he smiled. Not that he was sad or glum, just a busy and important man who had little time for frivolity in life.

"I am pleased to see you looking so well," he said with a stately nod.

She smiled. High praise, coming from him. He had never been cruel or unjust, just not overly warm when it came to his affections. He wasn't one to keep a genuine compliment from her, though she wasn't sure the same could be said of his interactions with Thomas.

"Thank you, Papa. I am feeling quite well."

It was an understatement. She was still fairly glowing with pleasure from Dering's visit. Yes, there was some sadness beneath the joy, knowing that the only other man she had ever kissed was her husband, but just as with the dancing, she felt peace in moving forward.

She nodded toward the entrance to the drawing room, where Hadley waited with Isabella at her hip. "I've brought your granddaughter. She's changed quite a bit since last you saw her."

The baby had been little more than five months old when he had made the journey to Cadgwith to visit last year. It had been a momentous occasion, only his second visit to her home since she'd moved there so long ago.

He lifted his chin to peer in the direction she pointed. "Very well. Bring her here."

Hadley hurried forward and handed Felicity her daughter before taking a quick, unobtrusive step back. Felicity turned and smiled at her father. "Isabella, this is your grandfather. Can you say *How do you do?*"

Suddenly shy, Bella buried her face into Felicity's neck. The earl compressed his lips as he considered the girl. "She looks very much like Lord Cadgwith. Her father, I mean, not the current baron. Though I suppose there is some resemblance there as well."

Felicity patted her daughter's back, willing her not to have another fit like she had had earlier. Heaven knew her father wouldn't approve. "She does indeed. I'm looking forward to discovering if she's inherited any of Ian's personality, as well."

He nodded. "I had hoped to see some resemblance to our side of the family, but she is a handsome enough child."

He shifted his gaze to Hadley. "Mrs. Keats will show you up to the nursery. It has been cleaned and aired out, and I'm sure she'll be quite comfortable."

Felicity frowned as she held Bella a bit tighter. His dismissal of her stung. Of course she knew that he felt interaction with young children should be kept to a minimum, but this was his only grandchild. "But, Papa, Percy hasn't met her yet. I thought now would be a good time, since we will all be here together."

He waved a hand. "There will be time enough for that later. Before your brothers join us for dinner tonight, I wish to speak with you privately."

She didn't like the sound of that. What would he have to say to her that couldn't be said in the company of her siblings? But she knew better than to argue. Nodding, she kissed Bella's cheeks before handing her back to Hadley. She almost smiled at how quickly the woman escaped to the corridor, where the housekeeper hovered near the door. Her father could be intimidating to many.

Papa extended a hand toward the chairs that faced where he'd been seated on the sofa before her arrival, and they both sat. "Now then. I'm most pleased that you decided to come to Bath. When Thomas sent word that you'd arrived, I took it as a positive sign of your recovery. I can see for myself that you have shed your mourning clothes, which is good."

She looked down at the apple-green gown she had

chosen for the visit and smiled. Yes, she was well and truly out of half mourning. She didn't want to think of the extraordinary kiss she'd shared with Gavin earlier, not with her father scrutinizing her, but still she felt warmth blooming on her cheeks.

"I felt the time was right." She didn't miss Ian any less, but she was so happy to finally feel that she was recapturing life again.

He nodded, clearly approving. "And so it is. You mourned him well and proper, as any spouse should. However, now that you have set aside your widow's weeds, I feel it is time to discuss your future."

Whether it was his intention or not, he had caught her completely off guard. She stiffened in her seat, blinking in confusion. "My future?"

Where exactly was he going with this?

He nodded, regarding her with a proper mix of detached sympathy and fatherly authority. The latter was something she hadn't seen in a decade, and it immediately put her guard up.

She was a widow now. She alone was responsible for her future, and the decisions regarding it.

"Indeed," he said gravely. "What are your plans, my dear?"

She shook her head, wary. "I have no plans other than to continue as I have. Cadgwith is home for both Isabella and me."

Besides being the place she felt most at home, the people there had known and loved Ian. She wanted Isabella to hear stories and anecdotes from others as she grew, so that in some way, she would know her father despite his absence.

He compressed his lips as he peered at her with something that looked suspiciously like sympathy. "Felicity, you must know that you cannot go on living in your brother-in-law's home, particularly now that he is wed. If you had borne a son, it would be another matter, but as things stand, such an arrangement is untenable."

The back of her neck tingled as she stared back at him, at a loss for words. Did he think she was taking advantage of Hugh and Charity, living off them like some sort of poor relation? "Papa, that house is my home—one that I am welcome in. There is more than enough room for Hugh, Charity, Isabella, and myself, as well as a whole host of others, if ever the need arose."

He reached over and patted her hand, as paternal a gesture as he had ever shown her. "Now, now, I am aware that you must feel attached to the place by now. But as kind as the baron and baroness may be, it is simply not fair to expect them to share their home. Your time for mourning is past, by your own admission, and it is time to move on."

His words were said with a pitying sense of kindness, as though he had only her best interests at heart, but that just seemed to make it worse.

Just because she had hung up her lilacs and lavenders, and had even enjoyed the attentions of another man, did not mean she had closed the door to her grief. She was moving forward, yes, but not without the remembrance of the past. For the first time since she and Gavin had kissed, the first hints of unease settled like fresh snow in her heart.

"Father, please listen to me. Hugh and Charity rather explicitly asked me to stay for as long as I wished. I initially planned to move to a cottage—I have a healthy widow portion, after all—but they insisted I was both welcome and wanted."

She set her jaw and lifted her chin, her pride smarting from his words. "Quite frankly, it is a matter that doesn't concern you."

His brow crumpled into a stern V. "You are my daughter, Felicity. In the absence of a husband, all matters concerning you, concern me."

Did he think her eighteen years old again? Some delicate debutante that needed a man to guide her through life? She was nearly thirty, for heaven's sake, raising a child of her own. "I hate to be blunt, but I'm afraid that simply isn't true. Not according to me, not according to the law, and not according to convention.

"Cadgwith is my home. Period. It is where I plan to live for the foreseeable future, particularly since it is where my daughter can be closest to those who knew her father."

"And what of her living family?" he countered. "She is the granddaughter of an earl, for God's sake. She should be raised accordingly."

What did he know about raising *her* daughter? He had seen Isabella exactly once before today, and he made no effort to keep up on her progress. Anything he knew about her was purely because Felicity chose to write with updates on a regular basis—updates he had certainly never asked for.

"Since when do you even care how I raise my daughter? You barely even looked at her just now."

"I don't need to see her to know what's best for her," he said, affecting the lord-of-the-manor tone that made her teeth grind. Setting his hands to either side of his jacket's lapels as though posing for a portrait, he pinned her with an authoritative look. "You should come back to Landowne Castle with us at the end of the summer.

"In the meantime," he continued, "I've taken the liberty of having a room made ready for you here. You'll see that it's the right thing to do, if you but ponder it for a moment."   ·

She was speechless. Staring back at him as she shook her head, she fumbled for what to say that would make him see that she wasn't going to bow down and pander to his whims.

Drawing a fortifying and calming breath, she offered him a polite but steely smile. "Thank you for the kind offer, but I'm afraid I cannot accept."

He shook his head, his eyes reflecting disappointment. "I don't believe you are thinking this through properly. Mrs. Potter wrote to me shortly before we left. I understand that you are interested in finding another husband, and I can tell you plainly that no man wants to think of his future wife as someone who lives on her former in-laws' forbearance."

Felicity nearly groaned aloud. Things were beginning to make a little more sense, not that it made her feel any better.

"Mrs. Potter needs to mind her own business. No, I am *not* looking for a husband. I am also not interested in what others think of how I choose to live my life. If ever there was any benefit to being a widow, because God knows they are few, it would be the freedom to live how best *I* choose. Not what others choose for me."

He pointed toward the direction in which Mrs. Keats

had disappeared. "Isabella is still very young. Would you deny her the opportunity to have a father figure? If not in me, then in a new husband?"

Her heart ached all over again with the truth that Ian would never be there to guide her. The peace that she had worked so hard to gain began to slip, and she placed her hand to her chest as though to stop it. "Hugh is a wonderful influence on her life."

"Until his own children arrive," he countered plainly. He stepped forward and laid a hand to her shoulder. "You need to think of the future, Felicity. You are young enough to still have a very good chance of marrying well. Making an advantageous match could be beneficial for both you and the family."

Ah yes. The age-old practice of aligning families through marriage. Though he had allowed her match with Ian, she knew he would have preferred someone of higher rank and influence. She was fortunate that the loss of her mother had softened him for a few years.

Meeting her father's gaze directly, she said, "If a new spouse is so important, why is it that you never married?"

He instantly dropped his hand and stepped away, his brow beetling. "That is completely different. If you children had been younger, I'm certain I would have."

For some reason, his answer surprised her. Had he ever considered marrying again? His marriage to Mama had been arranged, and she knew they shared a deep respect, but there was no great love between them. "You do realize that it is not too late. There is no reason why you shouldn't remarry, should you choose."

She thought of Sir Anthony, and his philosophy on marriage. How he felt people weren't meant to lead solitary lives. Despite what she had told her father about herself, she was starting to believe the baronet might have had a point.

Papa's ruddy complexion turned even more red. "You are in no position to lecture me on the topic." But instead of belligerence, his response showed more embarrassment than anything.

The sound of footsteps in the marble entry hall made them both glance to the doorway of the drawing room. Her father cleared his throat and turned back to her. "We can resume this conversation at a later time. In the interim, I expect us to have a civilized meal together tonight."

Civilized? After this whole disastrous discussion, not to mention how very fond Thomas and Percy were of each other? Still, it was family, and she had been raised to put on the proper face when necessary. "As you wish," she said stiffly.

She drew a bracing breath, attempting to shed her annoyance so she could properly greet Percy and be there to support Thomas.

"Felicity," her father said, drawing her attention as Percy approached the room. "I hope that you will think about what we've discussed. Regardless of our differences, I assure you that I have only your interests, and the interests of Isabella, at heart."

There was irony in that statement. Hadn't Gavin's mother claimed the same motivation? Well, just as Gavin had made clear earlier, no one could know what was best for her but her.

Just thinking of Gavin made her want to slide into his embrace and forget all of the doubt her father had just planted. Which, in itself, seemed problematic. Was she using him as a way to escape? Every time she was with him, she just felt so wonderful, but what, exactly, did their future hold? Soon she would be going back to Cadgwith, and he to his various homes and entertainments.

Should she be indulging in their relationship like this? Especially given the argument she had just had? Yes, he had been a huge part of her moving forward, of her getting over the paralyzing feeling of being afraid to let go. She was grateful for that, but did that mean they should carry on as they were?

She really needed some time to think. She didn't regret a single moment of her time with Gavin, but perhaps she should begin living her life in the way she intended to continue: a widowed mother taking joy in life while concentrating on her daughter.

The thought of stepping back from her connection with Gavin made dread pool deep within her, but she couldn't help but feel as though it were the right thing. She already knew that he had pulled away from much of what he loved for her.

As she trained her lips into a smile to greet her older brother, she couldn't help but think of the good-bye that she would have to say to the viscount sooner or later. Was it best to end things now, or to enjoy just a little more time with each other, knowing that it would be over soon?

She pressed her lips together. At that moment, neither option seemed ideal. It appeared she had *much* to think about.

Chapter Twenty

His mother was a crafty one, he'd give her that. As Miss Sellers clapped with all the enthusiasm of the nineteen-year-old girl she was, Dering shot a narrowed glance in his mother's direction over the girl's head. The countess simply smiled serenely back before offering up her own restrained applause for the Elizabethan-costumed singers bowing from the stage.

Oh yes, she had known exactly what she was about when she'd casually requested that he accompany her to the Pump Room to take the waters and promenade the room this morning. "How lovely to be seen on the arm of my handsome eldest son," she had said with an indulgent smile as they'd collected their glasses of mineral water.

He'd come with the hope of setting her straight regarding the debacle with Felicity, but before he could even broach the subject, Lady Sellers had just happened by with her dear, sweet, unmarried daughter Delilah. The girl truly did possess a lovely temperament, but she seemed so young, he had had to quell the desire to glance about for her governess.

As if scripted by the Bard himself, the two mothers

had proceeded to trap him quite handily into offering up the use of his box at the Theatre Royal for the much-anticipated *Shakespeare's Songs for a Midsummer's Night* performance.

He stifled a sigh. So here they were.

As the curtain went down for intermission, the roar of the audience immediately filled the cavernous, four-story theater. His young brunette companion turned to him with bright blue eyes and grinned. "Wasn't that magnificent? Oh, thank you so much for allowing us to join you in your box tonight. It is ever so much nicer than the gallery was last time."

He nodded as graciously as he could manage. "I am pleased that you and Lady Sellers could join us. If I had known that one of Mother's *dearest* friends was in town, I would have offered you the use of the box earlier." When he wasn't in it, preferably.

Oh, the girl was certainly a lovely young lady, and her mother wasn't nearly as pushy as, say, his own mother, but this was not his idea of an enjoyable evening. He preferred more mature company.

For perhaps the tenth time in as many minutes, his eyes darted to the box where Felicity sat with her stern-faced brother Percy on one side and Lady Effington on the other, with Lord and Lady Evansleigh behind them. It wasn't an easy angle, given their position far to his left with the stage to his right, but he had found himself craning his neck again and again.

Lady Sellers leaned into his field of vision and set her hand to her heart in a show of gratitude. "Lord Derington, you truly are a saint among men. Having missed the festival last year, we had no notion of how very well attended it would be. We might have hired a box ourselves, had we known. Now they are all sold out."

Just past the woman's shoulder, Dering saw Felicity rise. "Do you know," he said quickly, coming to his feet, "I believe I'll go see if I can't convince one of the waiters to see to our refreshments first. Pardon me just a moment, ladies."

Not giving any of them a chance to stop him—or worse, ask to accompany him—he hurried from the box, flapping the heavy velvet curtain aside as he dashed into the corridor. People were starting to fill the dimly lit space, either to make use of the retiring rooms, to mingle with friends, or to purchase refreshments.

The very first servant Dering saw, he held up a guinea, effectively capturing the man's undivided attention. After ordering a platter of food and a tray of drinks for the box, Dering rushed on toward where Felicity's box entrance was. A quick peek through the curtains revealed an empty seat where she had been, so he turned back around and began searching the hallways.

Every third person seemed to want to talk, but he simply smiled and waved and made vague gestures ahead of him. Finally, he caught a glimpse of her dark green gown as she emerged from the ladies' retiring room. When their eyes met, the air whooshed from his lungs on one long breath.

God, but she was beautiful.

Her eyes widened for a moment at the unexpected sight of him before she smiled and walked forward. "Good evening, my lord. How are you finding the singing?"

So formal. He smiled, rather liking the feeling that they were sharing a secret in the midst of all these

people. "Excellent, as expected." Leaning down closer
to her ear, he added, "The company, on the other hand,
could definitely be improved upon."

"Indeed? I would happily loan you Percy."

She was teasing, which was good, but he didn't miss
the reservation in her manner. She wasn't as comfortable as he liked to see her. Of course, he knew that she
was never terribly at ease in crowded spaces like this.

On a whim, he held out his elbow. "There is someone
I would like you to meet, if you have an extra moment
to spare."

Her gaze darted to his proffered arm before meeting
his. "I probably shouldn't. The others will wonder
where I've gotten off to."

"I'm certain they'll realize you're conversing with
some friend or another." Allowing a small private grin,
he added, "I promise to have you back by curtain rise."

He caught a hint of her gardenia scent and inhaled,
wishing like hell that he could slip his arms around her
and pull her close.

She hesitated for a moment before capitulating. "If
you insist," she said, setting her gloved fingers atop his
forearm. He led her to the stairs, earning an odd look
from her.

"There are more boxes upstairs," he explained as he
motioned for her to take the railing.

They ascended the two flights of stairs to the small
section at the top floor that overlooked the entire theater. But instead of pulling aside the curtain to the
seating area, he opened a narrow door to his right and
quickly pulled her through.

She gasped as they emerged onto the building's roof,
turning to him with wide eyes. "You—"

But he didn't let her finish the sentence. He tugged her flush against his chest and captured her lips in one smooth motion. She tasted exactly as he remembered, warm and sweet and distinctly *her*. After an initial moment of surprise, she responded, leaning into him in a way that made his pulse go from fluttering to galloping. He wrapped his arms securely around her as much in an effort to ward off the chilly dampness of the night as to draw her as close as possible.

Below them, the sounds of the street were distant and muted, echoing as they rose to the heavens. The soft glow of the city's light was dim enough to allow the intimacy of darkness with just enough illumination to let him see her lovely, familiar features.

After a minute he pulled back and smiled down at her. "Hercules."

Her brow wrinkled adorably as she peered up at him, confusion swimming in her softened gaze. "I beg your pardon?"

"I said I wanted you to meet someone." He pointed straight up to the clouds above. "Hercules. Unfortunately, the stars did not cooperate tonight. Hopefully I'll do in his stead."

As understanding dawned, she lifted one finely arched eyebrow. "I thought you *were* Hercules," she said, amusement painting her tone.

He grinned wolfishly and pulled her a little closer. "I am, aren't I? Lucky you."

"Something like that," she teased. The humor in her eyes quickly faded as she glanced to the door, and he knew she was thinking of how long they had been gone.

Kissing her on the lips again, he sighed. "God, but I've dreamed of kissing you beneath the stars. I wish it could be longer, but I suppose we'd best get back. I just couldn't bear not seeing you alone, if only for a moment. Will I have to wait until the trip to the ruins to see you again?"

It was two days away, but as he'd discovered in the two days since they'd last kissed, it could be an untenable amount of time. This feeling she gave him, that subtle frisson of energy that made his whole body come alive, was one that was hard to step away from.

She looked down for a moment before meeting his gaze again. "Yes, I think so. I have plans tomorrow, and I'm sure you'll be busy as well."

He slipped a finger beneath her chin and tilted her lips up for one more kiss. "I'm never too busy for you. However, if I must wait until Thursday, then so be it."

Pulling back with noticeable reluctance, she nodded. "I shall see you then."

Why must her body betray her every time he was near? She had been so determined to be aloof, to show that she could be pleasant and friendly without giving into that nearly overwhelming desire to touch him. To prove to herself that they could maintain the friendship she so valued, without stepping across that invisible line to something more than friendship.

But then, when she'd stepped out on the roof and the whole city had been at their feet, the whole universe at their heads, he'd pulled her to him, and she was lost.

Wholly and completely.

All of the promises she had made to herself to maintain her distance had crumbled beneath the first touch of his lips to hers. Heavens, but he knew how to kiss. He knew how to transport her from her thoughts and reservations, so completely that she hadn't even given a moment's thought to whether anyone might have seen them or what such a kiss might mean.

His mouth had opened to hers, and the rest of the world had ceased to exist.

Now, as she sat quietly between Percy and Lady Effington, her blood still thrummed from the lingering pleasure his kiss had stirred. Almost against her will, she was looking forward to their excursion. She wanted to be with him, to laugh and tease and touch him as casually as one breathed.

Part of her knew that she needed to say something to him. To give a name to what it was they were doing, and in the process, give it limitations. To be bluntly clear that this attraction could go no further. Lord knew if anyone reported back to her father that she was in the company of a man like that, she'd lose much of what she'd staked her argument on.

But part of her longed for the ambiguity just a little bit longer. The end would still be the same: her returning to her life, Gavin to his. She bit her lip and exhaled. The faint taste of him still remained, slight but unmistakable.

Thursday, the day of the excursion, would be both of their birthdays. Perhaps, for just that day, it wouldn't be so bad to indulge in his company.

Anticipation immediately slipped through her belly. As she settled back into her chair in the darkness, she turned her head just enough to see his box. Their eyes collided almost at once, and she smiled.

Yes, they definitely deserved one more day without rules.

And she had to believe that it would be enough.

Chapter Twenty-one

The place looked like a dream, just as Dering had envisioned. With one huge tent and two seating areas set up a hundred paces from the tumbled-down ruins of the old monastery, it was an eclectic combination of modern and ancient touches. His servants had gone above and beyond, laying out settings suitable for the king himself at each of the four round, folding French wine tables situated beneath the canopy.

Flowers spilled from tall vases at the center of each, a fragrant mix of roses, lavender, lilies, and a single white gardenia. Overhead, a small but elegant crystal chandelier hung from the center of the tent, though it was more for effect than usefulness. It was unlikely they would remain anytime close to sunset.

He'd had Cook create a veritable feast of cold meats and cheeses, fruits and breads, decadent puddings and a selection of small cakes in five different flavors. Wine, spirits, beer, and lemonade were arranged in an ice bath as cool refreshment for the warmth of the day.

Setting his hands to his hips, he shook his head and grinned to the three footmen who had been working for hours to set it all up. "Thank you, all," he said, truly meaning it. "Tomorrow, you may have the day off as a token of my appreciation."

As a cheer went up among them, Dering caught sight of the first carriage as it followed the narrow lane leading to the ruins. A fresh wave of anticipation went through him.

All of this had been to surprise Felicity. She'd always loved being outside in the country, away from the bustle of the city. He could still remember the night when they were about seventeen, lying side by side in the folly looking up at the stars, when she'd sighed and proclaimed that she would live there if she could. String up a chandelier or two, add a comfortable chair, a trunk of books, and a card table, and she'd be happy forever.

He'd almost told her then. He'd almost turned on his side, set his hand to her middle, and told her it could all be hers if she would but marry him someday.

If he had, perhaps things would have been different. Perhaps they would have married and had babies and she would never have known the pain of widowhood. And he would never have known the pain of heartbreak.

But then again, if that had been the case, neither of them would be the people they were today. He suspected that, given the chance, she would never have traded the time she'd had with her husband. The real question was, would he have traded his own experiences? Was he a better man for the loss? If nothing else, he had certainly learned to reach for what he wanted. The trick was keeping his heart protected in the process. He'd excelled at that over the years.

What he didn't know was where that left him now. Because, God help him, he wanted her. He couldn't bring himself to define what that really meant, because he didn't know if he was prepared for the repercussions. For the time being, he was content to be as close to her as possible in the time that they had here together.

There were too many questions with not enough answers, but today it didn't matter. Today was about taking their pleasures in the moment. It was about enjoying a day meant to celebrate them. It was about happiness.

He truly hoped this surprise made her smile.

He'd sent word yesterday evening that he would be traveling separately due to some business he needed to attend to, so none of them would know what he was up to. The ball on Saturday would be of little interest to her, so this was for her to feel special.

As those on horseback and the first carriage in the procession came to a halt, Dering spread his arms and grinned. "Welcome, everyone! I hope you don't mind a little civilization with your rustic outing."

Radcliffe, who had led the group, nodded as he looked around. "Not bad," he said, hopping to the ground from atop his speckled gray beast. He squinted as he took in the tent, the sitting areas, and the crumbling walls of the old monastery. Little remained other than the remnant of one three-story wall and a few glassless window openings that were square at the bottom and arched to peaks at the top.

Dering smiled as he gave a sound pat to his friend's back. "I hope it will make for a memorable outing."

Radcliffe snorted. "I'll admit, this wasn't what I was picturing. The ladies will be delighted."

Evansleigh pulled up beside them and dismounted. He lifted his hat and ran a hand over his hair before setting it back in place. "Well, you certainly know how to hold a party," he said with a wry shake of his head. "If anyone needs me, I shall be languishing in the shade with a bottle of whatever is chilling in the ice over there."

After a footman had opened the carriage door and unfolded the step, Sophie was the first to emerge. Her grin was huge as she waved an arm at the setup. "Dering, this is wonderful! I think I could live here and be perfectly happy all of my days."

Evan shook his head as he helped his wife down. "You say that, but I know how very fond you are of the extravagancies in life, such as walls and flooring."

"Well, I suppose there is that. I shall simply have to thoroughly enjoy myself today in order to get the most out of it."

Charity stepped down next, sending Dering a fond look. "Only you would know how to go about setting something like this up in the middle of nowhere. Do you own all of this, or do you simply know people who do?"

"A little of both," he admitted with a grin. If ever there was something he didn't have that he wanted, he always knew someone who did.

Thomas pulled up on his mount's reins while Cadgwith and May made their way out of the carriage.

"Capital," the vicar said on a laugh, suitably impressed. "This manages to put my party in the park last year to shame. Although I did manage to transport a pianoforte out there, so there's that," he said with a good-natured grin.

"Oh, that'll be here shortly," Dering deadpanned.

Thomas let out a sharp crack of laughter. "The devil you say."

"No, not really," he confessed, much to the man's amusement. He had considered it, though.

The second carriage rolled to a stop then, and Dering

strode toward it, hardly able to keep his eagerness in check. The two days since he'd seen and kissed Felicity had felt like weeks. All he had been able to think about was how they could have some time alone together to really explore things between them. A few rushed kisses weren't nearly enough.

To that end, he had some tricks up his sleeves. The surrounding woodland was a wonderful place to lose oneself with a beautiful and willing lady.

Felicity was the first to emerge, and pleasure flared in his chest at the way her golden brown eyes danced when she met his gaze. Despite an hour cooped up in the carriage, she looked as fresh and lovely as a summer marigold in the brilliant orange gown he remembered from the night of their dance.

"My lady," he said, holding out his hand. "You look stunning, particularly for a thirty-year-old."

She laughed aloud even as she shot him a mockingly disgruntled look. "A lady's age should never be mentioned in mixed company, my lord. Especially when I am quite certain that you are at least half a day older than me."

She allowed him to assist her down, and he gave her fingers a little squeeze before letting them go.

"Touché. Although I have it on good authority that women, like fine wine, only get better with time."

Lady Effington's raspy chuckle drew his attention back to the carriage. "That's a bag of moonshine, I can assure you. Enjoy your youth, my dears. It's far more fleeting than you can imagine."

"I shall do my level best," Dering said, winking as he helped her down.

Felicity leaned backed into the opening of the coach and held out her hands. "Come to Mama, sweet girl."

Dering blinked in surprise. She'd brought the baby all the way out here? But . . . what would the child do all day? The games and activities he had in mind didn't easily accommodate having a child at one's hip. Still, he knew better than to let his dismay show. Setting a smile on his lips, he greeted the girl as he assisted the nursemaid to the ground.

"Good morning, Miss Isabella."

She scowled at him a moment before holding her arms out to Lady Effington and grunting. The older woman kissed her hands and grinned. "Now, now, Miss Bella. We must always properly greet a man with a title. Say *How do you do, my lord?*"

The baby babbled back, perhaps getting a *how* in there somewhere. He really couldn't be sure. The viscountess smiled and said, "That's better. Now then, Grandmama will hold you later, once we sit down."

The soft grin Felicity gave her daughter was beyond lovely. It reminded him of just how very well he liked those lips. Clearing his throat, he turned his attention back to the group at large. He'd have more time for those particular thoughts later.

Raising his voice, he said, "I thought we could explore the grounds and ruins first, then have a light luncheon, and finally move on to some games I have planned for the group. Complete," he said, grinning hugely as he pulled a page of the newspaper from his breast pocket, "with a formal reading of Mr. Wright and Lord Cadgwith's very moving sonnets in ode to their recent defeat."

Thomas and the baron groaned loudly, as the others laughed and clapped. Dering had purposely refrained from reading the poems yet so to share the experience with his friends.

"Does this meet with everyone's approval?"

"That depends," Thomas said, screwing his face up in distaste. "Do we have free rein of the beverages? I'm feeling terribly parched all of a sudden."

Laughing, Dering slapped him on the back. "Indeed, my friend. Feel free to partake at will. I have a feeling you'll need it."

For the next half hour, the entire group wandered around the ruins, peering through the old windows and pacing off the length of the walls. Even the dowager joined in for a while before finally retiring to the tents.

"This place must have been huge for its day," Dering mused as he walked alongside Felicity. "It must have held a hundred people, at least."

"Where do you suppose they all came from? There's nothing but farmland and forest around for miles." She'd kept Isabella tucked along her hip, pointing out interesting formations and pretty flowers as they wandered.

"It used to be a monastery, so I imagine they would have had many living here. But legend has it there was a village nearby that was burned to the ground several centuries ago."

"How tragic," she said, frowning as she looked down the overgrown interior where the center aisle would have been. Grass, weeds, vines, and even trees grew where pews likely once stood, giving the whole place a rather eerie, ethereal feel.

As she started forward, she stumbled over something and pitched forward with a squeak. His hands shot out, catching her almost instantly. As he righted her, she blew out a breath, her eyes as wide as her startled daughter's. "Thank you. For a moment there, I was certain I would fall flat on my face."

He smiled, glad his reflexes had reacted so quickly. "Never fear when you are by my side. I'll always catch you before you fall."

"Ever my hero." Her eyes were warm as she switched her daughter to the other hip. "I should have been more careful with all these stones strewn about."

Smiling at her offhand compliment, he held out his hands. "Can I take her for you?" The baby might have been light by his standards, but after half an hour, she surely must have felt like a lead weight to Felicity by now.

She sent him a dubious look, raising a single blond brow. "Are you certain? Things didn't go so well the last time."

Ah yes, the infamous fit on the pavement. Still, Isabella had more or less been an angel this whole time, pointing and chattering away. Shrugging, he turned his attention to the baby and said, "Miss Isabella, may I hold you? The view is much better from up here."

For a moment, the girl looked back and forth between him and Felicity, clearly unsure. Felicity gave her a little jostle. "Go on, Bella. Just look how much taller you'll be than me when you are in his arms."

Grinning wide enough to reveal a mouthful of baby teeth, she threw out her hands. He couldn't help but smile back. She really was a cute little thing, even if she didn't look at all like her mother. He hoisted her up to sit on his shoulder so that she could look down on Felicity.

She squealed with laughter, her little body squirming with mirth as she waved down at her mother. It was . . . pleasant. Enjoyable, even. He rather liked the sound of her unfettered joy, and absolutely loved the delight it seemed to bring Felicity. The day hadn't started quite as he intended, but perhaps that wasn't such a bad thing after all.

Felicity shook her head in wonder as they approached the incredible arrangement Gavin had surprised them with. "How in heaven did you do all this?" she said, tightening her grip on his arm.

He had thought of everything, from silverware to colored lanterns to the elegant chandelier. Thoughtful details were everywhere, including the cozy little seating area situated on a wide blanket beneath the huge oak tree. Mostly there were pillows and wooden folding chairs, but a grand armchair complete with footstool dominated the space. There was even a little basket with an open lid revealing a handful of books.

"I have excellent servants and multiple vehicles," he responded with a wink. "What do you think, Bella?" he asked of the baby, melting Felicity's heart.

She loved how effortlessly he carried her daughter. She knew that he wasn't particularly comfortable around children, but this morning she had seen a glimpse into the father he would someday be. It made her heart swell to see how sweet he was with her, now that the two of them had gotten used to each other.

The baby bounced and clapped her hands as Gavin lowered her to the ground and let her explore the little seating area. Felicity laughed. "I think she is one very happy little girl. Thank you for carrying her. I think you made the outing more fun for both of us." Though she loved seeing Bella's personality come out more every day, she missed how tiny she was as a sweet little infant whom Felicity could hold for hours.

"My pleasure," he murmured, the words soft and deep. Hadley came forward then to take over, and Felicity and Gavin strolled to the tent, where the others had gathered.

Spreading his palms, he said, "I hope you all are hungry, because we have roughly enough food to last a fortnight out here. And," he added, pulling out the folded sheet of newspaper from his pocket, "we have mealtime entertainment."

"Your cruelness knows no bounds, old man," Hugh grumbled good-naturedly as he reluctantly accepted the paper. "Wasn't it enough to witness our defeat firsthand?"

Felicity shook her head. "Oh no. You would have gladly had us sing at church in front of half the city. The least you can do is stand up in front of a dozen of your *dearest* friends so that we may be properly entertained."

Charity grinned and rubbed her hands together. "I, for one, am very much looking forward to it. That's what he gets for betting such a thing in the first place."

"And to think I married you, you bloodthirsty wench," he responded, earning himself a smack on the shoulder. "Very well, I suppose it's best to get it over with sooner rather than later."

He stood, cleared his throat, and began.

"I played this night a game of cards
Though sense so common bid me refrain
But with the promise of victory in yonder stars
I bellied up to the baize with everything to gain

So sure was I as the cards were dealt
I laughed and bet more than any man should lose
Now here, this moment the pain is felt
As my pen scratches, down my throat with the booze
My congratulations to Lady F and to Lord Dering
For winning at cards, even whilst losing humility
Thou hast captured my pride, without a whit of caring
I'll just slink on my way, with a crisis of my ability
My lesson well learnt, at least I do hope most eagerly
From this moment on, I'll stick to bets much more
    meagerly."

Every last one of them was laughing by the time he
was done.

"Good God, man," the duke said, shaking his head
ruefully, "do you have any idea what meter is? Iambic
pentameter? Anything ring a bell?"

Hugh made a face. "It was late. My pride was
crushed. Give a person a break."

Wiping tears from her cheeks, Charity patted her husband's arm. "You are exceedingly fortunate that Dering
allowed you to withhold your name from the publication.
You would never have been able to live that down."

"Oh," Evan piped up, his pale eyes alight with
humor, "he's never living it down, regardless. That's
what friends are for, no?"

Chuckling despite himself, the baron thrust the
crumpled-up page to Thomas. "Your turn, my fellow
loser. At least I can have company in my misery."

Felicity rubbed her hands together in anticipation.
"Oh, this had better be good. You are, after all, quite the
accomplished orator."

"Why, thank you, sister. I shall do my best to impress."

Rattling the page dramatically, he tilted his head, lifted out a hand, and began his recitation.

"When to the sessions of sweet silent thought
I summon up remembrance of games past—"

"Wait just one second," Felicity said, snatching the paper from him. Reading the first few lines, she laughed and turned her finger at her brother. "This is Sonnet Thirty! You cannot just steal from Shakespeare and change a half dozen words to suit your purposes."

He bit back laughter even as he attempted to feign innocence. "What? Where was that rule when we made the bets? At least it was a genuine sonnet, *Cadgwith*."

May sat back in her seat, her blue eyes flashing with mirth. "You both deserve the brig, as far as I'm concerned. Crimes against the English language."

Hugh waved his hands. "It doesn't matter. If I had to read my terrible poem, then he must read his mangled one."

Snatching the paper back, Thomas nodded. "Thank you. There's genius in here, if you would but listen." Clearing his throat, he started again.

"I sigh the lack of many a thing I sought,
And with old woes new wail my dear time's waste:
Then can I drown an eye, unused to flow,
For precious cards hid in defeat's harsh night,
And weep afresh pride's long since cancelled woe,
And moan the expense of many a vanished sight:
Then can I grieve at lost bets foregone,
And heavily from woe to woe tell o'er
The sad account of losing hand moan,

Which I begrudge pay since not paid before.
But if the while I think on thee, dear friend,
All losses do sting with no sorrow's end."

May and Sophie booed through their laughter as
Gavin tossed a piece of bread at him. "Somebody grab
the hook. You, sir, don't deserve the stage."

The bantering carried on, making Felicity laugh
again and again. The day was rapidly becoming one of
the most wonderful birthdays she had ever spent. Good
friends, lively conversation, a quiet, beautiful venue—it
was all absolutely perfect.

And then there was Gavin, who sat beside her all the
while. Every now and then, his leg would brush against
hers beneath the table, sending a shiver down her spine.
She loved the feel of his solid presence so near to her. She
relished the quiet hum of tension between them, knowing
that he felt it, too.

He could be so sweet and generous, so mindful of the
enjoyment of others, she couldn't help but wish things
could be different between them. Outside of this enchant-
ing little summer they were sharing, they led such wholly
separate lives. There was part of her that wondered . . .
what if?

But the other, saner part of her knew that she should
simply enjoy the time that they had together.

Swallowing a bite of buttercream cake, she tapped
his foot with hers and grinned when he turned to her.
"I've planned a game for today as well."

"You have?" he said quietly, his brow lifting with
interest. While everyone was still conversing around
them, he leaned in so the moment seemed private.

"Indeed. Actually, it's as much a gift to you as anything."

Pleasure bloomed in his dark eyes. "Oh, really? I do like the sound of that. Any hints?"

Sending him an arch look, she straightened and clapped her hands to gain the others' attention. "As you all know, this day marks my thirtieth birthday, which seems utterly impossible. I'm fairly certain I was five-and-twenty only yesterday."

Her friends chuckled, exactly as she'd intended. Although, in truth, it did rather seem that way. It felt as though she blinked and her third decade had gone by in a flash. Pinning each of them with a look of expectation, she said, "So, seeing as it is my birthday and I am desperately in need of a distraction, I decree that the men should entertain us with some sporting events."

Sophie applauded, her smile rounding her apple cheeks. "Oh yes, I love that idea! Particularly when I can sit in the shade with friends, food, and cold beverages and watch you all compete for our favor."

Evan wrapped his arm around her and pulled her close for a kiss. "You, my love, already have my favor."

"Yes, but you must compete for *mine*," she teased, patting his cheek affectionately.

May nodded, turning her full attention to the duke. "Oh yes, I think it sounds like a wonderful idea. You won me far too easily the first time."

He sputtered in response, nearly choking on his drink. "If that was easy, I'd hate to see hard. It may well kill me."

After a few minutes' debate, they settled on three events: the hundred-stone relay, the log toss, and the three-legged race. The last event was purely because the idea of seeing the men hobbling around like the competitive fools they were made Felicity laugh just thinking about it.

The first two events, however, were chosen to give Gavin a chance to shine. She knew exactly how hard he worked at his fitness, and she rather liked the idea of giving him the opportunity to show off his skills. If it was at the expense of the other men's pride, well, as Evan had pointed out, that's what friends were for.

Of course, the idea hadn't been *solely* hatched for Gavin's benefit. Though she'd never say as much out loud, the idea of watching him perform the tasks, showing off his endurance and strength, was more than a little appealing.

As the group settled in for an hour of relaxation in order to give the men a chance to rest up after eating luncheon, anticipation tingled at the back of Felicity's neck. She was more than ready to see Gavin at his best.

Chapter Twenty-two

To say her idea was a good one would be a vast, vast understatement. Felicity tried not to hold her breath as she watched Gavin shrug out of his jacket, preparing for the first event. His muscles were clearly visible against the thin lawn of his shirt as he went about untying his cravat.

"I must say, I approve of your request," Charity said, watching her own husband prepare for the first event.

Hugh had worked so diligently these last few years to get to a place of good health, Felicity knew that he wouldn't push himself too hard. Still, with his frequent swims and stretches, she could see that he had filled out significantly since the darkest days of his illness. He looked hale and hearty, and it made her smile to see Charity's delight in watching him.

"I'm glad to hear it. I thought it sounded like good fun, especially since we ladies may sip lemonade from the shade whilst they battle for victory."

May, who had been nominated as the official, set her hands to her hips and addressed the men. "All right, gentlemen. The relay is simple: Whoever transports the full one hundred stones to their respective marker first, wins. One at a time, gentlemen, and no tripping one another up."

It sounded easy enough, but Felicity had presided over this particular game several times at the Flora Day Festival in Cadgwith. The sheer distance the men would eventually cover would be exhausting. It was all about endurance, not speed.

With a wide smile, May lifted a handkerchief, held it aloft for a moment to build anticipation, then tossed it in the air, signaling the start of the game.

Thomas took an early lead, sprinting out in front of the others. The women began cheering them all on—even Lady Effington and Bella joined in. Felicity shook her head at her brother's tactic. He would regret that pace soon enough. Evan and Hugh hung back in second and third place, while Gavin and the duke brought up the rear.

Settling back on her elbows, Felicity gave up any pretense of watching the other competitors. Her gaze followed the viscount as he trotted along, his stride long and confident. There was something so powerful about the way he moved, yet still with a certain grace. It was mesmerizing. He laughed and taunted the others, but she could see that his real focus was on the game.

As the pile of rocks grew larger and larger, the contestants became more and more visibly exhausted, their faces red and hair dampened with sweat. Thomas began holding his side about halfway through, puffing air through his pursed lips.

"Whose . . . idea . . . was . . . this?" he panted as he passed by the sitting area, his humor still firmly in place despite his flagging pace. Evan was now in front, then Thomas, followed by Radcliffe, Cadgwith, then Gavin still at the rear.

Even though he was still trailing, Felicity knew the viscount was merely biding his time. He had only just broken a light sweat, while most of the others' shirts had wide damp patches at their necks and arms. He was playing with them while they wore themselves out.

Each time he passed by, he'd meet her eyes with a grin, or a wink, or tip of his head, and she would smile in return. He wasn't even trying to disguise his attentions, but then again, neither was she. It was only natural, given the other couples and her own brother for a participant, that she would champion him.

She *wanted* to champion him. He had supported her again and again, helping to pull her from the shell she'd disappeared into after Ian's death. She liked being able to turn and offer that support back to him, even if it was for a silly event like this.

Bella crawled into her lap toward the end of the race, and Felicity clapped the girl's hands with her own, both of them cheering him on. It wasn't until the last five laps that he proved her suspicions right. While Thomas was barely jogging and Evan had paused at the end of the lap to brace his hands to his knees, Gavin surged forward with a burst of energy. She wouldn't call him a particularly fast runner, but the endurance that it took to have that much speed left in him at this point of the race was extraordinary.

Juggling Bella onto her side, Felicity jumped to her feet, shouting encouragements to him as the other women did likewise with their respective champions. Radcliffe put up a fight, dashing forward as well, but there was no way for him to compete with Gavin's strong and steady stride.

With a triumphant whoop, he tossed his last stone on the pile. He turned and smacked the hands of each of the other men as they finished their relay, a good sportsman through and through.

"That was remarkable," Sophie said, clapping unreservedly for the men. "I was exhausted just watching them—though, to be fair, we were cheering quite enthusiastically, which takes some amount of endurance given the length of the race. But to see Dering sprint to the end like that, as though he was fresh as a spring chicken, was really quite remarkable!"

May laughed out loud. "A spring chicken?" she repeated, wrinkling her nose.

Sophie's dark eyebrows hitched up. "Do you have a better term?"

"Many," she said with a wry grin. "But I will agree that he was phenomenal."

Exactly the word Felicity would use to describe him. Handing Bella back to the nursemaid, she waited impatiently as the other competitors congratulated him on the win before the lot of them came over to the sitting area.

She couldn't seem to take her eyes off him. By now, his white shirt clung damply to his skin, leaving very little to the imagination as to just how chiseled his upper body was. As he approached, his gaze locked with hers, triumph and pride lifting his chin.

She dipped her head, not even trying to keep the grin from her lips. "Well done, my lord. I do believe all your training has paid off."

"Why, thank you, my lady. I suppose I felt particularly motivated today."

As the servants passed out glasses of small ale, the men accepted praise and commiseration from the women. The sun was high in the sky, warming the air and brightening the day.

"Next time we do a horse race," Radcliffe rasped, shaking his head as he fell back into the closest chair.

Evan nodded. "Yes—in that I could give you a run for your money."

"Or an archery contest," Thomas quipped, lying flat on his back in the grass.

"We already did that," Charity reminded him. "And we won. Therefore I think it best we don't push our luck," she said with a wink. "Better to be champion than defending champion."

"Truth," he said, accepting a towel from a footman and dropping it over his face.

Hugh took a large gulp of his drink before saying, "Give me swimming or target shooting, and I'd have the sorry lot of you beat."

"I don't know what you are all complaining about," Gavin said with a mischievous grin. "I thought the relay was a great choice."

"Yes," the duke said, his tone as dry as tinder even as his gold eyes glinted with mirth, "just as I'm sure you'll *love* the log toss."

"Hoisting heavy objects and hurling them through the air? What's not to love?"

"Everything," Thomas said on a groan as he sat up. "I'm not sure log tosses were included in that whole I-can-do-all-things-through-Christ-who-strengthens-me verse."

Hugh gave him a hearty smack on the shoulder. "Well, there is no time like the present. Shall we get on with this? You and I shall be graceful losers together on this one."

The log toss went exactly as Felicity had predicted it would. While the duke and the earl both put in a good showing, Hugh and her brother decided to make a team effort of it, which did more harm than good for their chances. The laughter at their method, however, was well worth the loss.

And then it was Gavin's turn.

Felicity held her breath as he easily hoisted the six-foot log in his wide, capable hands. He bent down low, showing off his leg muscles to great advantage before rocketing up as though spring-loaded. The heavy timber hurled through the air in a wide arc, landing nearly twice as far away as any other try.

"Who would have thought all that bulk wasn't just for show," Lady Effington mused, earning hoots of laughter from them all.

Felicity smiled to herself, almost ridiculously proud of him. *She* had thought. She was well aware of his hard work and dedication, but more than that, she had felt the firm wall of his chest for herself. She'd felt those corded arms around her, had experienced the leashed strength of his body as he'd held her against him with unexpected tenderness.

The men moved directly on to the next event, the three-legged race. Hugh had already decided to sit that one out—too much jostling for his neck after the other exertions—so it was down to Evan and Radcliffe against her brother and Gavin.

The duke was actually of similar height to the earl, so they ended up being a much better pairing than Gavin and Thomas, who had about a four-inch difference between them. It was a hilarious race, with the pairs tumbling again and again as they tried to fall into rhythm with each other.

By the end of the race, they were all laughing so much

it was little wonder any of them made it to the finish line. Radcliffe and Evan emerged triumphant, but by little more than a nose.

As Gavin strode back to sitting area, butterflies fluttered to life deep in Felicity's belly. Despite the silliness and the loss of the last race, he looked as ruggedly handsome and triumphant as she had ever seen him. His shirt hugged his body while his forearms glistened in the early-afternoon sun. For someone who was always dressed to perfection, he looked deliciously unpolished and unrestrained.

And when his eyes met hers?

The promise she saw there was enough to make her shiver.

Nothing, absolutely nothing, was headier than winning. Victory filled Dering's every pore, straightening his spine and lifting his head. Striding back toward Felicity, he felt ten feet tall, especially when he saw the look in her eyes.

She was impressed. His chest swelled with the knowledge that she'd been able to see him at his best. All those hours spent in pursuit of improvement had been very well put to use indeed.

He paused to swipe a linen over his sweat-dampened brow before leaning down close. "Was the lady entertained?" he asked, his voice a low, seductive rumble even to his own ears.

She bit her lip and nodded as she held out a glass of ale. "Quite. I'm suddenly very glad that you didn't listen to your mother about giving up your lifting."

Her eyes fell to the open V of his shirt, and he had to forcefully shove away the desire to bend down and kiss her right then and there. It felt good to be triumphant, yes, but it was a thousand times better to have been so with her as witness.

He drew a mind-clearing breath before downing half the contents of his glass. The cold liquid did nothing to cool the ardor that heated his blood. He had enjoyed the day, but he didn't want to wait another minute to be alone with her.

"Are you game for a challenge?" he asked, allowing his fingers to graze the bare skin of her forearm. She gave a little shiver, making him smile.

"Perhaps. Would I be playing with you or against you?"

"Definitely *with* me."

Her lips slid into a private little smile. "Then I definitely am."

Lord have mercy.

Setting the drink on the table, he abruptly turned to the group at large. "After our manly sporting event, I thought we could use a game that we all had a chance of winning." He grinned as the men groaned and rolled their eyes. They knew a taunt when they heard one.

Walking over to a basket by the corner stake, Dering pulled out a stack of papers, each carefully transcribed by he himself last night. He should have been out enjoying the festival, but all he could think of was planning the perfect birthday for them both.

"A scavenger hunt, my friends. Four teams, each heading in a different cardinal direction. The first team to collect all the listed items will win the most coveted of all prizes, bragging rights for the rest of the summer."

"How shall we divide up teams?" Charity said, leaning back against the table. "There are nine of us, assuming Grandmama doesn't wish to participate."

Thomas waved a hand. "Sitting this out, thank you. After staying out a hair too late last night, I believe I shall lounge in the shade and enjoy a strong drink or two. Besides," he added, setting both hands over his heart, "my pride can't afford another loss just yet."

"Suit yourself," Dering said, pleased that the numbers would work out according to his plan. "Are the rest of you game?"

After a chorus of yeses, he handed out the sheets. The others could rush to collect the random list of objects he had come up with last night, which should take an hour at least. This was a game he had no intention of winning.

Chapter Twenty-three

Felicity had a feeling she knew what he was up to, but she had no intention of interfering as they paced off the required two hundred steps due north. By luck or design they had been pointed in the most heavily wooded direction, where the tree trunks were wide and damp and the shade made it hard to see past the tree line. In the distance, she could hear the faint babble of water, but the stream wasn't yet visible.

Glancing down to Gavin's hand, she purposely kept herself from reaching for it. She was finally getting time alone with him, and she didn't want to raise any suspicions from the others that would jeopardize that. She could wait, if only for a few more minutes.

She hadn't planned to leave Isabella alone today, but the baby was fast asleep on the pillows beside Lady Effington and Hedley when she'd left. There was no better time for Felicity to slip away, and she had eagerly seized the opportunity.

They moved in silence, neither one of them attempting to break the tension that had been building between them for most of the day. He'd not replaced his jacket before setting off, leaving one less layer between them. The thought of touching that spot where the muscled cords of his neck met the hard wall of his chest at his collarbone made her stomach tighten with anticipation.

She probably should have insisted he put his cravat back on when he'd donned his waistcoat. It was one thing to indulge in a few kisses; it was quite another to imagine the feel of his bare chest beneath her fingers. That was the sort of thought that could really get her in trouble.

The grass beneath her feet gave way to an old path, where the shade of the huge trees overhead inhibited the ground cover. The air was noticeably cooler as they entered into the forest itself.

They'd taken little more than a dozen steps past the tree line when Gavin seized her hand, sending a rush of excitement sizzling through her. In one fluid motion, he pulled her from the path and pressed her against the smooth bark of a large birch tree. The move was so fast, she'd barely had time to register what he was about before his mouth slanted across hers, hot and seeking.

Desire licked through her as she pressed her eyes closed and tilted her head back more fully, not hesitating to kiss him back. She wrapped her arms around his neck as he squeezed her waist with his hands. A soft, breathy moan escaped her. She'd never experienced anything so exhilarating in her life.

Entirely too soon, he pulled back and exhaled a pent-up breath. "God, Lissy, I've been dying to do that all day. All *week*," he amended.

She knew exactly how he felt. The sensations ricocheting around inside her were far more powerful than she even wanted to admit. Running her tongue along her lips, she looked up at him and said, "Then why did you stop?"

That made him grin. Raking a hand through his hair, he shook his head. "We should move a little deeper into the forest. I don't know about you, but I *really* don't want anyone stumbling upon us right now."

"Excellent point," she conceded with a nod. At least one of them was thinking properly. She allowed him to lace his fingers with hers and pull her along the path. His hands were as rough as ever, something that oddly thrilled her. Thank goodness she'd shed her gloves long ago.

"I'm glad you wore that gown again. It's nearly as gorgeous as you are."

The heat of a blush rose up her chest as she ran her free fingers over the fabric. "It was a bit of a silly choice, given our activities today, but I love the gown. I let myself get stupidly upset last time I wore it, and I wanted to reclaim the happiness it gave me. What better place than here, on my birthday, where I know no one is judging me?"

She thought a lot about reclaiming happiness these days. Before she came here, she wouldn't have thought it possible to feel this way again. Yes, she'd had many light moments and good times, but none of it seeped down into the deeper part of her soul.

Not until she'd reconnected with him.

His lips curled in a warm smile as he glanced down at her. "I love when you forget what others are expecting and just do what suits you. There's not enough of that in this world, I think."

He lifted her easily over a fallen log before setting her feet back on the path. She smiled up at him. "Sounds a lot like the girl you used to know. I know now how very fortunate I am that my parents were too preoccupied to pay attention to me."

Even as she said it, she knew *fortunate* wasn't quite the right word. If her mother had been well, Felicity would have had much less freedom—a price she would have willingly and happily paid. But she'd made the best of what her situation had been.

Not unlike now. She had certainly never expected to be a young widow, slipping away with the neighbor boy again like when they were young. Only now, she saw him in a whole new light. She had feelings for him now that had never been there before. What had changed?

"I've missed that girl," he said, his fingers tightening over hers. "Over the years, I mean."

"Have you?" She arched a brow as she met his gaze. "Well, maybe this time you'll keep in touch when I go back home."

He slowed as they came upon a small clearing beside the water. The stream was barely ten feet wide, and was shallow enough to walk across. Setting her hands to her hips, she said, "Give me a moment. I'll need to take my shoes off."

"Don't be ridiculous," he said, sending her a wolfish smile that she felt all the way to her toes. "I've been waiting years for an excuse to do this."

He slipped one arm behind her back and the other at her knees before swooping her up into his arms. She laughed aloud at the sensation, clinging to his neck even though she knew he'd never drop her. "It's terrifyingly high up here," she said through her mirth, loving the feel of being light as a feather in his arms.

"Mm, yes, best not to look down." He dipped his head and captured her lips in a quick, playful kiss. "Keep your eyes on me, and everything will be all right."

He was teasing, but she did as he instructed, flitting

her gaze over his strong, angled jaw and the straight line of his nose. He really was an exceptionally handsome man. Even though his face was dear enough to her that she'd love it either way, there was no denying that he was definitely attractive.

"I'm glad your nose is still as it was."

Stopping midstream, he looked to her with cautious good humor. "I beg your pardon?"

"Because of your boxing. I'm glad you've not broken it, because it is an exceedingly nice nose."

He chuckled, the sound purring through her as he moved forward again. "I'm glad you approve, but I'm equally as glad simply for the fact that a broken nose sounds very unpleasant indeed."

When they reached the other side, he didn't put her down right away, and she made no effort to move. "Have you ever broken anything?"

Nodding, he moved toward a sunny patch of grass. "A few ribs," he said, lowering them both to the ground. "Two of my fingers." He gently set her down, then sprawled out beside her, bracing himself on one elbow so he could look down at her. "My heart."

Her eyes widened at that. "Someone broke your heart," she breathed, hating the thought of him hurting.

Almost of their own volition, her fingers lifted to the V of his shirt, which, thanks to his position, gaped open a few inches. She grasped the smooth edge of the fabric between her thumb and first two fingers, then lightly slid her hand down. The backs of her fingers flirted with his chest, making her heart race.

He gave a light shrug, his lips only inches from hers now. "Just a girl I used to know," he murmured before leaning down and pressing his lips to hers.

Her pulse thundered at the contact, and she sucked in a deep breath through her nose. The smell of the water and grass mingled with the clean scent of his sweat-dampened skin. It was a heady combination. She lifted her chin to meet him more fully, relishing the kiss even as his words tumbled around in her head. *A girl I used to know.*

She moved her hand to his temple, plunging her fingers into his sleek dark hair. It was like warm silk against her skin. Still, his words wouldn't leave her, and snippets from their other conversations raced across her mind. *I've dreamed of kissing you beneath the stars. I've been waiting years for an excuse to do this.*

Making a soft sound in the back of her throat, she pulled back, meeting his heavy-lidded gaze. "Gavin, who broke your heart?"

He looked back at her for a moment, his eyes unfathomable in their darkness. "Lissy," he said, his voice raspy and low. "I promise you, there is no one else I'd rather be with in the world right now than you." He pressed a soft, sweet kiss against her mouth. "Please, please let us leave it at that."

She wanted both to argue and to simply just let it go. Did she need to know more? Did she *want* to? She felt as though she were poised on a precipice, afraid of making a choice that would change everything.

Blowing out a breath, she nodded. "As you wish."

Right then, all she wanted was to languish in his arms, to soak up his affections and offer up her own. He meant the world to her, and she wasn't ready to take the chance of ruining what they had.

He smiled, then rolled to his side and pulled her partially across him. "All I want is for you to be happy.

To enjoy every moment of our time together." He settled his hand at the small of her back. "Tell me what you want, Felicity."

His words still hadn't quite left her. A part of her warned that they couldn't keep doing this. It was too easy to fall. It was too easy for one of them to be hurt.

And it was too easy to want to never give it up.

Swallowing, she smiled softly. "This, exactly," she said, sliding a finger down his chest. "I want you to kiss me like it's the very last time. Like this is all we've got. I don't want there to be any regrets."

He lifted a hand and brushed her hair from her temple before allowing his palm to cup the side of her face. She leaned into it, loving the way they seemed to fit just right. The way it felt just then, being with him like this, she didn't want it to end.

"When it comes to kissing you, Felicity, I could never regret a single moment."

This was the way he had always imagined them.

Sprawled together on a carpet of grass, their bodies fitting together as though they were made for each other. He kissed her slowly, then. Pouring every ounce of passion he had ever felt for her into this perfect meeting of their lips. Her mouth was willing and pliant.

The kiss was achingly tender and deeply moving, taking his very breath with its perfection. He'd waited a lifetime for this, and he wasn't going to rush a single moment of it. His hands wandered across her back before gliding down her skirts, along the curve of her hip.

It was so much more than just a simple kiss. Her body moved with his, her leg sliding up along his while she pressed her hand to the tensed muscles of his chest.

His every sense was filled with her: the taste of her lips on his tongue, the sound of her whisper-soft moans filling his ears, the familiar floral scent of her teasing his nose, the incredibly alluring feel of her body stretched out along his.

This was what he had dreamed of since the very first night she had shown up at his home in Bath. Hell, this was what he had dreamed of since the moment his soul had awakened to her when he was fifteen.

As her tongue danced with his, his fingers squeezed the soft flesh of her hip, pulling her that much closer to him. If she wanted a kiss to last a lifetime, she would damn well get the kiss of a lifetime.

In the back of his mind, he knew the fantasy was there. She'd taste his passion and realize that she didn't want to live without it. That she didn't want to live without *him*.

He shifted their positions, sliding her to her back so that he could have full control. Not because he was taking it, but because she had given it to him. He started raining kisses down her throat, tasting the sweet and salty flavor of her, feeling the rapid flutter of her pulse beneath his seeking lips. She shivered at the sensation, encouraging him with her soft sighs of delight as she pulled him more fully against her.

His hands went to her waist, gently squeezing where it nipped in, wishing her dress and stays would disappear so he could feel her, all of her, beneath his questing fingers.

"Are you absolutely certain," he breathed as he kissed his way along the delicate curve of her collarbone, "that a kiss is all you desire?" His whole body was aflame for her, and he wanted her to feel the same way.

"Gavin," she said, his name little more than a sigh on her lips. It was half plea, half reluctance.

He could feel the desire thrumming through her, yet he wanted no uncertainty between them. He wanted nothing more than to bring her pleasure, but he could wait until she was ready. He'd waited a lifetime already, hadn't he? Shifting so he was poised above her, he pressed his lips to hers again in a kiss that was soft and undemanding, but infused with emotion.

The kiss heated by increments as she opened to him, letting go of any reluctance as her lips grew more and more insistent. Her hands plunged into his hair again, sending rivulets of sensation dancing down his back. This time, she broke the kiss, but instead of pulling away she turned his head and kissed her way to his ear. When her teeth found his earlobe, he closed his eyes and groaned with pleasure.

Dear God, but she would be the death of him.

Reaching down, he found the hem of her skirts, and he allowed his fingers to skim along the butter-soft skin of her leg. When he reached her knee, he hooked his hand beneath it and drew her leg up along him. They were as good as entwined together, like the lovers he'd always wished they could be, when something penetrated his haze of desire.

Her name. He hadn't said it; he had *heard* it. He froze, holding her tight against him as he listened. Crashing foliage, followed by a desperate shout.

"Felicity!"

Chapter Twenty-four

Felicity sat bolt upright, alarm flooding in a rush through her veins at the sound of her brother shouting her name. What the devil was he doing here? She scrambled to untangle her limbs and skirts from Gavin, her urgency making her clumsy.

Before they could get to their feet, Thomas burst through the woods into the clearing on the other side of the stream, his eyes wide with panic. *"Felicity,"* he rasped, desperation cloaking the word as he splashed through the water toward them.

Her body turned to ice as anxiety washed over her. Something was wrong. Very, very wrong. Even as Gavin hauled her to her feet, she reached for her brother, desperate to know. "What is it? What's happened?"

Beneath the flush of his exertion, Thomas's skin was pale as moonshine. "Bella," he panted. He shook his head, the words not seeming to come to his lips. "You must come, now. She's . . . hurt. I don't know."

Fear as she had never felt in her life burst forth within her, and she surged into motion. She didn't wait to hear more, didn't wait for them to follow. She wrenched up her skirts and ran. Through the stream, across the path, through the woods—she ran like she had never run in her life.

Through ringing ears she could hear the others crashing after her, and when they emerged from the forest, Gavin sprinted past her, his arms pumping with his effort. Tears streamed from her eyes and dampened her hair as she raced, her lungs burning and her muscles screaming.

Not Isabella, not Isabella, please not Isabella. The words were an uninterrupted stream of consciousness, crowding out all other thoughts.

As she crested the rise, she saw Lady Effington and Hadley bent over a tiny little body on the blanket. A footman rushed toward them with a pitcher of water that sloshed with every step.

When Gavin reached the blanket, he dove to his knees, skidding to a stop in front of them. His huge body obscured her view, making her sprint all the faster. She needed to see her baby. She needed to know what was wrong. When Hadley looked up at Felicity's approach, her wide eyes and tear-streaked face made Felicity's stomach plunge clear to her knees.

"I don't know, a bee, it stung her and then, I *don't know*," she cried, shaking her head over and over.

Felicity pushed her aside as she rushed to her baby, her heart pounding so hard spots crowded her vision. And there, on the blanket, Isabella lay, her eyes swollen shut, her top lip grotesquely large, wheezing as though her life depended on it.

"No," she gasped, lifting her daughter up and cradling her in her arms, even as the others tried to stop her.

She knew that sound. That horrible, desperate draw for air when the body was attacking itself. She'd heard it before, seventeen months ago, as the life had drained from her husband's beautiful blue eyes.

How could this happen again? She wept and rocked her back and forth as Gavin shouted for ice and linens, authority ringing in his voice. She could hear Thomas behind her, reciting a prayer with a seriousness she had never heard from him.

The footman brought a bundle of napkins and a cupful of hastily chipped ice. Gavin dunked the linens in the water, wrapped the ice into the center of it, and set it over Bella's swollen eyes. He wet another napkin and gently, urgently pressed it to her cheeks, the top of her head, her shoulders, and even her hands. He wet it again and again, carefully ministering to her as she weakly struggled.

The baby's skin was turning slightly blue, just the slightest tinge but enough to steal Felicity's own breath. She wasn't getting enough air. Desperate, Felicity began patting Isabella's cheeks, over and over, trying to keep her alert. "It's all right, baby. Breathe, baby. Breathe for Mama."

All of the images from that night with Ian that she'd managed to shove to some deep, dark corner of her mind came rushing back. The look of surprise. The coughing and pulling on his cravat. The dawning panic as his throat had closed like a shutting door. His last words: *I can't breathe.* She could still taste the metallic tinge of terror as she'd tried to wake him. She could feel the burning in her throat as she had screamed and cried and done everything possible to wake him.

But he was gone.

Felicity shook her head, squeezing her daughter to her chest as she begged her to stay here. To *live*.

"Come on, Bella," Gavin murmured, rubbing the baby's arm with one hand as he rearranged the ice over her eyes with the other. She flailed her arms a little more, her wheezing becoming louder but seemingly more productive.

"How long has she been like this?" Gavin demanded, his eyes on the nursemaid.

"I don't know," she said tearfully, so different from her normally unflappable self. "Less than ten minutes, I think. The swelling started so quickly. . . ."

Through the wheezing, the baby started to cry, raspy and broken, but still—a cry. "She's breathing," Felicity said, tears blurring her vision as she began rocking again, trying to soothe her daughter even as she prayed the sound would continue. Crying meant air; air meant life.

She was vaguely aware of the others arriving, their shock and worry coloring a flurry of activity behind her. Felicity ignored them all. She focused wholly on her daughter, watching as the pale blue tinge gave way to pink skin again, and the cries became louder and louder. As her breathing grew stronger, so did Felicity's hope. Isabella was so tiny, but she was strong. She was a fighter.

All the while, Gavin sat at Felicity's side, silently bathing Bella's skin and regularly tending to the ice. When at last, after what seemed like an eternity, the baby was able to crack one eye open, Felicity finally let go of the terror and wept with raw relief.

That precious blue gaze, the exact shade of her husband's eyes, stared back at her, full of life once again.

Gavin had never experienced fear like that in his entire life.

As it became clear that Bella would be all right, he collapsed back on his haunches, only now letting his iron control slip. His relief was almost too intense. He felt like a wrung-out old rag. He'd never seen anyone, let alone someone as tiny as Felicity's daughter, with a face that swollen.

It seemed a miracle that she had survived.

The only reason the ice had occurred to him was because of the memory of the time he'd ended up with a black eye from boxing one winter and one of the professional boxers had suggested he slap a handful of snow on it. He'd swapped it out for a side of beef once he'd gotten home, but the snow had seemed to really help.

There was no way of knowing if his small contribution had done anything at all to help, but at least it had given him something to *do*. For all of his training, for all of his strength, he had been just as powerless as the rest of them.

He dragged a hand through his hair. For as long as he lived, he would never forget the fear in Felicity's eyes, the way her whole face had been cloaked in grief so profound, it had stolen his breath just to see it. He never, ever wanted her to feel that way again, yet it was just another thing in life that was out of his control.

He exhaled the tension from his body and set a calming hand to Felicity's shoulder. "Can I escort you home?"

Cadgwith had already declared that they would leave immediately, and the coach was being driven round to meet them.

She didn't even look at him as she shook her head. Her eyes were still pinned on the baby, who was fussing in her arms. "No. Hugh will be with us. Thank you, though," she added, her voice betraying her exhaustion.

He wanted to wrap her up in a hug—wrap them *both* up—but he knew it was probably more than she could handle just then. "Will you be all right?"

At that, she did lift her gaze. "So long as I never have to let her go again."

One side of his mouth slanted up as he sighed and tenderly stroked a finger down the baby's still-swollen cheek. Poor, sweet thing. She looked measurably better, but the swelling was still painful to see. When he'd first arrived, the stinger had still been lodged in her forehead, and he had carefully slid his thumbnail over it to dislodge it. It was almost impossible to believe that such an insignificant tiny thing could cause so much damage.

Looking back to Felicity, he said quietly, "Take care of yourself, too. I'll be by this evening to check on you both."

"No, don't do that. I don't think I'll be up for visitors for a while."

He wanted to argue, but one look at her wan face told him she just needed peace tonight. Pressing his lips together, he nodded. "Very well. I'll have Cadgwith send a note to let me know how she's doing tonight."

It was hard, not having the right to be there. Not being able to insist that he be allowed to take care of them, to make sure they were both safe and well. But he cared for her enough to respect her wishes on this. Tomorrow would have to be soon enough.

The carriage arrived then, and everyone fussed with seeing them off safely and quickly. As he stood and watched them hurry off back to Bath, he had the odd sensation of feeling as though his heart was leaving without him.

Despite his best efforts, perhaps it was.

"May I come in?"

Felicity glanced up to see Thomas's blond head poking through the doorway of the nursery, his eyebrows raised in question.

She smiled in welcome and gestured for him to join her. "Yes, of course. I'm glad to see you."

Isabella slept soundly in her arms as she rocked, completely at peace. Felicity could barely look away from her. It had been well over a day since the sting, but she had yet to leave her daughter's side. Even now, as dusk faded to inky darkness outside and it was well past the baby's bedtime, she couldn't bring herself to go downstairs for dinner with the others.

"How is she today? No ill effects, I hope?"

"No, thank God. She's been fine since last night, when the last of the swelling receded." Only then had Felicity been able to draw a proper breath. No matter what the doctor had promised, no matter what the others said, she hadn't been able to fully release the dread until then.

"And you?"

She blew out a shaky breath. "Not sure I'll ever be the same. But relieved. Thankful." Today, Bella had laughed and played as though nothing had ever happened. Felicity wished she could be half so resilient.

He smiled as he paused beside her and ran a gentle hand over Isabella's dark hair. "I think she has an angel up there looking out for her."

"I concur," she murmured, thinking of Ian and his beautiful blue eyes.

Swallowing thickly, she shook her head and said, "And it's a good thing, since clearly I have fallen down on the job." As her fear had receded, guilt had crowded in to take its place. She'd been entirely too focused on herself and her own happiness of late. She'd allowed what was most important in life to come in second to the addictive company of a man and the way that he alone seemed to make her feel.

Thomas cocked his head as he sat on the chair beside them. "What do you mean? Isabella was in the care of three people who love her. You did nothing wrong. It's not as though you can or should spend every moment of the day with her."

Emotion welled up inside of her as the image of her daughter's swollen face assailed her. "I should have been there. She's my daughter. She's all I have, Thomas."

He leaned forward and placed a comforting hand to her knee. "First of all, you have many people who love and care for you—myself included. It was an accident. A freak one, at that. You likely couldn't have prevented it any more than we could. But it's all right. She's safe and sound tonight, and all of us were reminded of exactly how precious she is to us."

The rational part of her knew he was right, but the guilt was stronger than logic. While her baby had been in pain, Felicity had been wrapped up in Gavin's arms, blissfully pursuing her own pleasure.

Tears unaccountably came to her eyes. "Oh, Thomas,

what you must think of me, finding me in that state."
Embarrassment lodged in her chest, but she couldn't
pretend he hadn't surmised what they had been up to.

He sat back, surprise registering in his green eyes.
Shaking his head slowly, he said, "What must you think
of *me*, that you imagine I would begrudge you happiness or love? You may have been putting the cart before
the horse, but I'm bloody glad you decided to take an
outing."

He *approved*? She blinked, completely taken aback
by his sentiment. "Thomas, I'm not some carefree young
fool who is free to do as she chooses. I am a woman with
responsibilities. I'm a mother who has someone else to
think about other than herself. *Paramount* to herself."

When had she become a woman ruled by her passions? When had she decided she could toss aside caution and prudency and live life as though there were no
such things as repercussions? That was the girl she had
been, not the woman she was. She was thirty, for heav-
en's sake.

"Lissy," he said, leveling serious, sincere eyes on her,
"You are a human being before anything else. You
deserve happiness and then some. You've experienced
a terribly tragedy in your life, and it does my heart good
to think that you can move on from that and find love
again."

Why did he keep referring to love? Her cheeks
heated conspicuously as she rose and placed the baby
in her cot. She cared for Gavin—deeply, in fact—and
considered him to be one of her most cherished friends,
but what they had wasn't love. It couldn't be. She knew
what love felt like, and whatever it was between them
was nothing like that. Besides, it was far too soon for

her to even consider such a thing. She wasn't done healing yet.

Yesterday's incident had proven that.

"Gavin is a dear friend, Thomas, but nothing more.
We . . . got carried away. It certainly won't happen
again." There were many reasons for that, not the least
of which being that, in the aftermath of everything that
had happened yesterday, she had decided she needed
to go home. She felt as though she was farther away
than ever from where she needed to be: safely tucked
away in their own tiny corner of the world.

Her brother came to his feet and walked to her side.
"I'm sorry to hear that." He waited until she turned
around before pulling her into a brotherly hug. When
he drew back, he said, "Do me a favor, sister. Try not to let
a sad accident disrupt how far you've come. It wasn't punishment for finally having moved on."

She nodded, mostly because that was what was expected of her. When he left, her eyes drifted to the table
and chairs in the corner, and the gorgeous arrangement
of flowers situated at its center. Gavin had brought them
over, though she hadn't been able to bring herself to see
him. He'd left them along with a little doll for Bella and
a sweet note wishing them both well.

The decision to go back to Cadgwith so early wasn't
just for her. No matter what she said, it seemed clear
that he wouldn't focus on his own pursuits until she was
away from the festival. She suspected that, thanks to
their history, he felt some sort of responsibility toward
her. Yes, there was a clear attraction between them as
well, but it seemed to her that he was bound and determined to help his old friend.

She'd already quietly informed Hadley and her maid

of her intention to depart sooner rather than later. Depending on how quickly she could make arrangements, they could be on their way as early as Sunday morning.

The thought eased the ball of tension that had settled low in her belly since returning home last night, but at the same time, it made her heart ache. She couldn't think about that now. She had to do what was right for her little family, and right now, that meant going home.

Chapter Twenty-five

The ballroom of his parents' home was alive with music and laughter, dancing and celebration. It seemed that every person in Bath had come to fete Dering's birthday, raising their glasses and toasting him again and again as he made his way through the multiple rooms of revelers. He kept his smile firmly in place, even as he scanned the attendants for one very particular person.

She still wasn't here.

Blowing out a sharp breath, he resisted the urge to look to the clock again. After all, he was certain it had only been a handful of minutes since the last time. He moved on through the connecting public rooms, his gaze flitting over the people grouped around the refreshments and seated at the clustered conversation areas.

Charity and Hugh were not much help. When he'd found them dancing on the terrace in the darkness two hours earlier, they had simply said that she had planned to come a little later, after the baby went to sleep.

Well, it was nearing eleven o'clock. She should have come by now.

He hadn't been concerned when she'd declined to come down to see him when he called yesterday. He knew how upset she had been, and understood she might just be tired.

But to not come tonight? More serious worry was beginning to form a stone in his gut. Was this more than just Bella's accident? Did this have something to do with their time together in the forest?

Mother materialized out of the crowd then, her blue eyes sparkling with determination in the candlelight. "There you are, darling. Look who I've found," she exclaimed, turning to wave Miss Sellers and her mother over. The girl was very becomingly dressed in a pretty white frock. Ever the innocent lamb.

He offered a shallow bow, wishing he could tell his mother exactly what he thought of her efforts. "Good evening, ladies. I do hope you are enjoying the party."

"Oh yes," Miss Sellers responded, her excitement bubbling over. "The music is ever so lovely, as is the conversation. Your family is exceptionally accomplished at throwing a lovely ball."

"They've had years of practice," he said with a polite smile. "Do help yourselves to some of the cake. Mother went above and beyond with it this year." The cake was a six-tier monstrosity, complete with sparklers and a sugar-paste silhouette of his likeness framed on the bottom layer.

"But first," his mother said, her smile turning flinty, "you must dance with our dear Miss Sellers. I was just going on about how marvelous a dancer you are."

It was then that he caught sight of Felicity as she slipped into the room. His heart soared at the sight of her as the rest of the room seemed to recede. "I'm sorry," he murmured, not taking his eyes from her. "I'm afraid I've already promised this dance to another. If you'll excuse me."

His mother made a sound of dismay as he offered a brief bow, which Miss Sellers and her mother promptly returned with hurried curtsies. He left them without another word, striding through the crush like a man with a purpose.

And he was.

She was his purpose. She was all he had thought of all day. All week. For half of his life, really. Even when he had tried not to think of her, she'd shaped how he had lived his life.

When she saw him, she visibly relaxed and offered him a slight smile. "There you are."

"There *you* are," he returned, drinking in the sight of her. She wore a sapphire-blue gown, which was deceptively simple in design. Despite its lack of adornment, its sleek lines and rich color made it stand out among a roomful of overly fussy gowns. "I was beginning to worry that I'd have to fetch you."

Her golden brown eyes slid away for a moment as she lifted her shoulders. "I almost didn't come, but I had to see you."

His chest lifted at her words. "You did? What a coincidence—I felt exactly the same way about you."

Setting her gloved hand to his forearms, she said, "Can we go somewhere private? I'd like to speak with you alone."

His first thought was the folly, but of course that would be impossible. "My father's library," he said after a moment's thought. Since most of the rooms on this floor were open to guests, it was the most convenient place he could think of where they wouldn't be interrupted.

And he definitely didn't want to be interrupted.

He wanted to reassure himself that she was all right, and wrap her in his arms for a while. He hadn't had the opportunity to comfort her before, and he longed to do so now, even if she no longer needed it so much.

Nodding, she said, "Lead the way."

He loved having her by his side. As they made their way through the crush, he couldn't help but grin with the pleasure of having her on his arm. For once, he wanted the world to know that they were together. That she was with him, and only him.

The corridor leading to the library was mostly empty, with only a handful of guests conversing in the relative quiet. As the music receded behind them, he could hear the purposeful swish of her skirts as she walked along beside him. They were no longer furtive young people, sneaking away from the ball. They were adults seeking a moment alone, and anyone who had a problem with it could be damned.

As he let them into the peaceful confines of the library, he was glad to see that several lamps along the wall were still lit. Her slippers barely made any noise against the marble floor as she made her way into the room.

"Can I offer you a drink?"

She shook her head. "No, thank you. I'd prefer to have my head about me when alone in your presence."

He smiled as he walked over to join her. "I rather like it when you lose your head."

"Which is one of the reasons it is so easy for it to happen." Her small smile fell then, and the first breath of unease drifted over the back of his neck. She looked . . . anxious. Restless.

He reached out and slid a hand along her arm, his brow knitted in concern. "Is something the matter?"

Almost reluctantly, she shook her head. "No, nothing is the matter," she said, her voice soft in the emptiness of the room. "I simply felt I needed to tell you in person that I'm returning to Cadgwith tomorrow."

The words hit him like a punch to the gut. He straightened, trying to make sense of what she was saying. "What? You're leaving *tomorrow*?" Surely she was jesting. Surely she was teasing him and would laugh and remark blithely about how he should have seen the look on his face.

But she couldn't have looked more serious as she nodded. "I need to go home, Gavin. I've gotten so far away from the life I know, and I have to get back to it. I've gotten carried away here, and it's not acceptable."

Not acceptable? He stared back at her, dumbfounded by what she was saying. "You haven't gotten carried away. You've bloomed like a flower in the first light of spring. Coming here has been good for you, not bad."

Her beautiful face was marred with lines of tension as she shook her head. "Please don't argue with me. I'm so grateful to you for all that you've done, and for being the wonderful friend and person that you are, but I've lost sight of what is most important in my life. After almost losing Bella this week, everything has snapped back into focus for me."

The bee sting. Of course that was what this was about. He felt slightly more in control of his rioting emotions, knowing where she was coming from. If he knew the problem, he could address it and fix it.

Setting his hands on either side of her shoulders, he said gently, "Felicity, you've had a shock, and it's understandable that you should want to react to that. But if you'd simply take a breath and think about it for a minute, you'd see that you are overreacting."

She moved away, out of his reach. "I'm not overreacting. I have given it much thought, and this is the best thing for us."

Frustration prickled deep in his chest. Couldn't she see how out of proportion such a thing would be to the incident? "Running away is never the best thing for anyone."

"I'm not running away. I'm going *home*." She put her hands to her heart, her eyes imploring him to understand. "Cadgwith is where I belong. It's where Bella and I can go back to our quiet lives, where there is structure and routine and predictability to our days. She has to come first."

He drew in a steadying breath, attempting to be reasonable. "Focusing on your daughter does not mean forgetting yourself and your own needs. Your own life. You act as though Cadgwith is the only place that she'll be safe, but what happened this week could happen anywhere." Her own husband had died there, for God's sake, though he wasn't about to say that aloud.

"Of course it can. But I've become so distracted with my own interests here, I've lost sight of hers. I need to step away from that."

She was scared; he could see that. The incident this week had shaken her and she was burrowing back into the shell from which she had only just emerged.

He raked a hand through his hair, trying to figure out how to make her see reason. "Just because you're afraid, you can't run away from the good things in your life. You want to go back because it's easier. It feels safe. But you'll only be burying yourself if you do that."

"Gavin, I know I let things go too far between us, and I'm sorry. I truly did enjoy every moment we spent together. But no matter what happened between us this summer, it was never going to change the fact that at the end of it, we would both go back to our own homes, our own lives."

"Then give us until the end of summer. Let us have this time."

She shook her head, her eyes full of compassion and regret, but also determination. "I can't. It's just too easy for me to lose myself when I'm with you."

"Of course it is, because we're *good* together. We fit. You can't deny the draw between us." His heart began to pound hard against his ribs. He couldn't bear the thought of her just walking away.

He looked around at the library, realizing then the last time they had been in here together. That was the night she had walked away from him the first time. Here they were, right back to where they started.

"No, I can't deny its existence, but I *can* keep from getting swept away by it." She pressed her eyes closed for a moment before meeting his gaze again. He saw resignation in them. She was determined to do this. "I only came tonight because you deserved to hear it from me that I was leaving."

She came to him then and wrapped her arms around him in an embrace that threatened to undo him. "Thank you for everything. You are an extraordinary man, and I'm lucky to call you my friend."

He hugged her back, fiercely, only just keeping the dam of his emotions in check. When she drew back, he let her, a thousand words of protest poised on his tongue, but unable to utter a single one.

She turned and walked away then, her head bowed as she hurried from the room. He stood there, rooted in place, assaulted by all the old feelings he'd spent a decade avoiding.

He'd been gliding through life, never allowing himself to put his heart on the line again. But when she'd come along, all bets were off. He couldn't have kept from falling for her again any more than he could have stopped himself from breathing.

It was a truth that was suddenly crystal clear to him: He was in love with her, desperately so, all over again.

He didn't just want her to stay for the next few hours or weeks or months. He wanted her to stay forever. And not just her. He wanted both of them, Felicity *and* Isabella. Somewhere along the way, the little girl had stolen his heart as well. He wanted to love and protect them both. To make both of them happy.

He couldn't bear to go back to that life of superficial pleasures. The way he felt when he was with her, even when he *wasn't* with her, that's what life was about. He was in love with her, and it was damn well time he told her.

Felicity barely kept her emotions in check as she pushed her way through the throng of people. She had thought coming here was the right thing to do, but it had only served to further confuse and upset her. She was more than overwhelmed, and all she could think of was getting home to her daughter.

Tomorrow they would be on their way home. All of these rioting emotions inside of her would calm as they neared her quiet little seaside home. She was sure of it. That was where peace was to be found.

Still, the look on Gavin's face had nearly been her undoing. He didn't deserve to be hurt by her. He'd been the very best friend she could have hoped for. No, it wasn't fair to call him merely that. He had been more than that, so much more, but she just wasn't ready for this. She wasn't ready to have her life turned upside down by her own passions.

As she threaded her way through the ballroom, she kept her head down, not wanting anyone to thwart her escape. Because truly, that's what this was: an escape. Despite her insistence to the contrary, she was running away. Too much had changed in her in too short of a time, and after what had happened with Bella, she simply couldn't handle it.

In the space of a week, she felt as though she'd let down her daughter, Gavin, Ian, even herself. Oh, and her father, too. Mustn't forget that.

"Felicity, where are you going?"

Charity's voice brought her up short. Felicity blinked, startled, and glanced up to meet her friend's concerned gray eyes.

"Whatever is the matter?" she asked, putting a hand to Felicity's shoulder in much the way Gavin had earlier.

"I shouldn't have come. I need to get home to Isabella." She started to move forward when Gavin's voice stopped her in her tracks.

"Felicity, *wait*." His deep voice seemed to echo across the crowded ballroom, cutting through the music and conversation like a warm knife through clotted cream. It cut through *her*, making her breath catch and her heart leap.

She turned, eyes wide, as he plunged through the crush straight toward her. He looked as dark and imposing as a rogue pirate, but she saw only the charming man who had enthralled her for weeks. She knew the gentle spirit he possessed, the sweetness behind his nearly black eyes. Even now, as desperate as she was to escape, she couldn't have walked away if her life depended on it.

All around them, heads turned, eyes widened, and conversation died away as he strode through the room and came to a stop directly in front of her. The music played on, thank God, but as far as she could tell, that was the only sound.

Her pulse thundered as her eyes met his. They were insistent, seeking, impossible to look away from. *Too much, too much.* She wanted to escape, but she couldn't.

Shaking his head, he reached for her hand and squeezed it between both of his. "I've never truly risked anything in my life, but I'm risking it all right here, right now. I'm through with hiding the truth and burying my feelings. I love you, Felicity Faith Wright Danby. I've loved you for literally half my life, and I will love you for the rest of it as well.

"You're exactly the person I wish to be by my side every single day from here on out. Marry me. Let me love you, and Isabella, and however many children we are blessed with in the future. I'll do everything in my power to make you happy for the rest of your life. All you have to do is say yes."

Felicity stood there, dumbfounded, nearly paralyzed with the force of her shock. *I've loved you for literally half my life. . . . I've dreamed of kissing you beneath the stars . . . I've been waiting years for an excuse to do this.*

And then she remembered the conversation in the library, so many years ago.

"Gavin, I'm in love!"

"Me, too!"

All these years. All *those* years, when they'd been the closest of friends. When she'd been in love with her own husband. When Gavin had danced with her in the park and kissed her beneath the stars.

All that time, he'd been in love with her?

Her ears rang as she fought to draw a proper breath. It was too much, far too much. She opened her mouth, without having a clue what to say. Tears pricked at her eyes as she shook her head, unable to even think straight.

"I'm sorry," she choked out, the only words that would fit past the rising panic in her throat. Pulling her hand free, she turned and fled.

Chapter Twenty-six

The salt air caressed Felicity's cheeks as she faced the sea, watching the sun slip down below the horizon. The cry of the gulls as they winged on the rising current of warm air served as a familiar lullaby to Isabella, whose eyes drooped from her spot on the blanket beside her.

It was one of the most beautiful sights Felicity had ever seen, with the pinks and yellows of sunset marbling with the blues and purples of descending twilight in a watercolor blend as vast as the heavens itself. Truly spectacular.

The sea was peaceful today. The water lapped at the shore instead of crashing, and the wind embraced instead of battered. It was impossible to imagine a more tranquil moment, yet Felicity herself was restless.

Nothing was as it was supposed to be when she had returned last month. The villagers were still as wonderful as ever, the sea as therapeutic, and the house was ever had it had been. Only . . .

It no longer quite felt like home. For the first time, she felt as though she was living in someone else's house, despite the fact that Hugh and Charity weren't even home yet. They were due to return in the morning, and the closer it became, the more urgency Felicity felt to leave them to their own home. The seed her father had planted had bloomed, and she saw now that perhaps they did need the house to themselves, especially with the baby coming.

Even Mr. Anthorp had been unable to bring her the same comfort he once had. Their reunion had been subdued, with the closeness she had felt with him in the preceding months paling in comparison to what she had shared with Gavin. He was as kind and accommodating as ever, and she was thankful for the role he had played in her initial healing, but it was increasingly clear to her that he would always simply be a friend.

Friend. The word tugged at her heart and she closed her eyes. Lord, how she missed Gavin. The longer she was here, the more she realized that she'd made an enormous mistake by fleeing him. The problem was, how did one say that to a person whose advances had been rebuffed in the most dreadful, public way possible?

In the time since she'd been home, she'd come to a startling realization: She was absolutely in love with him. She hadn't believed she was because it had been so different from the love she had shared with Ian. But then it had dawned on her: Love could come in many forms. It didn't have to be the same to be just as meaningful and profound.

In a way, it was a relief. She never wanted anything to eclipse what she'd shared with her first husband. It was comforting to know that the special connection they had would always be unique to them.

Still, she couldn't help but feel that she had completely ruined things with Gavin. She couldn't regret her instincts—she had truly needed this time to sort out her feelings—but she desperately regretted the pain and embarrassment she knew she must have caused him. She'd penned a dozen letters to him, and had tossed just as many into the bin.

"I thought I might find you here."

Felicity startled at the sound of Charity's voice and whipped around to find her friend beaming at her from the path, her skin fairly glowing in the pink light.

Grinning, Felicity scrambled to her feet to give her a huge hug. "What are you doing here? I thought you were to arrive tomorrow."

Charity gave a little shrug as she bent down to pick up Isabella so she could cuddle her close, rousing the girl and eliciting a welcoming shriek of delight. "Excellent weather combined with a pregnant woman who was very much ready to be home made for a few long but productive days of travel."

"Are you feeling well these days? How are Hugh and Lady Effington?"

"I feel well at this moment, and we will leave it at that," she said with a wry grin as they settled back down on the blanket. "Hugh and Grandmama are exhausted but well. We are all quite happy to be home."

Felicity smiled, though not as brightly as she might have. She only wished she could recapture that feeling of being exactly where she was supposed to be.

Charity sent her an appraising look as she kissed the top of Isabella's head. "And how are you?"

Hollow. "I am well enough." She paused, but couldn't hold back the question that burned at the back of her throat. "How is Gavin? Is he all right?"

Pursing her lips, Charity glanced to the water for a

moment before answering her. "He is about as well as one might expect, I suppose. He withdrew from much of the festival, spending some time with his brothers instead."

"That's good, I suppose." She hated to think of him giving up the energy and noise of the entertainments he so seemed to enjoy, but spending time with his brothers was a very good alternative.

At Charity's silence, Felicity cut her gaze back to her. "What is it?"

Her reluctance was tangible. "He's decided to join the *Anna Britannia* on its latest journey to India. He said he needed to get away for a while."

Felicity's heart shuddered to a stop before roaring back at double speed. "He's going to *India*? When?"

"He and the duke were headed to Portsmouth with Captain Bradford, May's father, the same day we left. I believe they were spending the week preparing for the journey before setting sail on Sunday."

So soon? But it was already Thursday night. She couldn't possibly reach him before then. Yet everything inside her rebelled at the idea of him leaving for such a long and dangerous journey. And what if he decided to stay in India for a while? Many an Englishman of his age and status had.

But what could she do? It was at least two hundred and fifty miles to Portsmouth.

She knew now that she should have written sooner. She should have told him just how sorry she was, and begged for his forgiveness. To let him know that, if he would still have her, she would happily consent to be his wife. That's the conclusion she had been coming to all these weeks, as she struggled with sorting out what it was that she truly wanted in life—for her and her daughter.

She had spent so much time worrying about Isabella not being her top priority, she had failed to realize that Isabella thrived best when her mother was happy and at peace. The child could sense her emotions as surely as she could the weather changes.

Charity set her arm around Felicity's shoulders and pulled her close. "I'm sorry. I know this whole experience has been difficult for you."

She shook her head, pulling away and coming to her feet. "Oh, Charity, I am such a fool. I love him. I love him so very much, and I've ruined any chance I ever had to be with him."

Surprise lifted her friend's copper eyebrows. "Goodness. I had suspected before, but after the, um, incident at the ball, I thought I was terribly mistaken." After a moment she stood, brushing off her skirts before bending to pick up Bella. "Well, perhaps not all is lost."

"What do you mean? I can't possibly travel that far in so little time."

"You can't, but an express messenger can. What if you were to send a letter? At least it would be something to let him know of your change of heart."

Felicity ran a hand over her hair, her stomach dancing with hope and fear and a thousand other emotions. What she could possibly say in a letter to convey to him her feelings? It seemed so unfair to thrust this upon him like this, just before he planned to depart.

An idea came to her then. She drew a sharp breath, inflating her lungs with the bracing salty air. If what he wanted was to go to India, she didn't want to selfishly ruin his plans. She'd already mucked up enough things between them.

But if he could just know that her mind had been not

so much changed as transformed, would he choose to give her a chance?

"I've got to go," she said urgently, needing to put pen to paper before she lost the courage. "Have you got her?" she asked, tipping her chin to her daughter.

Charity nodded quickly, shooing her with her free hand. "Yes, go. Hurry! You write the letter, and I'll have Hugh hire the messenger."

The last of her sentence was swallowed up by the whooshing of wind past Felicity's ears as she sprinted toward the house. Perhaps she had a chance at happiness after all, if only she could find the proper words.

Dering had never been on a ship before. At least not at sea—he'd walked the decks several times while the *Anna Britannia* had been at port. The true sway and rock of the vessel at sea was a *vastly* different experience.

"Ahoy there, Lord Derington," Captain Bradford shouted, his mouth tilted up in a grin beneath his graying beard. "Haven't quite acquired the old sea legs, I see."

Dering grinned back at the man, shaking his head. "Not quite. I figure by the horn of Africa I should have the hang of it."

He held tight to the railing as the captain came to join him. Bradford was as surefooted as if he were walking on land, his body moving easily with the roll and tilt of the deck beneath their feet, even with the satchel he held in one hand.

The old man laughed, the sound as raspy as sandpaper. "If you're lucky, lad. Just wait till we're on the true open ocean, with nary a coastline to be seen."

That idea had held quite a bit more appeal for Dering two days ago, when they were still safely moored at

Portsmouth. But this was an adventure, and he was confident that he would adjust. He needed a change of scenery. A change of *life*.

After what had happened with Felicity, he'd been rocked to his core. The parties and events of the festival had lost their allure, and he couldn't help but look at his life in the harsh light of reality. His old life simply wasn't good enough for him now.

He needed more.

More honest friendships like the ones he had with Radcliffe and Cadgwith. More time with his family, even if his mother was still smarting from his ballroom disaster. She'd confessed days after the debacle that she'd always suspected that Felicity had been the one to break his heart, and she had attempted to prevent it from happening again. Though he still wasn't happy with her interference, he could at least sympathize with her intentions.

Above all, he needed more meaning in the things he chose to spend his time on.

When Radcliffe had mentioned his intention to accompany his father-in-law to Portsmouth, the idea had come nearly fully formed. By sailing to India, he would have better firsthand knowledge of his investments, a broader understanding of the world at large, and hopefully, in all the time away, he could figure out what he was going to do next.

Now, if he could just get used to the queasiness, that would really help to recapture his enthusiasm. Tipping his chin toward the shoreline in the not so far distance, Dering said, "How long until we reach that open water? I'd have thought we'd be there by now."

The shore was actually quite a bit closer than it had

been only an hour ago. He could easily make out the ragged shoreline and weathered trees atop the erratic cliffs. A huge house perched on a rise not far from what looked to be a tiny little fishing town clustered around a narrow cove.

Leaning against the railing, the captain pursed his lips. "Not long now. We're coming close to the very tip of jolly ol' England as we speak. Which is why I've come to find you."

Dering's brows came together as he turned a questioning gaze on the man. "You have need of me?"

"No, my lord. But there is someone who does. I'm about to weigh anchor for a few hours. Two of my men will row you to shore. They'll be back to get you in two hours' time. If, for whatever reason, you choose not to return, they'll have your things ready and waiting."

Dering blinked in astonishment, trying to make sense of the bizarre order. "Are you afraid I can't make the journey?"

The captain put a hand to his shoulder, his eyes softening. "No, lad. But I am hoping you decide you don't want to." He gave him two firm thwacks on the shoulder before stepping back and holding out the satchel. "I thought you might like a change of clothes. Just in case."

With that, he gave a wink, then turned to walk away, leaving Dering utterly lost behind him.

An hour later, as the tiny rowboat approached shore, he was no closer to understanding the point of the exercise. Shielding his eyes from the midday sunshine, he glanced around at the little town. There were several thatched-roof buildings, some with natural stone and others whitewashed. A handful of boats were pulled up on shore, and people bustled this way and that.

It was then that he noticed the woman who wasn't moving. She stood beside the massive boulders lining the left side of the cove, one hand shielding her eyes and the other holding a baby to her hip.

His heart squeezed as he drew in a sharp, astonished breath. *Felicity.* Her golden curls were uncovered despite the wind and sun, shining like silk in the bright light. She stood, motionless, waiting as the boat drew nearer and nearer to shore.

He swallowed against the surge of emotions that threatened to clog his throat. Oh, to see that beloved face again. He'd resigned himself to the fact that it could be years—if ever—before he saw her again.

His pulse began to pound with every swipe of the oars, and it was all he could do not to yank them from the men and paddle them himself. How was this happening? What forces had conspired to bring him back to her, just when he thought he couldn't be any farther away?

When the boat finally scraped bottom, he vaulted into the water and waded the last few feet to shore. The pebbles crunched and shifted beneath his boots as he found his footing and strode the last few yards to her. When he was only a handful of feet away, he stopped, drinking in the sight of her and her sweet baby.

He could see the rapid rise and fall of her chest as her eyes roamed his face. "Gavin," she said at last, her voice desperately earnest. "I'm so sorry. So very, very sorry for the way we parted."

She stepped forward, closing the distance between them by half. He savored the sight of her, refilling the well of his memories. He never wanted to forget the way she looked now, so soft and sweet and looking back at him with an expression that made his heart swell with hope.

"Felicity—"

"No, please," she said, shaking her head. "Let me say what I've been dying to say for weeks now, but couldn't find the courage. When you told me you loved me, I was too overwhelmed to respond properly. I needed time, and because of that, I'm afraid I hurt you in a way you never deserved."

She drew a deep breath and wet her lips, and he realized just how nervous she was. He wanted so badly to reach out to her, to comfort her, but she had asked him to wait, and he would. He wanted to know what this was all about. Desperately wanted to know. Was this all to apologize, or was there something more?

Holding out her hand, she said, "Will you come with me?"

He held his breath, looking down at her ungloved fingers. Slowly, with his heart hammering in his chest, he slid his fingers into hers. The feel of her soft skin against his was sweet, sweet torture.

Without another word, she turned and led them up the beach to a small walkway. The path took them around the side of the large stone building fronting the beach. Her fingers were chilled in his hands, and he resisted the urge to stop her so that he could properly warm them. She had a clear purpose, and he wouldn't waylay her plans.

When they walked around to the front of the building, he came to an abrupt stop, shocked at the sight that greeted him. It seemed as though the whole town had come out, with several dozen men, women, and children filling the small village square. As Felicity pulled him toward the center of it all, he saw Cadgwith and Charity standing off to the side, holding hands and grinning hugely. Lady Effington stood beside them, her mouth pressed together in an indulgent smile and her eyes glittering with delight.

"What is all this?" he asked, unable to contain his curiosity any longer.

"This," she said, pausing when Charity came forward to take Isabella from her, "is my very public declaration."

All eyes were on them as she released his hand and turned to face him fully. "This time, the gamble is mine. Gavin, I thought I could never bear to fall in love again. The idea of risking heartbreak after what I had been through was too scary to consider."

She shook her head and offered him a look of such sweetness, he longed to reach out for her. "But then you came back into my life. You showed me compassion and kindness, thoughtfulness and patience, passion and, indeed, you showed me love. It was only when I pushed you away that I realized the truth: The risk of *not* loving is far worse."

She stepped closer, taking both of his hands and peering up at him with those beautiful brown eyes of hers. He caught the first hint of gardenia on the sea air and smiled, so full of hope and buoyant optimism he could barely contain it.

"I've come to realize, Gavin Theodore Stark, that I am quite desperately, madly—no, *happily*—in love with you. Will you mar—"

He cut her off there, pressing his lips to hers in a quick but searing kiss. "I'll let you have anything you want in life, but I won't let you say those words," he said.

She tilted her head, confused. Smiling as he squeezed her fingers, he said. "I insist on being the one to ask."

Still holding her hands, he dropped to one knee,

right there in the middle of Cadgwith's town square, with the village as witness, and said, "My sweet Felicity, will you and Isabella marry me?"

A cheer went up as she nodded vigorously, tears pooling in her eyes. He stood and kissed her properly then, not caring a whit if the whole world was there to watch. When he pulled away, the people around them were clapping and music seemed to come from nowhere. A fiddler emerged, playing a lively tune as Dering escorted his beloved betrothed to their friends.

He held out his hands to Isabella, and the little girl didn't hesitate to raise her arms to him. He pulled her into his arms, kissing her cheeks and silently giving thanks to the man he had never met, but whose love had brought her into this world.

After accepting copious felicitations from the celebrating townsfolk, he leaned down and whispered in Felicity's ear, hoping for a little privacy. After handing the baby back to Charity, they slipped away to a little area of the beach that was obscured by the rugged boulders.

"However did you make this happen?" he asked, unable to contain his curiosity anymore.

Her lips stretched in a small secret grin as she slipped her arms around him. "A little luck, a very dedicated messenger, and a certain sea captain who I happen to know is a sucker for love."

He laughed, amazed the old man had kept him so effectively in the dark. It was fortuitous—serendipitous, even—that their trade route would pass by so close to her home. "Remind me to give him a raise."

Contentment seemed to fill every inch of his body as he looked down at the woman he had loved for so very long, but only now could call his own. "Are you certain you'll be comfortable with leaving Cadgwith? As lovely as it is, we won't be able to live here."

Her eyes strayed to the sea as she nodded, her expression peaceful. "I know. This place will always be very special to me. It was a wonderful home, but I know now that it's time to move on. I'm *ready* to move on."

He slid his arms around her waist and pulled her close for a kiss, but she stopped him at the very last minute.

"Yes?"

"I do have one request," she said. "I'd like to visit for the Flora Day Festival each year. I want Bella to know and love the place her father and I called home."

"Is that all? If we're bargaining, you might as well lay out all of your requests now," he teased.

"Hmm," she said, her eyes dancing with mirth. She glanced heavenward as though considering what she might want. "You must never defeat me at billiards, you must kiss me beneath the stars as often as possible, and you must always, always tell me you love me."

"Deal," he said, capturing her lips in a kiss even as she laughed. When they finally came up for air, he smiled and said softly, "I love you more than I can even express, Felicity. Say that you will marry me as soon as I can procure a special license."

"Oh no," she said, emphatically shaking her head. "I will not be responsible for robbing your mother of the wedding of her firstborn. It's going to be hard enough winning her over as it is, after the spectacle we created at the ball."

He sighed nosily. "I suppose you're right. About the wedding, that is. Mother will be thrilled to have you as a daughter-in-law for no other reason than it will keep me from sailing away."

"Mmm, let us hope so."

Chuckling, he pulled her back to him for a long embrace, happier than he could ever remember being.

"Gavin?"

"Yes?" he replied, dropping a kiss to the velvety skin just above her collarbone. It made his blood rush to think of kissing the rest of her someday very soon.

"I really am sorry for what happened in the ballroom. It was a magnificent gesture, and I hate that I ruined it for you."

He pulled away, lifting his eyebrows. "Look at me, Lissy. I'm holding my future wife in my arms after a lifetime of waiting. I'd say it was a risk that paid off pretty handsomely in the end."

"Really?" she said, sending him a very promising smile. "Then how is it that I feel as though I'm the one who won?"

He lifted his hands to cup either side of her face. "In this, my love, I'd say neither one of us could ever lose."

Epilogue

"Papa, look," Isabella exclaimed, holding up a pebble as though it were a lost treasure of the deep. Her dark curls ruffled in the wind, loosening themselves from the ribbon Felicity had just retied ten minutes ago.

Gavin bent down on his haunches, carefully examining the rock as though there weren't a hundred more just like it underfoot. "How absolutely marvelous, my dear. How did you find it?"

"I looked . . . and there it was!" She spread her hands in wonder, as though it had been placed there just for her to find.

"How clever you are! You must go show Mama," he said, sending an indulgent grin Felicity's way.

Smiling back at him, she placed a hand to her rounded belly, her opal-and-diamond wedding ring throwing tiny prisms of colored light across the fabric of her gown. She was only five months along, but she was already exhausted from the short walk to the beach. She waited, eyebrows raised in expectation as Bella ran toward her, the rock held out in front of her.

Felicity gave the thing due consideration, complimenting her daughter on her excellent find and adding it to their growing collection of pebbles, shells, coral, and even a piece of sea glass.

"Can you go find me something else pretty? And tell Papa to come see me for a moment, please?"

Nodding with excitement, Bella ran back over to Gavin, her hair streaming out behind her now. Well, tidiness was completely overrated when one was at the beach. She rather loved to see both her husband and her daughter with tousled hair and sandy feet.

Leaving Bella to dig in a small pile of rocks nearby, Gavin strode over to the blanket and sat down beside her. Leaning over, he brushed a lingering kiss across her lips that made her pulse skip a beat. Lord, but he was handsome. And strong, and sweet, and doting, and . . .

"You summoned?" he murmured, placing a warm hand to her belly.

"Just wondering if there were any stars out yet." She smiled innocently, trusting him to know exactly what she meant. These days, the stars were for much more than kissing.

His lips turned up in a suitably wolfish grin as love shone from his gorgeous chocolate gaze. "I have it on good authority that the stars will be out in force tonight."

She couldn't help but laugh at the way he waggled his eyebrows before kissing her again. Oh, how she loved him. How she loved *them* together. With him, she'd found love, peace, and the sort of contentment she had once feared she'd never know again.

Happiness. That's what she felt most of all. Shaking her head, she said, "Have I told you today how very much I love you?"

"Indeed," he answered, the sound a low rumble in his chest. "But feel free to say it again, my love. I waited years to hear those words, and I promise I shall never grow tired of them."

"I love you," she said, simply and honestly. "I love you, I love you, I love you."

"You, Felicity Stark, took the words right out of my mouth."

Don't miss the first book in the
Prelude to a Kiss series,

The Baron Next Door

Available now from Signet Eclipse!

H ell and damnation. Was he to have no peace at all?
Hugh Danby, the new and exceedingly reluctant
Baron Cadgwith, pressed the heels of his hands into his
eye sockets, pushing back against the fresh pounding
the godforsaken noise next door had reawakened.

"Go to Bath," his sister-in-law had said. "It's practically deserted in the summer. Think of the peace and
quiet you'll have."

Bloody hogwash. This torture was about as far from
peace as one could get. Not that he blamed Felicity;
clearly the news of the first annual Summer Serenade in
Somerset festival hadn't made it to their tiny little corner of England when she offered her seemingly useful

suggestion. Still, he'd love to get his hands on the person who thought it was a good idea to organize the damn thing.

He tugged the pillow from the empty spot beside him and crammed it over his head, trying to muffle the jaunty pianoforte music filtering through the shared wall of his bedchamber. The notes were high and fast, like a foal prancing in a springtime meadow. Or, more aptly, a foal prancing on his eardrums.

There was no hope for it. There would be no more sleep for him now.

Tossing aside the useless pillow, he rolled to his side, bracing himself for the wave of nausea that always greeted him on mornings like this. *Ah, there it is.* He gritted his teeth until it passed, then dragged himself up into a sitting position and glanced about the room.

The curtains were closed tight, but the late-morning sunlight still forced its way around the edges, causing a white-hot seam that managed to burn straight through his retinas. He squinted and looked away, focusing instead on the dark burgundy-and-brown Aubusson rug on the floor. His clothes were still scattered in a trail leading to the bed, and several empty glasses lined his nightstand.

Ah, thank God—not *all* were empty.

He reached for the one still holding a good finger of liquid and brought it to his nose. *Brandy.* With a shrug, he drained the glass, squeezing his eyes against the burn.

Still the music, if one could call it that, continued. Must the blasted pianoforte player have such a love affair with the brain-cracking high notes? Though he'd yet to meet the neighbors who occupied the adjoining townhouse, he knew without question the musician was a female. No self-respecting male would have the time, inclination, or enthusiasm to play such musical drivel.

Setting the tumbler back down on the nightstand, he scrubbed both hands over his face, willing the alcohol to deaden the pounding in his brain. The notes grew louder and faster, rising to a crescendo that could surely be heard all the way back at his home in Cadgwith, some two hundred miles away.

And then . . . *blessed silence.*

He closed his eyes and breathed out a long breath. The hush settled over him like a balm, quieting the ache and lowering his blood pressure. Thank God. He'd rather walk barefoot through glass than—

The music roared back to life, pounding the nails back into his skull with the relentlessness of waves hitting the beach at high tide. *Damn it all to hell.* Grimacing, he tossed aside the counterpane and came to his feet, ignoring the violent protest of his head. Reaching for his clothes, he yanked them on with enough force to rip the seams, had they been of any lesser quality.

It was bloody well time he met his neighbors.

Freedom in D Minor.

Charity Effington grinned at the words she had scrawled at the top of the rumpled foolscap, above the torrent of hastily drawn notes that danced up and down the static five-lined staff.

The title could not be more perfect.

Sighing with contentment, she set down her pencil on the burled oak surface of her pianoforte and stretched.

Whenever she had days like this, when the music seemed to pour from her soul like water from a upturned pitcher, her shoulders and back inevitably paid the price.

She unfurled her fingers, reaching toward the unlit chandelier that hung above her. The room was almost too warm, with sunlight pouring through the sheers that covered the wide windows facing the private gardens behind the house, but she didn't mind. She'd much rather be here in the stifling heat than up north with her parents and their stifling expectations.

And Grandmama couldn't have chosen a more perfect townhouse to rent. With soaring ceilings, airy rooms, and generous windows lining both the front and back—not to mention the gorgeous pianoforte she now sat at—it was a wonderful little musical retreat.

Exactly what Charity needed after the awfulness of the past Season.

Dropping her hands to the keys once more, she closed her eyes and purged all thoughts of that particular topic from her mind. It was never good for creativity to focus on stressful topics. Exhaling, she stretched her fingers over the cool ivory keys, finding her way by touch.

Bliss. The pianoforte was perfectly tuned, the notes floating through the air like wisps of steam curling from the Baths. Light and airy, the music reflected the joy filling her every pore. Here she had freedom.

Free from her mother and her relentless matchmaking. Free from the gossip that seemed to follow her like a fog. Free from all the strict rules every young lady must abide by during the Season.

The notes rose higher as her right hand swept up the scale, tapping the keys with the quickness of a flitting hummingbird. Her left hand provided counterbalance with low, smooth notes that anchored the song.

A sudden noise from the doorway startled her from her trance, abruptly stopping the flow of music and engulfing the room in an echoing silence. Jeffers, Grandmama's ancient butler, stood in the doorway, his stooped shoulders oddly rigid.

"I do beg your pardon, Miss Effington. Lady Effington requests your presence in the drawing room."

Now? Just when she was truly finding her stride? But Charity wasn't about to make the woman wait—not after she had singlehandedly saved Charity from a summer of tedium in Durham with her disgruntled parents. "Thank you, Jeffers," she said, coming to her feet.

She headed down the stairs, humming the beginning of her new creation. Her steps were in time with the music in her mind, which had her moving light and fast on her feet. The townhouse was medium sized, with more than enough room for the two of them and the handful of servants Grandmama had brought, so it took her only a minute to reach the spacious drawing room from the music room.

Breezing through the doorway with a ready smile on her face, Charity came up short when the person before her was most definitely *not* her four-foot-eleven, silver-haired grandmother.

Mercy!

She only just managed to contain her squeak of surprise at the sight of the tall, lanky man standing in the middle of the room, his dark rumpled clothes in stark contrast to the cheery soft blues and golds of the immaculate drawing room. She swallowed, working to keep her expression passive as her mind raced to figure out who on earth the man was.

Charity had never seen him before—of that she was absolutely sure. It would be impossible to forget the distinctive scars crisscrossing his left temple and disappearing into his dark blond hair. One of the puckered white lines cut through his eyebrow, dividing it neatly in half before ending perilously close to one of his vividly green—and terribly bloodshot—eyes.

He was watching her unflinchingly, accepting her inspection. Or perhaps he was simply indifferent to it. It was . . . disconcerting.

"There you are," Grandmama said, snapping Charity's attention away from the stranger. Sitting primly at her usual spot on the overstuffed sofa centered in the room, her grandmother offered Charity a soft smile. "Charity, Lord Cadgwith has kindly come over to introduce himself. He is to be our neighbor for the summer."

Kindly? Charity couldn't help her raised eyebrow. The man had come over without invitation or introduction, and Grandmama had actually allowed it?

Correctly interpreting Charity's reaction, the older woman chuckled, clasping her hands over the black fabric of her skirts. "Yes, I realize we are not strictly adhering to the rules, but it is summer, is it not? Exceptions can be made, especially when the good baron overheard your playing and so wished to meet the musician." Her gray eyes sparkled as she smiled at their guest.

It was all Charity could do not to gape at the woman. Yes, no one was more proud of Charity's playing than her grandmother, but this was beyond the pale. Good gracious, if Mama and Papa knew how much Grandmama's formerly strict nature had been changed by her extended illness, they never would have allowed Charity to accompany her to Bath without them.

The baron bowed, the movement crisp despite his slightly disheveled appearance. "A pleasure to make your acquaintance, Miss Effington," he said, his voice low and a little raspy, like the low register of a flute.

Despite the perfectly proper greeting, something about him seemed a little untamed. Must be the scars, the origin of which she couldn't help but wonder about. War wounds? Carriage accident? A duel? Setting aside her curiosity, she arranged her lips in a polite smile. "And you as well, Lord Cadgwith. Are you here for the festival?"

"Please don't mumble, my dear," Grandmama cut in, her whispered reprimand loud and clear. Charity cringed—the older woman insisted that her hearing was fine, and that any problem in understanding lay in the enunciation of those around her.

"Yes, ma'am," she responded in elevated, carefully pronounced tones. "Lord Cadgwith, are you here for the festival?" Heat stole up her cheeks, despite her effort to keep the blush at bay. She had never liked standing out—when away from her pianoforte, of course—and practically shouting in the presence of their neighbor was beyond awkward. One would think she'd have come to terms with the easy blushes her ginger hair and pale freckled skin lent itself to, but no. Knowing her cheeks were warming only made her blush that much more violently.

It certainly didn't help that the man was by far the most attractive male to ever stand in her drawing room, scars or no. She swallowed against the unexpected rush of butterflies that flitted through her.

For his part, Lord Cadgwith did not look amused. "No, actually. I had no knowledge of the event until my arrival." He made the effort to speak in a way that Grandmama would hear, his dark, deep voice carrying easily through the room. A man used to being heard, she'd guess. A military man, perhaps?

"Well, what a happy surprise it must have been when you arrived," her grandmother said, smiling easily. "Charity is planning to sign up for the Musicale series later this afternoon. There are a limited number of slots, but I have no doubt our Charity will earn a place."

And . . . more blushing. Charity gritted her teeth as she smiled demurely at her grandmother. Music was the one thing for which Charity had no need for false modesty, but sharing her plans with the virtual stranger standing in their drawing room felt oddly invasive. "I'm sure Lord Cadgwith isn't interested in my playing, Grandmama."

"On the contrary," he said, his voice rough but carrying. "It is, after all, your music that prompted me to visit in the first place."

Her mouth fell open in a little "Oh" of surprise before she got her wits about her and snapped it shut. Still, pleasure, warm and fizzy, poured through her. Her music had called this incredibly handsome man to her? Not her looks (such as they were), not her father's station, not curiosity from the gossip. No, he had sought her out because her playing touched him. Pride mingled with the pleasure, bringing an irrepressible grin to her lips.

Grandmama beamed, her shrewd gaze flitting back and forth between them. "Well, I do hope you'll stay for tea, my lord."

His smile was oddly sharp. "Unfortunately, I must be off. I just wanted to introduce myself after being serenaded this morning. Lady Effington, thank you for your indulgence of my whim."

She nodded regally, pleasure clear in the pink tinge of the normally papery white skin of her cheeks. He turned to face Charity, his green eyes meeting hers levelly. "Miss Effington," he said, lowering his voice to a much more intimate tone as he bent his head in acknowledgment. "Do please have a care for your captive audience in the adjoining townhouses, and keep the infernal racket to a minimum."

Lost as she was in the vivid dark green of his eyes, it took a moment before his words sank in. She blinked several times in quick succession, trying to make sense of his gentle tone and bitingly rude words. He couldn't possibly have just said . . . "I beg your pardon?"

"Pardon granted. Good day, Miss Effington."

And just like that, the baron turned on his heel and strode from the room. It was then that she caught the fleeting hint of spirits, faint but unmistakable, in his wake. A few seconds later, the sound of the front door opening and closing reached her burning ears. *Of all the insufferable, boorish, rude—*

"My goodness, but he was a delightful young man." Grandmama's sweet voice broke through Charity's fury, just before she was about to explode. The older woman looked so happy, so utterly pleased with the encounter, that Charity forced herself to bite her tongue. It wouldn't do to upset her—not after she was only just now recovering from her illness. The currish baron wasn't worth the strife it would cause.

Forcing a brittle smile to her lips, she nodded. "Mmhmm. And you know what? I think I'll go play an *extra*enthusiastic composition just for him."

With that, she marched from the room, directly back to her pianoforte bench. The baron could have been pleasant. He could have kindly asked her to play more quietly, or perhaps less frequently. But, no, he had chosen to go about it in the most uncivilized, humiliating way possible. It was his decision to throw down the gauntlet as though they were enemies instead of neighbors.

She plopped down on her bench with a complete lack of elegance and paused only long enough to lace her hands together and stretch out her muscles. Then she spread her fingers out over the keys and smiled.

This, Lord Cadgwith, means war.